TRAMPLING IN THE LAND OF WOE
Hellbound – Book 1
Copyright © 2021 by William LJ Galaini
(Original First Edition Copyright © 2015 William Galaini)

SECOND EDITION SOFTCOVER
ISBN: 1622535359
ISBN-13: 978-1-62253-535-4

Editor: Lane Diamond
Cover Designer: Kabir Shah, with images by Aleks Dochkin
Interior Designer: Lane Diamond, with images by Bruce Brenneise

EVOLVED PUBLISHING™

www.EvolvedPub.com
Evolved Publishing LLC
Butler, Wisconsin, USA

Printed in Book Antiqua font.

BOOKS BY
WILLIAM LJ GALAINI

HELLBOUND
Book 1: *Trampling in the Land of Woe*
Book 2: *Sparks from a Cruel Grindstone*
Book 3: *Patron Saint of Wrong*
Book 4: *An End to Ice and Sorrow* [2022]
Book 5: *Beneath the Titan's Stride* [2022]

The Line

DEDICATION

For those of us who fail to let go.

THE CIRCLES
OF
HELL

NEW DIS
LUST
GLUTTONY
HOARDERS
OLD DIS RUINS
RIVER STYX
SUICIDE WOOD
PHLEGETHON
FROZEN WASTES
COCYTUS

CHAPTER 1

Waves of floundering bodies, naked and desperate, clawed at the ship's unyielding sides as it crushed through their groaning and gurgling masses. Despite having a tall iron-riveted hull, the *Bonny Sweetheart* teetered sickeningly from side to side. An imposing ship, she stood thirty feet high from wave crest to main deck, with two paddlewheels grinding away at her sides. The bow lurched upward and forward in the black Sea of the Damned as her smoke stacks spewed into the starless sky above.

A ship of the ages, this magnificent ship-of-the-line boasted a pointed bow and elegant bulging sides, but as technology trickled down from the living world into the afterlife, she'd evolved and mutated into a steam-powered hulk with an armored hide, deck guns, and a red-iron ram at the front. Each of the *Bonny Sweetheart's* owners had made their own modifications, and her spacious cargo holds now brimmed with Hell's fire—her burning belly would power her steam engines for eternity.

Some of those floundering bodies around them clung to the wiring of the protective cage that housed the massive paddle wheels, but if any of the destitute wretches climbed too high from the water, the vigilant crew promptly gunned them down.

Hephaestion gripped the railing, white-knuckled, as he scanned the mewling sea of bodies for just the right one. He needed a specific body type for his plan to work—tall and massive in girth, approximately 20 stone in weight and perhaps seventeen hands in height. Man or woman would do, and other factors, such as skin tone and hair, meant nothing.

They'd been searching for three months, and had yet to yield anything but impatience and distaste among the *Bonny Sweetheart's* crew. Whenever Hephaestion stood or walked near one of the sailors, he took care to stand straight and make eye contact, punctuating his passing presence with a firm nod.

The deck consistently bustled with sailors, each in their sleeveless leather tunics, clumped in teams and dangling long metal poles over the sides of the ship, poking at the surges of wailing and water-logged humans. The ship's occupants remained focused and dedicated, but Hephaestion could tell from their sidelong glances that they'd rather be enjoying their afterlives than searching in the waters that lapped Hell's shore.

The deck's planking creaked behind him. "I know, I know...." Hephaestion sighed over his shoulder. "We're here longer than I promised."

"You don't have to placate me," Ulfric chimed. Even on a ship in a turbulent sea of wailing damned, Ulfric still managed to be cheery. The man's disposition glowed as brightly as his blond hair and braided blond beard. Leaning against the railing next to Hephaestion, the Viking's presence provided comfort.

"I don't thank you nearly enough," Hephaestion confessed.

"Not nearly."

"How is the crew holding up?"

"A few of them have been lost in this very ocean, and they remember vividly their long swim to shore with only Hell to look forward to. I asked a lot of those men and women *specifically* to return here to help. Their knowledge has been helpful, and they've muscled through the memory of being here just to help."

"I didn't know that. I'd never expect someone to come back here, but like I said—"

"They insisted. They knew the waters and they knew what to expect." Ulfric made a sweeping gesture with his open hand.

In the distance, Hephaestion could see endless cresting mounds of miserable, tangled bodies. Silent lightning strikes in the distance lit up the horizon, casting a spotlight on tormented humanity as far as the eye could see.

"Some stay out here, you know," Ulfric said. "Some try and avoid the current pulling them in because they suspect greater punishment awaits them."

Hephaestion silently searched for a retort, but Alex's face came to his mind instead. "I won't find peace until I find *him*," he said stonily to his large friend.

"Don't I know it." Ulfric straightened up to leave. "The crew will do their part, regardless of their feelings on the matter. You asked me for this, so I asked them. You'll have it."

"I'm sorry.," Hephaestion turned away from the rolling waves, steadying himself by grabbing the railing.

With his usual disarming grin, Ulfric looked back. "The hell you are! You wouldn't be doing this if you were sorry. You're just obsessed."

Hephaestion couldn't help but smirk back; that insuppressible grin of Ulfric's could melt all negativity. Indeed, Ulfric had given him the very same smile when they first met.

Hephaestion had been clinging to jutting rocks as the raging currents of Purgatory pummeled him, nearly a thousand years ago. Up above him flickered Ulfric's blond hair, dancing about like a lighthouse's flaming beacon. The huge man was all grin and open hands, reaching down for Hephaestion to pluck him from the battering waters.

Gratitude. This was the first word that always came to mind when he thought of Ulfric. The man provided unyielding and unrelenting kindness. Still, Ulfric was right: Hephaestion had asked a lot of the crew, and a lot of Ulfric himself. It didn't matter, though, because Hephaestion had committed to perhaps one of the greatest endeavors imaginable.

He planned to get beyond Minos.

He intended to descend into the Pit.

He would rescue Alexander the Great from Hell.

CHAPTER 2

If days could be judged on a sunless sea of wailing dead, then surely many had passed. Within the guts of the *Bonny Sweetheart*, several hourglasses kept time, as well as a giant mechanical clock powered by the ships growling Hellfire furnace, but Hephaestion rarely descended below deck. He obsessively scanned the swells of bodies for his quarry, unwilling to leave the search solely in the hands of Ulfric's crew.

Time meant little to most in the afterlife, but it meant nearly *nothing* to Hephaestion. He'd spent centuries on the rolling hills of the infinite mountain Purgatory, upon the other side of the underworld, serving Ulfric and aiding others. All those centuries had marched on at the same, unperceivable rate, and all the while Hephaestion pined for his heart's core.

He permitted himself a moment of mental rest, and his eyes drifted closed, shielding him from the wailing cacophony and distant flashes of lightning. He sighed and thought of Alexander. Despite the hundreds of years, he could easily remember his youth.

Alex romped in the stables attached to his father's palace, and flopped in the hay, laughing as he often did. Hephaestion was taller than his king-to-be, even then, but Alex was always the rambunctious

one. The boys, still under Aristotle's tutelage, sparred every afternoon with training swords and wooden shields. As they did before each round, they banged them together three times to indicate they were ready to fight, restraining their laughter while they whimsically stared at each other.

Training, roughhousing, and daring horse-jumps had filled their summer that year, and between lessons from their tutors, they often ran and hid in the stables.

Alex liked to pick fights. He now jabbed at Hephaestion, more a sharp slap than a punch, and would continue to do so until Hephaestion's temper, as it always did, got the better of him. Alex could always manipulate his friend's feverish fury.

"Come on, lanky!" Alex taunted between smacks. "Girls like me better. Don't matter how pretty you are."

"Hard *not* to like the heir better than the sidekick!" Hephaestion snapped back, his guard up as he bobbed and dodged his friend's annoyances.

"I might leave a girl for you, when we're older." Alex grinned. "Let you have kids. Bet they'll be pretty, too."

"Stop calling me pretty!"

"I'm sure some famous horse lords were pretty," Alex said while delivering an echoing, open-palmed smack across Hephaestion's face.

Hephaestion, teeth clenched, *flattened* Alex. He landed a knuckle-first jab and heard Alex's nose 'pop' as his dirty blond head snapped back.

Alex staggered on his heels for a moment, slumped backward into some hay, and stared at the wooden beams above. "You broke my nose," he marveled, half stunned.

Hephaestion put his hands over his mouth in shocked shame. The prince, son of King Philip, had blood pouring down from his nose onto his lips as his green eyes gazed into the heavens beyond the roof of the stables. Fifteen-year-old Hephaestion felt certain he would never see the age of sixteen now.

"You broke my nose!" Alex screeched with pubescent delight. "That's perfect! Now I'll look like a soldier!"

"What?"

"Yeah! And even *with* a crooked nose, I'll still get more girls than you!"

Hephaestion pounced on him, pinning Alex's shoulders with his knees, and proceeded to set his prince's nose back into proper place.

"Stop!" Alex protested while flailing. "Quit it! I want it!"

"You're being a jackass!" Hephaestion snarled. "I won't get the rod because you were a jackass. Let me at least.... *Ow!*" He leapt back as Alex nipped at his fingers like an ornery horse.

Alex grinned through red teeth. "I get a broken nose, and you get a finger missing. We'll both be warriors!"

The boys collided and tumbled as they gnawed and kicked and bit in the dust. The horses snorted and stamped and tossed about while watching the spectacle. Hephaestion knew he would lose, but he honestly didn't mind it.

Alex always wanted the fight more, wanted the victory more, and nothing pleased Alex more than winning.

But as Alexander bit down on Hephaestion's ring finger, he did so without severing intent. Alex instead nibbled, and he soon pursed his lips and suckled on the end of Hephaestion's finger.

A jolt shot down his spine, paralyzing Hephaestion with sensation. He gasped, face agape while he watched Alexander worship his entire hand with an eager mouth. Soon the two boys collapsed into each other, interested in far more than just fingers and noses, and the horses calmed.

Hephaestion smiled, eyes down, thoughts in a distant place. He would have his Alexander again. Alexander was his Earth, and his thoughts orbited him like the moon. He would hold him again, and his eternity of being incomplete would be over.

"Ho!" cried one of the crew, her raspy voice piercing the din. As soon as her cry hit the ears of her fellow crew, they each tossed their heads back and echoed the call.

Ulfric jumped back on deck within an instant, his eyes keen. "Hepher!" he hollered over all other voices. "Someone speared a whale for you!"

Hephaestion ran and arrived at the port stern just in time to see an enormous, pale man flopped onto the deck.

The man's eyes were red from duress, and his hair had been torn from his head in clumps, ripped out by the fellow damned that drifted

with him. The wheezing and frothing coming from his mouth and nose were a product of his endless gasping, his sudden exposure to solid ground, and the agony of having a barbed spear haul him in. Tall but thick-limbed, the man was so large that his fat moved almost like a separate entity from his skeleton. His body blobbed on the ship's deck, rolling about with each swell, only given shape by his pallid skin. The spear lodged in his midsection, a jagged and clumsy-looking weapon, caused yellow fat and dark blood to pool in its quarry's folds.

Hephaestion did the man a small mercy, and immediately drove a dagger deep into the back of his skull.

The man is perfect!

Hephaestion needed a human being large enough that he himself could fit inside, and that was a rarity among humanity.

"We've got about two days before he revives," he said. "If he heals up faster than that, just be at the ready with a knife."

The surrounding crew nodded, and Ulfric clapped his coarse hands twice. The crew responded by binding their new passenger with thick hauling rope. Several men grunted as they dragged him into the deck's upper cabin.

A tinge of remorse hit Hephaestion, his shoulders and brow lowering involuntarily. It was an imperceptible and unconscious gesture, but nothing slipped past Ulfric.

"See?" Ulfric accused him when the others were out of earshot. "You feel like shit for that. I know *you* know this is an idiotic idea."

"I was quick!" Hephaestion protested. "He won't suffer unduly by my hands. We'll gut him, I'll get myself and my kit inside him, and when he heals up, he'll be right back in the water."

"For you to then wait *how many* decades for him to wash in?"

"You know the docks aren't an option with my face. Someone will spot me before I even get off a boat. Damn it, stop trying to talk me out of this at the last minute!"

While Ulfric had been amazingly supportive in this rescue operation, he'd challenged each of Hephaestion's decisions long after he'd made them. For centuries, Ulfric had quietly, and sometimes *loudly*, urged Hephaestion to stow his longing for Alexander and simply focus on himself. A man should not be stuck in Purgatory for so many centuries, but when it eventually became clear that Hephaestion would not be moving on without Alexander, Ulfric ceded to help in the rescue. In Ulfric's eyes, any direction was best for Hephaestion, regardless of 'up' or 'down.'

Ulfric's posture eased from argumentative to attentive. He remained silent, gently listening.

"He needs me, Ulf. And you know I need *this*. A part of me is down there... and this is the only way I can think of to do this. I'm done waiting. I'm done feeling broken."

Ulfric nodded his understanding, and then hugged Hephaestion tightly. "All right, maybe I'm just being selfish." He clapped both his weathered hands on Hephaestion's shoulders. "Maybe I don't want you to go, and maybe you have a totally different path than I'd hoped for you, but this Trojan horse of yours is a man—a man in there waiting to be gutted by—"

"A glutton, Ulf. The man is a glutton aimed for Hell, and I'm going to piggy-back on him to get down there. Just as I have my own path, he has his." Hephaestion gently pulled away. "And you have yours."

"Don't define people by their sins, Hepher."

"He put himself here, and I'm going to use his horrible choices in life to my ends, to rescue Alex. Yes, it's cruel how I'm going to do it. I know. I do feel bad, all right? I do. But that man is a glutton and he earned a place down there."

"Like Alexander earned his?"

Hephaestion's gaze lost all warmth, and he evaluated Ulfric coolly. Without a word, he turned on his heels, and prepared to set about his savage task of disemboweling the gluttonous man.

CHAPTER 3

"Keep him bound up tight at each limb and pull his arms and legs downward. It'll stretch the torso a bit more," Hephaestion commanded his two assistants. The oil lamps above swung lazily from side to side with the ship, as he gave his gutting blade a last drag on the sharpening stone. The floor was grated to drain out blood and viscera, and Hephaestion hung up his tunic next to the other two already hanging there. As messy as things would get, Hephaestion thought it ideal that he and his assistants be naked for their work.

He paused for a moment and looked at the dead man's blank gaze, his pupils unresponsive to the light dancing in the room. Most people, depending on the severity of their wound, remained dead only for a few days in the afterlife. For some, it was a brief respite in oblivion, a reprieve from suffering or sorrow. Often referred to as 'afterdeath,' Hephaestion had experienced it several times, and always by accident, either while training or rock climbing on the cliffs in Purgatory. Afterdeath was often preferable to dismemberment or severe bone breaks, because at least in afterdeath you were spared the pain of the injury, or worse still, the pain of healing.

He'd sold Ulfric on the idea of using a gluttonous hellbound soul to sneak into Hell.

Ulfric was against it at first, stating, "We aren't demons or torturers, Hepher. You're asking something nasty."

Hephaestion kept at him, though, making the case that the initial pain would be minimal. It took many decades, but he wore Ulfric down.

Reminding himself that the person before him was just meat, Hephaestion cut into the glutton's right side, near the lowest rib, with a

ragged sigh. He drew a deep, bloody smile all the way across the lower belly, sawing through skin, fat, and tissue until striking muscle.

His assistants pulled the opening wide with hooks, and each man was soon standing on top of the quivering body, their bare feet slick. Suddenly, the whole ship lurched. One assistant fell off, the other dug his knee under the chin of the body, and Hephaestion drove his left calf deep into the man's guts.

"Was that another one?" the man on the floor asked, sliding about as he tried to climb the table again.

"Most likely," Hephaestion answered through his teeth, correcting his grip on his knife. "Sometimes the new damned just boil up in big pockets from below."

"Seems to be happening a lot more than expected."

"War...." Hephaestion continued vacantly, continuing his gutting. He was now reaching in under the sternum to slice loose the lungs. "War back on Earth, in Europe, like no war ever seen before—tens of thousands dead every day. They call it the Great War."

"Fucking idiots...."

The three men fell silent as they sliced and severed and scooped the glutton clean, and after many hours' work, his entire midsection consisted of empty skin, a spinal column, and the limp red fist of muscle that was the heart dangling from its arteries.

After dousing themselves clean with buckets of salty water, the two assistants slid their tunics back on and got their cord and needles ready. Each needle was the length of a finger and thick enough to puncture a cured animal hide.

Ulfric wandered in and leaned against the near wall.

Hephaestion was still angry, and tried to ignore him, but there was no avoiding Ulfric's presence. When Ulfric wanted a person's eye contact, he got it.

"Give us a few minutes, if you two would?" Ulfric asked of the men, who at any rate were grateful to stretch their legs and be away from their gory work for a bit. Soon, only Ulfric and Hephaestion remained.

Instead of waiting for Ulfric to speak again, Hephaestion dove in. "I'm insane," he confessed.

"Lord Almighty, you are." Ulfric smirked.

"Trying to reason with me on this is a waste of time, especially now, as we're in the sea with the body right on this table. I'm going down there and I'm getting Alex."

"I know. A part of me hoped we wouldn't find anyone fat and tall enough."

"You underestimate how delinquent people can be with themselves."

"I hate it when you judge people, Hepher."

"You hate it when I judge people more harshly than *you do*."

"Which is *always*."

The two men stared at each other silently, the remaining fat on the glutton gently rolling to and fro with the ship.

"I've got your kit ready to go outside the door, here," Ulfric offered. "But I know I'll hate myself, and always wonder, if I don't make one last plea for you not to do this. Alexander lived a life according to how he wanted, and he is in Hell for it. You followed him and loved him and served him, and somehow that merely got you Purgatory."

"Not all of us just wake up in Heaven, Ulf."

"Yet I choose to hang out in Purgatory helping people like you ascend, because... well, you know my thoughts on Heaven." Ulfric made it regularly clear to anyone within earshot how boring Heaven was. "But if you go down there, and some devils or monstrous people get a hold of you, they might gnaw on you for all eternity. They'll pluck your heart out, stick it in a jar, and you'll never regenerate. You won't think, or remember anything, and only know suffering and imprisonment. Hell, you might get charred into ash and sprinkled to the wind. Maybe something will eat you and shit you out. How long would it take to regenerate from that kind of thing?"

"That's why I'm going as prepared as possible, and I've trained — *we've* trained — for this for decades."

"You might not come back, Hepher."

"I know."

"You're one of the ones worth saving and working with, to get upstairs."

"And I appreciate that. I truly, truly do."

Suddenly a shift in Ulfric's voice filled the cabin with anger. "I wouldn't have done any of this for Alexander the Great."

Hephaestion couldn't meet his friend's eyes, but he felt them burning on him.

"But...." Ulfric's voice eased. "I'd do it for Hephaestion the Good. I'll miss you." The man crossed the room in a blink and smothered Hephaestion in another hug.

"I'll miss you, too, but you'll come and rescue me if Lucifer gets me."

Ulfric's body jerked with a snicker. "Jackass!" He banged on the wall to summon the two men back from outside, then returned to his spot against the wall and let everyone work.

Naked except for leather greaves, Hephaestion strapped the two separate halves of his hoplon shield to his back, a compact and collapsible design from Ulfric. In the center of the shield was the simple design of a heart—he felt it fitting that when the shield was whole, the heart was also whole.

Next came the three parts of Hephaestion's dory spear. Each spear segment would screw in to the next, turning three two-foot sections into a six-foot-tall thrusting weapon.

Hephaestion curled into a face-down fetal ball, head in the glutton's pelvis, and placed the spear portions between his knees along his host's spine. While gruesome, he maintained his perspective by recalling that he'd done many horrible things to many horrible people, and this was not a singular occurrence. This body provided a means to an end, and through it he would reach his first goal.

Elbows and knees in tight, he took deep gasping breaths, knowing that it would be the last time he would taste air for a possible eternity.

"I'm ready! Sew me up!"

The assistants went about their work.

"Remember, Hepher," Ulfric said. "If you do get through, and get your man, you head downward. Just keep going until everything is frozen, farthest from the light of Heaven. Find the Devil's Spine. Get through there, be worthy, and once out, you'll see the first two stars man ever saw. Look for *those stars*."

Hephaestion nodded as best he could. Soon the loose skin lay over him, slapping against his bare, arched back. The men stitched furiously and swore, but sound became more muffled to Hephaestion's ears.

The work was done. The glutton would regenerate, but with Hephaestion in the way his lungs and intestines would grow back malformed and entangling, creating a terrible mess.

To Hephaestion's benefit, however, was the simple fact that without air, he would drift into a death-like dream state. It wasn't uncommon that when a soul wanted to recede into oblivion, they would hang themselves from a tree in Purgatory, a chiseled stone often nearby asking passersby not to cut them down. Hephaestion hoped it would be a place where he could dream, adrift inside a warm body in an ocean of wretches.

He heard muffled grunts and shouts, and felt the body being tugged at and rolled about by rope and pulley. He ran his fingers along the wooden shafts of his dory, imagining how glorious it would feel to drive its piercing edge into the heart of whatever beast tormented Alexander. There was no power greater in Earth's history than a Greek and his spear.

The ropes twanged and the pulley's arm creaked.

After so many centuries pining, and so many decades planning, it all came down to this moment. What if the seams tore? What if Minos detected something was amiss while judging the glutton? What if the man he hid within had committed greater crimes than gluttony, and was sent elsewhere? What if the man was a suicide? A suicide would circumvent Minos's judgment altogether and be cast down into the forest to sprout into a red tree. If that happened, would Hephaestion spend an eternity encased in bleeding bark and moaning wood?

Yet he could not turn back, and calmed himself once again by thinking of Alexander's laugh, his vibrant eyes, and his sandy-blond hair. He thought of them both riding Bucephalus together, as they led 35,000 Grecians marching across Achaemenidian fields of wild flowers, the huge horse sniffing at the blossoms casually, its powerful weight shifting between their knees.

Rocking back and forth as he was lowered down the side of the *Bonny Sweetheart*, Hephaestion tried to reach a peaceful state of mind.

The cries and screams and gargling coughs grew louder and louder.

Clawing fingers tugged at the glutton, and Hephaestion felt like a morsel being lowered to starved dogs.

Alexander's laugh grew silent in the mayhem.

Gravity eased, and water began to seep in through the stitching. Howls and cries and lamentation rose all around him, and Hephaestion tried his best to close it out, but it filled him with terror. The battering eased as the water engulfed him, and soon everything was submerged.

He despised the sensation of drowning—a helpless kind of death. No matter how hard one tried to remain dignified while doing it, the soul's body refused to go easily. Ulfric had run him through, bashed his head in, and sliced him up during their training sessions, to prepare him for this journey. With each death, his earthly life felt farther away.

Drowning was still the worst. No human in the afterlife truly needed food, air, or sleep, but very few conquered their need of *any* of them, and rarely did a person conquer all three. Food and sleep were relatively simple, but the lung's desire for air was so primordially anchored in the soul, it was by far the most difficult to overcome.

He'd spent decades developing the discipline to suppress his need for air, but it was always a brutal challenge. With convulsions, the salty water ran into his nose and slithered down his throat into his burning lungs. He clutched his dory as tightly as possible, desperately trying to remember that a Grecian with his spear can and *will* shape the world.

That was his last cohesive thought before blacking out into suspended oblivion, awash in the sea of angry and terrified condemned.

CHAPTER
4

Hephaestion dreamt—if that's what it could be called during death—about the cruel and white-tipped swells of the Hydaspes, a river as far East as any Greek had ever ventured. Its rippling current had claimed wagons, carts, horses, livestock, and men.

All those centuries ago, tasked yet again to find a way across another brutal river, he sat on its bank and stared into its hypnotic swirl. His ears filled with the long, sustained note of the river's rushing rumble, occasionally punctuated by the staccato of mallets that drove stakes into the ground around him.

Teams of men dragged ferryboats, wide and flat on the bottom, through cleared paths in the forest behind him, all the while singing a song of back-bending motivation.

Hephaestion had ordered the construction of several long, slender docks, so the boats could load quickly before launching. This gave the enemy less time to react in the event they spotted Alexander's army crossing the river. The idea was to get as many hoplite and cavalry across the Hydaspes as possible, and flank the enemy's ranged troops guarding the far bank to the north, where the bulk of their army resided.

For Alexander to directly charge the river here with his Companions would mean absolute death. The water to the north was more shallow, however, and the heavy cavalry was making a good show of trying to attempt to cross without endangering the men, in order to keep the Punjabi army occupied. If King Porus and his slingers expected an attack from the south, Hephaestion's ferryboats wouldn't

get their divisions of foot soldiers, phalanx, and light cavalry across for Alexander to lead into the enemy.

Hephaestion, not a strong military tactician, had always been slow with making decisions, and Alexander had often critiqued his technique as being far too conservative for large-scale battle. Nonetheless, Hephaestion was a logistical master, and no one else could haul twelve ferry-boats across seventy miles of land and trees in two weeks. The enemy had no idea, and didn't fathom such a river crossing possible, since the mouth of the river and the bends farther to the south had villages that never spied so much as a Grecian oar in their waters.

While Alexander provided the ideas and the battle plans, Hephaestion provided the support.

Everyone had received their instructions, and Hephaestion had trained and prepared his underlings so minutely that they carried out their duties while he simply sat back and watched the river taunt him.

The men used pulleys and rope to raise the boats closest to the water's edge onto thick tree trunks, from trees felled in the night. They wheeled hot cauldrons of oil from their fires, and sailors smeared it under each ship's belly to glide them out into the water with greater ease.

They'd built the docks themselves only this morning, each section previously assembled to exact specifications. Their hasty construction had been a gamble, but to not move quickly would have ended the India Campaign's prospects definitively.

Several men, waist deep in white water and bound by safety cords under their arms, adjusted and positioned the posts for the docks. One of the posts started to buckle, and several men cried out for help.

Hephaestion, up and running in a single motion, ran into the river. He high-stepped as deep as he could, and then proceeded at a full swim. Someone threw him an encircled cord, and he frantically wrangled himself into it. He reached the dock's weakening spot and added his shoulder to the others.

The men held fast. One man's head had sunk beneath the water line but his hands still held firm.

Hephaestion was concerned for the man's safety, but also moved by his dedication.

More men came barreling into the water to help. They clung to each other and called reassurances to their companions as the whole body of men began pushing the dock into a more stable position.

The songs from the bank changed rhythm, and the gathering crowd chanted music of empowerment in unison. A surge went through the water-logged men and the dock straightened. A cheer went out, but was quickly hushed by prudent reminders from the sergeants. Men with reinforcing stakes bundled to their backs waded into the water with teams of divers to aid in the dock's repair.

Hephaestion stayed and held his portion of the dock for over an hour, until it had become steady. He was nearly the last man to let go, but due to the exhaustion, the cold, and the joint lock, his body simply didn't respond to his brain, and he fell limp into the current.

Water flew up his nose and into his throat, and everything turned to a muffled, frigid white. He possessed no power, his limbs worthless as they flopped about like loose cloth from his body.

He couldn't tell if the current was dragging him down river or carrying him into another dock. If the latter, his head would surely crack open upon impacting a post at the speed the river moved. Hephaestion was too exhausted to care at that point.

"Patty!" he heard. "*Patty!*" And suddenly the sky appeared.

Several men had caught him by the cord, one of which was Alexander, and they hauled him to slower, shallow waters.

Alexander beamed down at him, a wide hand over Hephaestion's heart. "You know, I told you I'd take you swimming when we get to Shahar, but *no*... you just couldn't be patient."

They dragged Hephaestion out of the river, his lungs containing more water than air, and pounded his back as he lay on his side. Alexander ordered a fire for him, and Hephaestion sat huddled with several other waterlogged men to watch the rest of his work unfold. Alexander himself brought blankets and hot sideritis tea.

They sipped tea in silence, as Alexander gently rubbed Hephaestion's back, giving warmth. The other recovering men kept to themselves, in order to give their leaders a moment.

"Thought I lost you there. No more being a hero," Alexander whispered into Hephaestion's ear.

"You charge first into every cavalry advance, and you want *me* to not be a hero?" Hephaestion croaked, his voice quivering as he suppressed a coughing fit.

"I'll be a hero enough for both of us. If I die, the army mourns. If *you* die, the army crumbles and no one gets home." Alexander tilted his head onto Hephaestion's shoulder and sighed. "Just be careful, all

right? I don't want to worry about you more than I already do. We all need you. *I* need you."

Hephaestion snickered. "Is that why you gave me the Companions?"

"They're the best, and they all have standing orders to sit on you if you're under threat."

"Fucker," Hephaestion said, playfully nudging Alexander in the ribs.

"This is brilliant, Patty." Alexander presented the docks and longboats with a sweeping hand.

The nickname 'Patty' had been Hephaestion's since their visit at Troy. Alexander was certain of his lineage to Achilles, and therefore he surmised that Hephaestion was his Patroclus.

"These boats will *glide* across the water," Alexander said. "This time tomorrow, we'll order the Heavies North and cross here."

The battle that came the following day was a brutal one, and Alexander suffered great losses, but still they emerged victorious.

While soldiers buried their dead and wept from the adrenaline withdrawal, Hephaestion was still coughing the last of the river from inside his chest. The river's ensnarement, however recent, already haunted Hephaestion. Perhaps it always would.

CHAPTER 5

Yitzhak Isserles avoided making eye-contact with Prior Albrecht. Yitzhak didn't fear or particularly dislike the man, he just thought Albrecht could *talk*, and Yitzhak wanted a quiet day of spectating and gambling without a constant stream of repeated nonsense pouring into his ear.

Alas, it wasn't to be. Despite getting to the bidding ring early, and his red leather wingback chair half-hiding him, the awkward and socially inept Albrecht still spotted him.

"What a good day to you!" the prior began.

Yitz pretended not to hear, but a chubby hand landed on his shoulder.

"What a good day to you!" the prior persisted.

"Oh, hello Albrecht." Yitz kept his gaze transfixed on the wagering paddle in his hands—a tall stick with an icon of a dove on each of the broad, flat sides.

"Lovely weather!" the prior spouted for the infinitieth time as he took his seat next to Yitzhak. He seemed to love that particular joke. Hell's sky remained the same in perpetuity, a dark, swirling bleakness that seemed to hang so low you could reach up and touch it.

The two men had paid a substantial sum for the privileges of their view, but not because of the ashen sky. A tall, stadium-angled ring had been constructed of black volcanic rock, and each seat faced toward its center. Yitz's chair was not as costly as those closer to the action, but it still cost several lifetimes' worth of prudently-earned income to afford.

His wife, Adina, had given him an earful about his gambling pastime yet again this morning. He'd never thought of a proper rebuttal for her, whenever they had a spat, partly because she was far more articulate, but also because, in the corners of his heart, he was a tiny bit afraid of her.

A pang of regret hit him. He'd left Adina at the craftsman's market to come and lay his wages, and now sat stuck next to this annoying man. She'd wanted him to skip out of the day's sin, but Yitz had sulked and pouted in his usual manner, and in the end, after a terse confrontation, he got his way. This gambling event occurred only four times a year, and during the days in between he thrilled at the thought of it.

The point of this gambling event was fairly simple: guess the sin of the sinner before Minos passed down his judgment of them. A freshly damned soul is dragged before the court below, after which everyone cranes their necks in their chairs, and then shouts their bets with their icons raised. Sometimes, as an example, what might appear to be a murderous soul is, in fact, a sexual predator, and the promissory notes change hands quickly, before the next sinner is presented.

"I wonder what we'll see today!" Albrecht babbled, murdering any chance of silence. "Do you think we'll see some sinners?"

"That... was that actually a question?" Yitz replied, so dumbfounded that he was lulled into eye contact with the buffoon.

"Well, certainly. Do you think we'll see some sinners? Well, not just sinners, but *proper* sinners that will run the pens dry? Someone truly evil from the war that's ending all war, or maybe a king skewered by his own people? I always enjoy those. Remember when Tellamore jumped out of his seat because he recognized King Stephon's great grandson? Oh, the wagers that flew in those few minutes! I made a fortune!"

Prior Albrecht had. Once everyone knew that the King of Hungaria's descendant stood before Minos for his tormental judgment in Hell, the entire betting circle had erupted. Dozens of gamblers surged out of their chairs, waving their wagering icons and placing their money. Most claimed he was going to boil in the currents of Phlegethon for murder, and some others placed bets on him being a false council, earning him a place in the frigid wastelands of lowest Hell.

As legend had it, Prior Albrecht had detected something the others didn't in the man. Apparently, Prior Albrecht sensed heartbreak and obsession.

"Lust!" the prior had screeched, waving his icon above his head, arm outstretched like a child eager to be called upon in catechism. His wager, which had been every pebble of wealth he possessed, was scribbled down by The Peruvian's men. And sure enough, Minos delivered the very judgment Albrecht had anticipated.

"Yes," Yitz replied dryly, fidgeting with his yarmulke on his head. "Given that this is Hell, and we're going to watch sinners being brought in one at a time for judgments, I think we'll see a few sinners."

"Big ones? Like country-ruining sinners? Traitors of family? I always like those. They cry the most, especially those that sexually prey on their nephews and nieces. So remorseful... as if it matters!" Albrecht beamed, Yitz's sarcasm seemingly lost to him.

The man's desire to constantly talk still baffled Yitz. The prior could afford a better seat, one closer to the judgments, but for some reason he stayed put. Yitz wondered if his own seat was so cheap because of it.

He committed to apologizing to his wife when he got home.

Later.

He looked down into the stadium's center and examined the giant, closed iris that sealed away the judgment chamber below. Within it, currently beyond sight, waited Minos. The creature looked like a long dinosaur, fashioned almost entirely out of spiny limbs, with a huge, coiled tail. Its hundreds of arms each held quills firmly within a claw at the end, and the quills' feathered ends squiggled furiously as each sin and transgression was recorded. After each soul had been thoroughly categorized, Minos reached a final calculation that condemned a sinner to their eternity.

At regular intervals, a naked body was dragged by metal meat hooks before Minos, fresh from the sea of tears. Two large, monstrous-looking men did this, acting as ushers, and they wickedly adored their task. Minos would then bend its long, rigid head down, and with its giant milky eyes and pale skin, sniff the person over. Sometimes, Minos would even give the subject a poke or two with one of its many claws.

Finally, the beast's tail would coil several times, indicating which circle of Hell the subject would be condemned to. The various scribbling hands, each with an apparent mind of their own, would talc their parchments to dry the ink, and file everything away as they dragged in the next subject.

This happened always and unendingly, but the actual bidding would be overseen by The Peruvian, and nobody dared place a bid

without his consent and oversight. Ever. When he sat in the highest chair at the farthest spot on the rim of the circle, he did so not to watch the sinners before judgment, but the gamblers at his feet.

The Peruvian would be arriving soon, and Yitz knew that he had to come away with a decent haul today. New Dis was an expensive place to live in comfort, and he wanted the best for himself and Adina as they waited for their son to finish his time in the pit.

...Assuming he ever would.

With his ear growing hotter from the prior's yammering, Yitz continued to nod vacantly while each chair filled. One could learn a lot from each spectator simply by examining their choice of chair. Some chairs were simple and unassuming, while others were lavish and built to be as thrones. Several people, enamored that they could afford a seat closer to the action, used chairs with tall backs with the intention of blocking the views of their rival gamblers. It had essentially evolved into an arms race of sorts, each chair its own vain, sovereign nation asserting itself within the pack.

Finally, the Peruvian arrived with his entourage of intimidating manservants. They were small men, and narrow of shoulder, but each carried an assortment of bindings and blades designed to subdue or tear down anyone who hesitated to pay their due. Rumor had it that the Peruvian employed several dozen such men, each wearing the same red, puffy-cheeked cherub masks, and that they took shifts skinning those delinquent in their payments back in his villa. Some whispered that the Peruvian draped entire rooms in the skins of unfortunate gamblers, and that he kept those subjects chained up, patiently waiting for their skin to grow back, so he could continue to furnish his home in new couches and shoji screens. Apparently, he employed an architect from the ancient Indus civilization to shape the walls of the room like a tall bowl, in order to channel and pipe the victim's screams throughout the palatial home as evening music.

Yitz wasn't as disturbed by such violent thoughts as most, partly due to his wife. Even the Peruvian could be persuaded by her particular skillset and power, but the thought of Adina rescuing him from a chained dungeon made his guilt swell to the surface again.

He swallowed hard, trying to validate his childish tantrum in the market. The money was for his family—wife and prodigal son—not for his love of gambling.

The chairs were now filled and the crowd buzzed with anticipation of the day's wagers. The Peruvian sat high in his throne on the outer

rim of the bettors' circle, sipped a nameless wine from an Aegean decanter, and pulled the long lever next to his throne.

The iris yawned open, its ancient gears screeching, and below stood Minos and its flurry of quills, scribbling away as a bloody and whimpering woman received her judgment. The ushers, their hooks still skewered through her ankles, dragged her away to her fate while she wept—all her misery and sin laid bare.

Yitz hated that moment every time. Still, this remained the best place in all of New Dis to make a fortune, gambling the only way to make money without being the direct subject of another. Employment contracts in New Dis were not for the faint of heart.

Next came the first official bet of the day. It proved a disappointment, because the man dragged before Minos was so extraordinarily fat and misshapen that he required three ushers.

"Gluttony... no one is going to be placing bets on this one," Albrecht uttered.

Yitz was inclined to agree, fumbling his icon in his hands.

They dragged the bulbous man to the same spot as all the others—a rancid spot wet with tears, blood, and sorrow. The ushers groaned under their jagged steel masks, straightening themselves to their full, towering height. They were gladiatorial-looking, beastly men, twisted with tusked teeth, possessing hulking shoulders like buffalo. Over time, as with all other locals of the afterlife, self-perception gradually altered outward appearance. These men saw themselves as brutish monsters, and they gradually became as much during the course of thousands of years.

Minos's quills furiously scratched on their parchments as he bowed down his head and eyed the fat, seizuring man. Something seemed off. Something was wrong.

One of the ushers kicked the man's midsection, and the sinner spewed foam from his nose and mouth. His belly moved independently, as though he were pregnant with a rambunctious fetus.

Yitz cocked an eyebrow.

Albrecht's face lit up with excitement.

And then, proverbially, all hell broke loose.

CHAPTER 6

Hephaestion, jolted awake by the usher's ferocious kick, knew he had been made. Through clenched teeth, he permitted himself a sputtering moment to curse himself for his plan failing. Guttural grunts and snorts conversed from outside his host, and he knew that, whoever they were, they'd gotten curious about the misshapen belly.

A foot poked his back.

The flat of a metal weapon slapped against his left shoulder.

With eyes clenched tightly, Hephaestion steadied his senses as best he could as he held the remaining un-drained water in his lungs. It sloshed inside him maddeningly, but the last thing he needed now was to break into convulsions from coughing it out.

He listened to the steps of one shuffling about near his head, and the other two seemed to be making conversation of some kind below his feet on the opposite side. Suddenly, the body was rolled over, belly exposed to the air, and Hephaestion found his sense of direction seriously disoriented. He knew that any intense light would blind him, so he had to make the most of his first blind strike.

Working his fingers furiously, Hephaestion fumbled with the bladed end of his segmented spear shaft and shoved the other two segments away, intending to use the spear tip as a close-range stabbing weapon. He hoped the collapsed shield on his back might provide limited protection, but it would be of no use against a well-armed assailant in front of him.

They grew louder, and he heard a metal *thwack* against the head of his host. He could wait no longer, and decided to lash out at the two

enemies that were closest together. Hopefully, he would at least injure one of them, or perhaps even make them fall into each other.

He exploded in an upward shove and jutted himself to his full height, spear point first as he pierced his way out of his host's belly. Stabbing wildly, his eyes clenched shut against the torchlight, he swung and twisted his spearhead about, and felt it snag and bite into someone's legs.

Shouts of alarm went up, but not only among the three enemies around him. It sounded like an entire crowd suddenly roared.

He had to move immediately, so Hephaestion rolled out of the slick gore that had encased him, bloody and awkward like a newborn calf. He tumbled to his knees, head down, with his ears open and hands shaking, and his chest could take no more. The sea water erupted from him violently, bending him in half on the cold railing.

He heard a foot land—just one—near him, and recognized it as the footfall right before a downward strike. He presumed the arc would most likely be high, guessing that these weren't trained fighters, so he scrambled up and jabbed with his truncated spear. The tip caught into something's belly. He lifted with his legs, stood himself up halfway, and drove his weapon up into a rib cage and through the gurgling of a heaving sternum, and with a twist, he cracked open their chest. As the body slumped against him, he realized their inhuman bulk. These people were *huge*.

The other two moved at the same time, fanning out behind him, and he returned to a crouching position, still coughing. His legs still couldn't manage his entire weight yet.

Hephaestion hazarded opening one eye, and peered about to give his brain a moment's picture.

Two hulks lumbered toward him—armored 'men,' if the word could be applied liberally.

But there was something else, something long and primal, possibly a creature of ancient myth. Hephaestion's atrophied eye could only handle a glimpse, but it looked like a giant winged beast or sea monster that Ulfric would occasionally sing drunken songs about.

Hephaestion knew what it was, and realized he might have been exposed in the absolute worst place he could imagine.

The two men flanked him and charged rapidly.

Hephaestion picked the nearest and less massive of the two, and sprung for him the moment he'd come within range. He collided into him like a meteor and drove his spear into the man's throat. He then

scrambled up onto his target, his heels driving down and inward into the beastly man's hips, and dug his blade around while leaning high over his enemy's head, brought him up slightly, and drove him down backward with a bloody and frothy thump.

While doing so, Hephaestion felt a jagged blade drive into his lower back near his spine, the jolt of the impact driving a gasp from him. Vise-like fingers closed in around his shoulder, but luckily the remains of his host's gore allowed him to slip free. As the giant pawed at him futilely, Hephaestion shoved himself downward and under his groping enemy. With both hands gripping the dory, knuckles white and teeth grinding, Hephaestion stabbed rapidly and repeatedly upward into the giant's torso. The usher groaned and buckled under its weight, nearly pinning Hephaestion as he scurried away.

His enemies dead, Hephaestion brought himself to his full height as best he could.

Four bodies lay splayed about on the floor, one face-down in his entrails, another with his chest cracked open, and a third with his throat open. A fourth body, the one of his host, looked like a deflated meat sack, moaning and coughing up sea water.

Hephaestion stood naked, bloody and covered in grime, his shoulders slumped in exhaustion as he finally opened his lungs for full breaths.

Minos stood over the whole scene, ancient and primal, the entire scene reflecting in its tiny, dead-white eyes. It leaned in, teeth peeking from its closed jaws, and examined him with its nostrils wide in curiosity. A thousand quills remained still in its army of hands.

Hephaestion had hoped to avoid Minos's gaze and get beyond into the pit, but plans occasionally go awry in Hell, as they do on Earth.

The shouting noise of a crowd didn't seem as distant anymore, and Hephaestion chanced a glance upward. Men of all time periods and nations stood waving small paddles with icons on them: a star, a castle, a sword, a rabbit, a crescent moon....

Yitz gazed about at the gamblers, who now stood on the ground or on the cushions of their chairs, shouting their wagers to the Peruvian's men.

"He's a Satan worshiper," one yelled, "trying to sneak into Hell! Minos will send him to the Malebolge! I pledge an eighth!"

It was the highest bet placed in years, an eighth of a talent a huge sum.

"One fourth! I place a fourth on him being a betrayer!" came a rebuttal. "He's avoiding the lake! One fourth!"

The bids escalated as the men wagered that Hephaestion was either a slayer of men gone completely mad, or a human so vile that he was trying to cheat the fires of Hell itself, even in the afterlife. One man even wagered that Hephaestion would attack Minos directly.

Only two men remained calm in the entire crowd. They looked down at Hephaestion wide-eyed amid the hollering din of their peers.

Yitz turned to Albrecht, and saw that he was thinking the same thing.

Albrecht nodded knowingly, for once not using an avalanche of words to express his thoughts.

Time was running out as Minos's quills erupted in activity, recording all sins.

Yitz and Albrecht raised their icons together, having both recognized something in Hephaestion. He was too calm and controlled to have come here carelessly, and both men quickly deduced that to sneak into the body of another, armed with a blade and a collapsed shield of some kind, took not only extraordinary will but also logistics and vision.

No casual sinner, this man—he had purpose and intentions. He had a mission.

"Hey!" Albrecht shouted, and a nearby manservant heard him.

Yitz saw the Peruvian cock an eyebrow.

"He's not the damned!" Albrecht continued. "He isn't condemned! Yitz and I wager... *two talents*!"

Everyone turned their way, jaws dropped and eyes wide. Nobody knew if the two men could be good for that much, even if they had an eternity to earn it.

Yitz's mouth went dry as the prior, the insecure and rambling prior, was suddenly in his element and confident. Yitz inched closer to him, hoping that his presence would shield him from the Peruvian's gaze.

The only sound pervading this new silence was the scratch of old quill tips, and everyone turned their eyes downward again. Minos's hands flew in a flurry, papers crinkling and talc sifting.

Hephaestion stood as a stone, shoulders low, head forward, still trying to decide whether to strike or run. His breathing became labored and intense, as his strength drained from the seeping wound in his lower back.

Yet as he gazed about in preparation to choose between his two options, it became clear he had to do neither.

The papers were filed, the pens dipped for the next person, but the tail did *not* coil. With no ushers up to drag him away, the man below staggered on wobbly knees as he gathered up his leather-bound satchel and spear fragments from his host's innards, and found his way out through a steel-riveted side door. Clearly, this man didn't register as being Hellbound at all.

Minos tapped a hundred fingers patiently for more beastly ushers to arrive with another subject.

No cheers rose... not a peep came from anyone.

Yitz didn't dare turn around and look his fellow gamblers in the eye. His fingers instinctively tugged at the prior's robes like a frightened child.

"Albrecht!" he pleaded out of the side of his mouth. "We might have been better off if we had lost!"

Oblivious of the danger, Prior Albrecht spun about with an enormous grin on his face. With a holler of triumph, he raised his hands toward the Peruvian with glee, his round chin jiggling with joy.

The Peruvian's eyebrow was no longer cocked.

"We thank you all!" shouted Albrecht. "What an amazing day! We'll retire for now, but see you next time! Be well, and go with God!" Albrecht proclaimed.

Like a baby elephant clinging to its mother's tail, Yitz gripped the prior's robe as they bobbed and weaved, between each chair and dumbfounded individual, to the door.

CHAPTER 7

Albrecht smiled, feeling lighter than he'd felt for a long time.

"We're going to die! *A lot!*" Yitz practically screamed.

They cleared the exit door into a cobblestone alley. All the spectators took this path, its center worn down into a smooth and gradual depression from centuries of shuffling boots and sandals. Lit by bright, dripping torches, the shadows of the two men danced wildly about in excitement.

"Relax." Albrecht laid his hand on Yitz's shoulder. "You've just made a fortune equivalent to the Peruvian himself. Nations don't have that kind of wealth back on Earth. Your only concern now should really be how to store and manage several tons of gold."

"I would feel much better if we just got out of here and headed toward the market before the Peruvian decides to skin us for eternity and keep the money for himself."

"Don't worry about him. He'll be fine after this." Albrecht casually strolled forward, a song in his voice. "When people all over New Dis hear that the largest wager in human history just occurred under his establishment, he'll never be for want again. He can charge anything for those seats now."

"And what about our cohorts? Our contemporaries? They'll want their money back from us after it filters through the Peruvian, hmmm? What, you don't think we aren't in danger of getting our hearts minced and ground into meal? I have a wife. I have a son. I've never met my great-great-grandchildren!"

Yitz bordered on hysterics, huffing, his eyes pained and his hands fumbling about Albrecht's collar.

Albrecht smiled knowingly, and was about to offer comfort, but the door they'd just exited slid open, and into the torchlight came the man who'd indirectly made them so rich.

The man slouched, leaned a shoulder against the wall, and feebly motioned for them to step aside, to which both men did as commanded.

Albrecht stood in awe of the wounded warrior. Up close, he could see his skin pulled taut against his skull, his eyes sunken from what might have been years of being adrift inside the body of that bulbous glutton. This man was barely hanging on, and his satchel hung loosely in his hands, his adrenaline having now burned away.

His feet plopped forward, one at a time, each step a shaky victory as he winced from each rasping inhalation. From under his blood-soaked hair and gore-plastered face, the man's vibrant eyes stood wide, fixed in the distance.

Albrecht and Yitz watched him closely as he transcended the alleyway heading toward the main avenue.

"He's not going to last," Albrecht whispered.

Yitz didn't know what to say. Clearly, this man had brought himself here of his own choosing, and hadn't been condemned to Hell. He may have been a good sort, even—a man of Heaven—so why the charade of attempting to sneak past Minos?

"So?" Yitz finally found his words. "Damned or not, he's doing something he most likely *shouldn't*. I get in enough trouble without anyone else's help!"

From behind the door came a snarl and an indecipherable shout.

"Ushers," Albrecht gasped. "I'll stall them. You go get our man to safety!"

"*Our* man?" Yitz hissed, trying to keep his voice low.

There was no steering Albrecht away, however, and the prior swung the door open and bolted inside. Through the door, Yitz could hear his aggravating ally's voice yammering away in an effort to distract the brutes.

The strange warrior had almost reached the alley, his leather satchel on the ground behind him, his spear tip dragging against the worn stone as it dangled loosely in his limp hand.

Yitz sighed and shook his head.

I could just walk away... collect my share... cite the laws of New Dis... take anyone resisting their payments to the Peruvian. I could drag any others indebted to me to court, or even to Sun Tzu, if the Peruvian himself couldn't persuade them to pay up.

Yitz had been waiting for this — the ultimate score. With this fortune, he and Adina could wait out their son's damnation in comfort and security. He would now be a legend among any gambling man or woman who ever walked in the afterlife.

He knew the smart thing to do — the prudent thing, the correct thing. Instead, he lifted the man's one free arm by the wrist, and hoisted the man to his feet from the wall. Though thin and weathered, the man still had enough meat on him to make Yitz groan.

"Hey!" he snapped, shaking the floppy man. "Hey, we have to move. Now! More of those Ushers are coming."

Just as Yitz dragged the man out of the alleyway into the avenue, the exit door in the distance burst open. Three well adorned men poured out, each a wealthy spectator that Yitz knew vaguely, and they pointed at him.

They snarled, shouted, and gave chase.

"Move!" Yitz pleaded, dragging the man's toes. The avenue was alive at this time of day, filled with steam-powered carriages and wandering crowds as they moved about the buildings. The structures of New Dis mirrored those of all civilizations and time periods: a Deutsch mortar and stone storefront here; a wide Chinese opera house there; all towered over by an ivory Egyptian obelisk. The older the structure, the more it influenced the renovations of the buildings around them, creating odd, mutant evolutions in architecture: a Sri Lankan hut not made of wood, but sandstone and red iron; a Buddhist Temple with gothic gargoyles.

Ahead lay an Arabic bazaar with alabaster Greek fountains, exactly where Yitz was headed with his limp cargo.

Wearing the warrior like a backpack, a weary arm over each of his shoulders, Yitz charged forward through the busy street of grumbling steam cars and bustling crowds. The wealthy and powerful of New Dis traveled with flamboyant entourages, which Yitz was especially careful to avoid. Bodyguards were brutal, and they would disembowel a stray soul that wandered too close, simply out of precaution.

Brushing against people rudely, Yitz profusely apologized in a frantic mantra to everyone in his path. A metal *clang* rang out near his

feet as his cargo finally lost all consciousness, the man's spear slipping free of his fingers.

The men behind them shouted out that they'd been victims of a thief.

"Stop the Jew!" one screeched. "With the dead man!"

Yitz felt eyes training on him as he reached the far side of the road and shoved his way through the bazaar's polished brass gate.

The refreshing tinkle of water and pluck of a harp greeted all those who entered. Well-clothed men, women, and indentured servants wandered about selecting pottery, painting supplies, and fabric. Some held the goods to the electric lamplight for examination, their fingers evaluating quality and durability.

"Adina!" Yitz pleaded into the crowd, heads turning to him. "*Adina!*" His voice silenced the harp and echoed into the pools of the fountains.

The men were right behind him now, crossing into the bazaar through the gate.

The crowd parted and Yitz saw her — Adina, his lovely and passionate Adina. She was slight of frame with eyes a little too close together and an unflattering overbite. She kept her dark, rambunctious hair bound in a humble tichel, and it flopped over her shoulder when she spun to face the commotion.

Yitz was grateful, on rare occasions such as these, that Adina was always ready for a fight.

Everyone ran behind a cart or flattened themselves into the cobblestone.

Yitz rolled with his new companion into a fountain, and dove underwater.

Adina's eyes alighted like a pyre as she spotted the three men charging into the bazaar, daggers and pistols drawn. She summoned her power to its full apex.

The three men, clearly comprehending the impending horror from the distant, lone woman, turned on their heels to flee. But there was no fleeing the searing slivers of burning salt from the flame-wreathed hands of a furious Jewess protecting her husband.

With precision, three long lances of white crystal fire sizzled through the air and impaled each of the men, careening them off their feet. One smacked into the gate, and the other two smashed to the ground. With limbs flailing, they flopped about hollering for mercy and quick deaths as their clothing burst into flame and their innards cooked from the Heavenly heat.

Few from the crowd chanced looking at the bright demise of the men, their bodies gradually disintegrating into little more than charred bone and evaporated viscera.

Adina walked casually up to her gory handiwork, frowned one of her infamous and wilting frowns, then drove her hands into the nearest fountain in an effort to cool them off in a gust of steam.

Yitz lurched up into the air at that moment, water splashing and his yarmulke dangling from his disheveled hair.

"Hello, husband," Adina said with poorly masked frustration, Yitz unworthy of her direct eye contact.

"It wasn't for me. It wasn't me! I didn't do it!"

"Mmmhmmm."

"It was *this* man." Yitz lifted his charge as best he could, clumsily flopping the Grecian over the pool's lip.

Adina's eyes narrowed on the unconscious man, his naked skin stretched thin over his starved muscle. Despite the impromptu washing, his wounds made themselves apparent again with their continued bleeding.

She conceded reluctantly, huffing a sigh that blew her loose bangs about. "You'd best carry him home, at least."

CHAPTER 8

Hephaestion woke with his skin feeling fresh and his nostrils delighted by an enticing fragrance. Suppressing the impulse to jolt upright, he continued to play unconscious. Through a barely cracked eyelid, he scanned the tiny room in which he was bedded, and found it warm and vibrant with draped silks, spools of delicate brass chains, and dimly burning oil lamps dangling from the low ceiling. His mattress was small but generously feathered, and though his feet dangled off the end, it was still the most physical comfort he could recall since his straw cot back in Ulfric's mead hall.

Searching his fuzzy recent memory, Hephaestion immediately thought of the man that saved him—a tiny man with a trimmed beard who'd tried to carry him through the street—and figured this must be the man's home.

With a sob of relief, he enclosed his face with his hands, for he'd known that the mission of sneaking past Minos would be a long shot. Everyone had told him he would meet his doom. Ulfric had given warning after warning, implying for Hephaestion to simply 'let *go*' and move on with his afterlife. The Ushers could have ripped out Hephaestion's heart and hidden it away in a jar for an eternity of stifling pain and suffering.

Yet here he was, warm and safe, able to collect his thoughts among sweet-smelling linens. He'd gotten this far, and the risks had been worth it. Even if they'd slaughtered him on the spot, the risks would have still been worth it. He'd completed only the first step, and had reached the rim of Hell, in New Dis somewhere, and he still had a chance of getting to Alexander.

But how? And why? Why did Minos let me pass? Who was it that helped me get clear of Minos's court? Will I owe them now? Am I indebted? Indentured? Do they have my satchel and spear?

A red door next to his bed was close enough for him to touch, and through it, muffled voices conversed. Hephaestion slipped his crisp linens off and struggled to sit upright, his feet sinking into a thick wool carpet. His toes, engulfed by its welcoming touch, tingled with limited feeling. Lacking the strength to stand, he merely leaned his forehead forward against the center of the nearby door to listen.

"And then what happened?" he heard a stern woman's voice calmly demand.

"We won. Albrecht called it," a man's voice calmly answered. "He made it all happen. He and I were thinking the same thing, but I was too scared to wager alone. But we won, and then we ran." It was clear from the inflections that the two knew each other and were close, perhaps husband and wife.

"The Peruvian will still honor the winnings," she replied. "He always does. So, when did Tellamore and his ilk start chasing after you?"

"As soon as I grabbed the crazy man."

Hephaestion found the energy for a smirk; Ulfric would agree with the male voice's assertion of his madness.

"It makes sense that they would chase you," she said.

"Ha! You think?"

"Yes, I've learned that *one* of us has to, at least!" Her voice escalated. "They were most likely fleeing the Peruvian because, thanks to you, they owed him more than they could pay. When they *saw* you, they decided to save face. Think about it, there's no way they could casually walk out of there without securing their payments through him. Who leaves Minos's court early when he's presiding over the wagers? Nobody! Whenever *you* go there, you're gone all day. Those men were fleeing, they saw you, and just gave chase because they are dumb and angry *men*. If you'd used your brain, you'd have stayed *put* under the protection of the Peruvian. His little monsters would have kept you safe from Tellamore and those like him."

Silence ensued, and Hephaestion could hear their breathing. He lifted his head, slowly undid the door's latch, swung it open a sliver, and woozily positioned his head to take a peek at his hosts.

The man's gaze was on the floor, his toes inward with a teacup and saucer in his lap. His fingers paddled its chipped edges.

Leaning forward opposite him sat a woman of smaller frame with vibrant energy in her eyes. "So, this crazy man," she prodded. "You took him into your care and ran with him.... Why?"

Like a remorseful child, the man shrugged. "It felt right."

A wry smirk crept across her face. "So you did something right, after all." Her smirk expanded into a full smile as she stood up and walked to him, and she placed a tender kiss onto his forehead, her lips looking full and warm.

"We'll be giving the money away," she added, stroking his shoulder.

"I figured. Well, *most* of it."

"*All* of it."

"But you normally let me keep some to make our way here!"

"This one feels wrong. You profited off that man, a man you risked yourself for. Be altruistic."

"Maybe *he* wants the money, or even *needs* it! Surely, we'll give most of it away, but I'd rather wait until we know this fellow better."

With a dangerous eyebrow cocked, she turned her head to examine her husband much like Minos would.

"You aren't just saying that in an effort to eventually change my mind?"

"No! I think New Dis could use a university and a historical archive, perhaps a refurbished government center, but I also want us safe and sound. Besides, we can control the money that would be in the paws of the Tellamore Estate, or worse. We can apply it and make sure it does some good for everyone who needs it—no more homeless street folk being cast into the pit!"

She nodded, seemingly buying his argument at present.

"And the crazy man, no doubt wanted by the Ushers and perhaps the guard.... What of him? They will come for him."

"We can deal with both parties, most likely. The guard can be bought, and the ushers are complete savages, so I doubt we'll hear from them anyhow. I don't think they're even allowed outside of their compound."

She sighed with disappointment. "It feels dirty. This place pollutes me—bribery as an option...."

The man took her hand and kissed her palm. "Which is why you went to Heaven, and I to Purgatory."

"Should have left you there."

"You should have."

"Loving you is a pain."

"I know."

"I could have married the Ashkenazi boy."

"He had a beak for a nose."

"I doubt he gambled."

"He was boring."

"Mmmmmmmm."

The man gently pulled his wife into his lap, and she instinctively leaned in. "You saved me," he whispered, and they lost themselves in a kiss.

Hephaestion slipped the door closed, silently returned under the sheets, and permitted himself more rest.

CHAPTER 9

"Why?"

Hephaestion heard the question, and it stirred him from his dreams. His body remained weak, but he could focus his eyes more easily now. With effort, he pushed his body back on the feather mattress and sat himself up against the headboard.

Blinking away his bleary vision, Hephaestion focused on the small man sitting compactly next to the bed, beard trimmed and perfect, with a tray of tea for two in his lap. It smelled freshly brewed and filled the room with a hint of cinnamon.

"Why?" the man persisted.

"Why what?"

"Greek? You speak Classical Greek." The man's eyes trailed off to his lower right, deep in thought.

In the afterlife, the language barrier ceases to exist. Everyone typically retains their earthly languages and tongue, but once a person has crossed over the threshold into death, all ears understand all languages. When one person in the afterlife speaks to another, they want to be understood. The connection between the speaker and listener is a simple relationship that emulates the connection between people overall. When people wish to commune, intentionally or otherwise, they do so.

The written word is an entirely different matter, however.

"You say 'Classical' Greek as if there's any other," Hephaestion returned.

"All languages change, especially the language of conquerors. The people they conquer redraft them. Who *are* you?"

"Where am I?"

"Who are you?"

"Where *am* I? And who are *you?*"

The man sat back with an exasperated huff. "You are in a tiny room in a tiny home of a tiny family that is keeping you safe and warm. You can call me Yitz. However, if you feel the need to gut me like you did Minos's ushers, know that my wife is in the next room, and nothing would spare you from her wrath. She *loves* this carpet, and if you ruined it with my innards, you'd wish Minos had flung you to the pit directly. Now, answer my damned questions, for you are at the mercy of our hospitality!"

Hephaestion remained silent, eyes locked onto his host.

Yitz poured the tea. "Here, drink your goddamned tea. It will bring your strength back. Adina saved this special brew for occasions like this. It's imported from Purgatory."

"Adina... your wife?"

Yitz nodded.

Hephaestion took the saucer and sniffed at it. His nostrils widened at the spicy warmth. He recognized cinnamon from Purgatory, and after his first sip, he found a pleasant fruity aftertaste.

Yitz savored his own cup. "Suffering a bastard like you is worth it if it means she breaks out the good tea. So, just answer our questions, will you? You don't realize the trouble you've caused us—are *still* causing us, by being in our home. I would have left you in the gutter if not for my wife and a certain annoying Christian, so out with it. Who are you, and why did you pop out of a fat man at Minos's feet?"

"I am Hephaestion, son of Amyntor, nobleman of Macedonia and general in the greatest army that walked the Earth."

Yitz stopped mid-sip, eyes examining Hephaestion's face for any indications of falsehood. "You're *shitting me*." He smirked.

"No. I am Alexander of Macedonia's right hand, and I am the *weapon* in that hand. And I am here to get into the pit to find him."

"Well," Yitz said, the smirk fading. "Had you not heard of the docks on the shores of the sea? Did you not know that New Dis had a healthy import and export business with the hamlets and coastal towns of Mt. Purgatory? You could have booked passage on a boat—"

"Well, I didn't *swim* all the way from the mountain. I had a boat, but I wanted to avoid being seen. I'd heard Jesuits guarded and monitored the docks... zealously."

"So instead you popped out of a fat sinner like an angry baby and began stabbing everything in sight?"

"I didn't know there would be an audience. I was going to chance Minos's judgment instead of the Jesuits," Hephaestion retorted, exasperated. "My things — my satchel and jerkin and spear — where are they? Do you have them?"

"Lost, mostly. You have your shin guards, which Adina is fixing. They need new leather straps. Your shield is fine too — it stayed on your back — but your little spear and bag are gone, lost during the pursuit."

Hephaestion's shoulders folded inward, but he gathered his voice to ask, "Pursuit?"

"People ran after you. The prior and I got you clear to Adina, where she protected us."

"Who is the prior? Is that the annoying Christian?"

"Albrecht is his name, and yes. The man can chat like no one on Earth or after, but he saved you — us — as did Adina. When you meet them, you will be grateful to them both. I don't care what your opinions are of Jews or Christians. You will be *polite*."

Hephaestion nodded knowingly. "Of course."

"So, you're the legendary Hephaestion, the man whose face has been carved in stone more than any other in history. And you snuck into Minos's court to get into Hell by hiding inside a poor, bloated soul. You killed three ushers, each of whom will surely hate you eternally once they revive, and you are now naked with little to no physical resources as you sip tea in our guest bed. Did you have a contact in New Dis, someone to meet up with?"

"No, I didn't want any communication channels to lead to me. I intended to get past Minos and head directly into the pit as fast as able."

"With no food or provisions."

"Food is a luxury in the afterlife, one we can all do without."

"Says the man enjoying a cup of the best tea he's ever tasted. So, you would go and find Alexander, and.... What then? Reunion?"

"Rescue."

Yitz's smirk returned, but larger this time. His stool creaked as he leaned back. "Aaaahhhhhh... so that's it. That's what's got them riled, the Jesuits. They see that sort of thing as a direct affront to God. They'd never permit it. They would sooner jar your heart and put it on a shelf with a plaque."

"Like you said, few faces were set in stone as often as mine. I was even on the currency of the empire. I would have been recognized by the dock masters immediately."

"But they wouldn't have known you were going to... to.... You could have just been a visitor. We get *lots* of famous visitors."

"I would have been followed. I would have been too high-profile."

Yitz chuckled helplessly and rubbed his eyes. "Sadly, you happened to cross Minos's path just when the Peruvian was holding court. Not only have you set the streets atwitter with your heroics, but you've also managed to make me and that annoying Christian two of the richest people in The After. So you couldn't possibly be *higher* profile. Adina has been turning away people pleading for loans. We had to put a sign up in every language we could write telling callers to go away. We haven't had a moment's peace since yesterday, when you plopped onto the floor."

"You're *blaming* me for your sudden fortune? Well then, I'm so sorry for your wealth."

"Oh *please*."

"But then, thanks to me, you have the resources to aid me. I need proper armor, maps to replace those lost, and a spear—a spear fit for Greek hands."

"You're making demands while lying naked between our linens and sipping our tea?"

"I would *stand* and make them, but this room is too small."

The door swung open, jolting the tea tray as Adina's head poked in, her brow furrowed in stern disapproval. "You two fools stop it, or I'll come in there." Her head withdrew and the door slammed shut again.

The two men sat in cowed silence, blinking at each other in alarm.

"That is my lovely Adina," Yitz proclaimed, knowing she could hear everything.

"She does seem lovely, and she makes a wonderful cup of tea," Hephaestion offered.

"The men chasing us are piles of ash. She burned them with divine fire manifested from her faith."

"I've heard that the Heavenbound can do feats like that."

"So be nice to her."

"What of the men she incinerated? Will they or their kin come for revenge?"

"Likely not. Family or servants from their estates brushed them up with dust pans, and in about forty years, when they re-congeal, they'll be by to apologize to her."

"Seriously?"

"You don't know my wife. They'll be bringing wine from their private stores, if we're lucky."

"*Dinner is ready!*" Adina called from behind the door. "Get that man some proper clothes!"

Yitz rolled his eyes. "You'll forgive me. The only thing that will fit you is my bathing robe, but it still will go down to your thighs, at least." Yitz stood and fetched a garish, paper-thin linen with green leaves embroidered into the collar. "Not that you really need bother. Adina spent an inordinate amount of time dressing your wounds and bathing you," he whispered contentiously.

"If you have a problem, dear husband, with my tending to our guest, then perhaps you'd like to discuss it *over dinner!*" she shrilled from beyond.

"Damn!"

Hephaestion understood his good fortune. A complete stroke of luck had befallen him as, despite the failure at Minos's court, he'd managed to land among friendly people. Ulfric had warned endlessly of the streets of New Dis and its brutal politics, such that Hephaestion had planned to circumvent the place altogether. By traveling within the body of a glutton, Hephaestion had hoped to already be several circles down into the pit by now. "Beware, Hepher," Ulfric would prattle while they sat by the fire, looking at the constellations above in the crisp night sky of Purgatory. "People in that city would snatch you up to ransom off to Alexander's Earthly enemies. You think kings get over having their nations taken from them by two boys?"

The gown felt awkward, and when Hephaestion sat at the dinner table, it rode up high, the slit in the side nearly to his hip. Being naked would have been more comfortable for him, but he wasn't sure that would be a good idea given Yitz's voiced concerns.

Adina '*tsked*' as she set a large brass pot with a wooden ladle-handle sticking out at the center of the table. "You two will be going shopping for men's clothes. I've adjusted the budget conservatively to accommodate for my husband's despicable winnings—a proper suit or two and whatever you might need for your journey."

Yitz's eyes lit up.

Hephaestion said to Adina, "You listened at the door to all of our conversation, then?" He grinned.

"You're in my house. Every drape and stick of furniture reports back to *me*," she said slyly while setting a fresh kettle to boil. "I'm glad you like the tea."

The three ate in silence, tender lamb soaked in a peachy spice Hephaestion had never tasted before. "I used to eat lamb back at home."

"Home being Purgatory?" Adina asked, careful to swallow first.

"Yes. You're Heavenbound? My friend, Ulfric, is also Heavenbound. He pulled me off of some rocks at the base of the mountain and took me in."

"People taking you in seems to be a theme, Lord Hephaestion. Are you always in need of rescue?"

"Darling," Yitz pleaded casually, mouth full. "Please be mindful and be polite to our guest. He murders people. Lots of them."

"But he's a good sort. He's going to rescue his commander and king. Out of duty?" Her eyes keened when she asked the question.

Hephaestion's eyebrows gave a confession and the corners of his mouth crooked into a grin.

"Lovers," Adina continued, satisfied. "Some say you two outgrew it, but others say that Roxana only conceived because both of you were in the bed chamber."

"Woman!" roared Yitz, meat and vegetable spewing and dangling. "Despite being a heavenly creature, you occasionally *don't act like one!*"

"And aren't *you* grateful for it, husband?" she fired back at him saucily. "I think it noble, and understandable, but foolish... this endeavor of yours, Lord Hephaestion. Naive. I think that, even after two thousand years, you haven't learned much in Purgatory. Maybe your Heavenbound sponsor is to blame. Maybe you're just that stubborn and stuck in the past. Either way, you're going into the pit with or without our help, so you might as well have it."

Hephaestion sat up, set his fork down, and gave a grateful nod to her.

Yitz patted Hephaestion's knee in affirmation. "But you're going to do something for *us*." Yitz picked up where his wife had left off. Clearly they'd discussed this during his recovery. "We have a son down in the pit. You'll find him and tell him that we love him and wait for him. Do not free him. He must finish his time and solve his own soul's dilemma. But you must find him. Perhaps the nudge from a stranger, the reminder that he is, even now, still adored, will be enough to speed his salvation."

It would add another layer of difficulty to his quest, and the closer he got to knowing that Alexander would be in his arms, the farther it seemed to feel. Still, these people had been kind, and they offered more than Hephaestion could have hoped for.

"I'll need maps, gear," he said, "and real steel—a spear. I'll also need to know everything I can about your boy, and where to find him."

"He... uh... betrayed his synagogue," Yitz confessed, his voice small, and he gazed at Adina's fleeting eyes before returning to him. "He embezzled money, and burned down the synagogue to hide the evidence. He was never caught on Earth. We know only that he's in the pit, but we're unsure of where, and on what circle, he resides, though betrayers...."

Hephaestion gave a nod of sympathy to spare Yitz from finishing the sentence. "Let's take it a step at a time, then. I need my strength back, and I'm useless without a spear."

CHAPTER 10

The following day, a courier came to the door, a polite, short man in simple dress, armed with flintlock pistols tucked into his belt. The envelope he delivered contained a promise of future payment from the Peruvian for seven talents of gold, to be delivered over a two-hundred-year period.

Adina went pale, and Yitz fainted. The home became busy with plans and future enterprises.

As for Hephaestion, after several days of roasted meats, crisp vegetables, and soothing tea, he could get about on his own with the aid of a cane—a plain, thin walking stick adorned with a bone handle. It stood only half his height, but it felt empowering to have *something* in his grip again.

"We'll keep you bundled up a bit," Adina cooed, doting over Hephaestion. "And here's a hood to keep you hidden. Are you warm enough? You still barely have enough meat on you."

"Woman!" Yitz protested. "You wouldn't preen him if you'd seen him opening people up like I did."

"I don't mind a little preening," Hephaestion playfully confessed.

"Of course you don't. We all need it from time to time, even codgerly old gamblers," she said, throwing a sly look towards Yitz. "Still, we want to keep you under wraps. I have two friends who will go to the tailor's with us. They'll keep you safe, and most will keep their distance from us as we make our way there and back. Oh, and if you're feeling weak in the knees, just lean on Yitz."

"Per usual," Yitz grumbled.

The stairwell leading down to the street was narrow and creaky, the wood bright and oaken, like the boards of The Bonny Sweetheart. Thinking of Ulfric, Hephaestion wondered if he should hire a messenger to bear a letter to Purgatory, in the hopes that it might put the Viking's worries at ease.

While still deep in thought, the door to the street opened, and Hephaestion was immediately met with a short woman in a crimson niqab embroidered with geometric patterns that tessellated into butterflies. Down both sleeves appeared a writing Hephaestion couldn't read, but it reminded him of the ancient language of the Persians. Through the narrow opening in the face, the only place where her olive skin could be seen, the woman's eyes beamed out a vibrant green.

Hephaestion was arrested by the sight and nearly dropped his cane.

"This is Minu," Yitz said. "Minu, this is Hephaestion."

"Yes, I know. Yitz, it seems your friends have started to become handsome. Perhaps your loathsome hobby of gambling isn't the sin we thought it was?" She chided with a rich, youthful voice from under her concealment as, nudging herself between Yitz and Hephaestion, she hooked both her hands around Hephaestion's elbow. "I'll help you along, young warrior. Yitz should hold hands with his wife. It's only right. And you won't be needing the cane." She gingerly snagged the item from Hephaestion's grasp before he could protest. "Just one foot in front of the other. This is hardly the first time you've died now, is it?"

Within a moment, they seemed to glide across the street, her hands gently resting on his arm, but somehow keeping him steady. His legs seemed alive and aware, and each of his steps seemed to carry less gravity than he was accustomed to feeling. Minu's eyes never left his face, and a welcome warmth radiated from them.

The street wasn't particularly busy. Although the city of New Dis never slept, it did have its down times. A few stragglers roamed about, pushing carts or hurrying from one bit of business to another.

Minu helped Hephaestion effortlessly transcend the berm, where standing before him was a second woman, tall and muscled with blue swirls all over her pale skin. A mass of brown hair, braided thick and high, crowned the top of her otherwise shaved head. She was imposing and appeared as mighty as any sword hand he'd ever seen. From a quick glance, he counted four blades sheathed on her body, the largest of them a gladius on her left hip, hilt forward. The design of the scabbard appeared Roman, but he couldn't know the blade's design for certain unless he saw it drawn. He wasn't eager to ask her to do so.

"Boudica, meet Hephaestion, lover and chief Companion to Alexander the Great." Minu patted Hephaestion's arm tenderly.

Boudica's eyes narrowed as she eyed him over. "I'm not impressed with conquerors," she said flatly. "But Adina likes you, and that's good enough for me. For now."

Yitz and Adina, their joined hands swinging between the two of them, mounted the berm soon after.

Adina looked about and quietly said, "We're going to head down the street three blocks and then go right. We're headed to Ancien Tailoring."

Both women nodded in agreement. Boudica spun on her heel and marched ahead at least forty paces, and then held a steady rhythm with her gaze shifting gradually side to side. Minu and Hephaestion followed her just within earshot, and soon after them Adina and Yitz straggled along.

Whereas Boudica moved like a soldier on parade, and Yitz and Adina tensely walked while looking all around, Minu seemed oblivious to any concerns, and seemingly strolled, her fingers locked on Hephaestion's elbow.

"If I know my history correctly," she said, "you were married?"

"Yes, just before I died I was married to a lovely woman named Drypetis. She was royalty."

"How is she?"

"She is in Heaven, I believe."

"And why are you not striving to be with her?"

Hephaestion was caught for words. Minu's tone was so innocent and curious, he couldn't determine if she was testing him or merely inquisitive.

"The love of my life is down there, and he needs me."

"How does your wife feel about this?"

"Drypetis knew of this when we married. Our marriage was political."

She nodded thoughtfully, her eyes giving away nothing. "Will he be glad to see you? Alexander?"

"Of course he will. He is the Achilles to my Patroclus."

"What if he isn't ready to leave?"

"I... what do you mean?" The question truly baffled him. "Of course he'll come with me. I'll take him back to Purgatory, where we'll live at Ulfric's hall and plan our future from there."

Minu's gaze locked onto him. Despite being considerably shorter than Hephaestion, she suddenly intimidated him.

"Please be careful, Hephaestion," she said finally, sweetness still in her voice. "You seem to be a man with good intentions, and while I'm sure you're familiar with the phrase, I'll say it to you: the road to Hell is paved with good intentions. Beware, Hephaestion." Her eyes looked forward into the distance, her hand stroking his arm gently once more.

They walked on, passing two blocks and reaching the third. Sputtering carriages and delivery bicycles wheeled about in front of them, only stopping for the occasional gaggle of well-dressed women with parasols twirling in displays of color.

"Lavender is very much in style," Minu said with a tinge of jealousy. "But if I kept up with style, I'd be sewing endlessly. I'll stay with red."

"What does your robing say? In the stitching?" Hephaestion inquired.

"It says, 'Allah is my anvil. Faith is my hammer. I am my steel.' It is my creed."

"I've never heard anything like that before. What does it mean? Allah is God, so I understand that God is constant and unmoving, like an anvil. But I don't get the rest."

There was a break in traffic and Boudica crossed first, glaring down any motorist or driver who might get in their way. Minu and Hephaestion followed with Adina and Yitz just behind.

Minu said, "You understand anvil: the notion of God's unending power, passive might. Our faith we wield, striking the iron. Some wield faith poorly, weakly striking the iron, perhaps missing the iron entirely. We're responsible for the hammer's motion. We're responsible for how we wield faith. As for the iron, well... some iron is just poor—brittle, filled with black pockets, or nonmalleable. In the end, what we forge ourselves into is a synthesis of the iron, the hammer, and the anvil."

"So, what have you forged *yourself* into?" Hephaestion pried, enjoying the philosophy of the metaphor.

"I haven't cooled on the anvil... yet. I've been out of the fire for some time, but I remain hot because I keep striking with my faith. Perhaps I'll decide on a final form while I'm here, in New Dis. Maybe a cane, perhaps? I seem to be doing the job well enough."

Hephaestion nodded in grateful agreement.

"Or a bladed weapon, maybe," she continued. "We often forge ourselves into what we think is needed, now, don't we, Hephaestion? A lover, a warrior, a general, a savior, an infiltrator.... The question you must ask is: how will you know your hammer is done striking? Will you be able to temper your steel? Willing to?"

Silence lingered as Hephaestion searched the ground for what to say next. After a moment, he opted for no response as the correct one, but considered the question for a bit longer. Was he a spearhead? Did he have a faith driving the steel against the anvil, or was it desire and desperation? Was he really holding the hammer, or did he hand the hammer over to circumstance? Was Alexander swinging the hammer, even after centuries?

"We're here," Boudica announced bluntly. "I'll wait outside. You four go do your shopping. I'll call if there's an issue out here." She jerked her thumb over her shoulder.

Adina thanked her with a nod, and led everyone inside.

A tiny bell over the door, silver so polished it was nearly white, announced their entrance cheerfully. The floors of the antechamber before them were of polished white stone with red mortar. Inviting furniture of spiraling brass and plush cushions graced the room. Fleur de lis were patterned in gold thread on the tapestries that lined the walls, tassels dripping to the floor.

Their arrival had been anticipated, as evidenced by the two servants who greeted them, both wigged and richly dressed in elegant white blouses and brocade waist coats, holding trays with wine.

Adina and Yitz nodded their approval and took a glass each, but when Hephaestion saw Minu decline, he did the same. Her eyes twinkled at him.

"Sip wine if you wish, Grecian," she whispered playfully. "Your people nearly invented it, but don't mention that here. These people are *French* and show no signs of recovering."

One servant led Adina and Minu to the salon, offering the ladies cards, tea, cheese, and hors d'oeuvres.

The remaining servant approached Yitz and said, "The lady Adina has opened an account here, sir. She said you two are to be outfitted in quality, but subtle, menswear in line with modern conservative fashion."

Yitz nodded. "Yes, and we'll need shoes, too. Nice shoes."

"Nice?" A boisterous voice boomed in robust French from behind a curtained doorway.

An elegant walking cane erupted through, heaved the curtain to one side, and out stepped the most flamboyantly dressed man Hephaestion had ever seen. His skin was black as onyx, each feature chiseled perfectly, as if with conscious intention. The white of his curled wig startled in contrast, making his eyes seem all the larger for it. The

buckles on his shoes boasted the same polished silver as the bell above the door, and when the tip of his cane rested near his feet, it was clear that it matched as well.

"Gentlemen," he said, "I shall tell you that 'nice' has no place here. We only deal with the exquisite!" He approached with arms open. "I've decided that lavender has become the new delight of New Dis's fashion sensitivities. Hence my lovely lavender overcoat. It's a difficult color to dye properly. Sometimes the dye is too coarse, but I'll tell you a secret." He suddenly moved in, dominating Yitz's personal space. "The Chinese can dye anything. Any color you can fathom. They just keep inventing colors for me to pick from."

With a sharp swivel of his head, the man suddenly noticed Hephaestion as though he'd been previously invisible. "Monsieur Yitzhak, you have brought a poor man in from the cold, it seems. How valorous. This poor fellow, I *must* see him, but not here inside the parlor. Please, come, come! And call me Adam. We're all friends here."

Through the curtain they strolled, and it flopped closed behind them. The main tailor's shop was much larger than the antechamber, the hardwood floors stained a deep red that made the thousands of vibrantly-colored suits and dresses leap off of their racks and hooks. Adam led the men to the center of it all, walking them up a spiraling ramp that terminated onto a flat surface several men's heights into the air.

All the while, something gnawed at Hephaestion, like an angry whisper in his ear.

"From here let your eyes wander!" Adam swelled with pride, his arm out and canvassing the scene before them. "We can get changed up here in privacy, while maintaining a perfect view of all the stock. If there's a coat you'd like a better look at, just tell me and I'll shout for a boy to bring it to us. Now, before we dive into your suit selection, Yitzhak, I simply must get a better look at this comely devil you brought into my store. I cannot *wait* to see my work on him. He'll be the talk of the entire ward. Don't be shy, good sir. Please disrobe, if you would."

Hephaestion did so, slipping off his cover and standing naked.

Adam looked disapprovingly and then called down below. "Garçon, please bring us up some pate with bread. Our guest needs to fill out a bit more." He looked back to Hephaestion. "Please do not be insulted, good sir. I just feel obligated to make you at home and fulfilled. May I take some measurements?"

Hephaestion nodded vacantly.

Yitz was lost browsing the attire, his finger working through the racks as he mumbled joyfully.

Hephaestion wondered if the ladies were playing chess, and suddenly longed to be with them.

Adam darted about Hephaestion, lifting an arm by the wrist or measuring the thickness of a thigh, while occasionally tapping his chin with '*hmmmm*' emerging from behind his pursed lips. "You're a tall man with a broad chest and a long torso. What a delight it will be to build for you. Also, you're simply not permitted to leave in that rag. Not only would it be awful having *that* worn by a patron leaving Ancien, but again I feel obligated to rescue you from such a tragically functional garment. Do you like velvet? Pinstripes are what I'm thinking for Monsieur Yitzhak, here, but you're too tall for a pattern like that, so I'm considering texture for you, good sir. And speaking of good sir!" Adam suddenly squawked. "What is your name? Have you a status?"

"Hephaestion. General."

Adam paused, eyes alight. "General! General Hephaestion, forgive my informality, but we're all friends here. Let's look at your feet!" Diving down, Adam began taking measurements of Hephaestion's ankles and arch.

As Adam did so, Hephaestion's gnawing came back, and his eyes wandered not among the clothes and dresses on the racks, or the servants standing by, but up to the ceiling. Lit by bright electric chandeliers, the ceiling had been constructed of the same deep red wood as the floors. It was an all-too-familiar shade of crimson, but Hephaestion had trouble identifying why it bothered him so.

A servant arrived with the pate, held high in his left hand while he carried a fold-out tray in the right.

"Please eat," Adam said. "Please! And allow me to remove this unsightly *thing* you came in wearing. It's beneath you and unworthy of your magnificent stature."

Adam provided a small stool, its cushion of white silk, and Hephaestion felt awkward sitting on it naked. He wasn't sure how to voice his concerns, though, so he simply hoped for the best and settled in.

The pate was delicious, even with his appetite blunted by his mind's unrest.

Yitz however, seemed completely at home. "While he's eating," he said, "should we measure me?"

"No need, kind sir," Adam chirped. "Your lovely lady Adina provided all measurements, as well as expectations regarding what you wish to purchase. Your wife said you needed one suit and a pair of shoes for today."

Yitz looked crushed.

"And next week she has booked our attention yet again, to select an additional two suits with another pair of shoes."

Yitz brightened considerably. In fact, he appeared giddy beyond any shade of self-respect.

Hephaestion set his spoon down and looked up at the ceiling once more, and his stool creaked under him.

It's the wood. The floor. The ceiling. The wood. Something about the wood....

"What kind of tree is this?" he inquired. "Hickory? In Purgatory, we had some woods that were red, but not like that. Did you dye them?"

"Oh, our lovely varnished red floors and ceiling? The wood helps with moisture for the stock. It isn't easy to come by, and almost no one ever uses it for construction, given how slick it gets. The real expense is dragging the lumber up from —"

Hephaestion leapt to his feet, knocking over the soup and stool. "*Suicides!*" he snarled, veins bulging from his neck. "You built your shop from suicides?"

"General," Adam pleaded. "I assure you it's just wood like any —"

"It is *people!*" Hephaestion used his full, unrestrained voice, the one that had called over the battlefield and led cavalry charges. His words boomed off the planks above and below. "Suicides fall right past Minos and plow into the forest. Each tree is a suicide. Each tree is a *person.* And you cut them down and build your home!"

"Now, now, let's not get carried away with things, General. The branches and trunks grow back just like any other tree. Please, sir, we're clearly getting off on the wrong —"

Hephaestion stormed past Adam and trotted down the ramp in a rage, the servants below giving him a wide birth. Tearing the curtain loose, he ripped into the antechamber. "Adina!" he shouted. "*Adina!*"

The salon door flew open and Adina charged out with Minu at her side.

The front door burst open too, cracking on its hinges, and a wild-eyed Boudica stood holding a blade in each hand.

"What? What is it?" Adina asked frantically, looking about for the danger.

"This shop is built from suicide wood! *People!* This place is a... a... flagrant and *trite* thing built from the bodies of suicides!"

Understanding crossed her face, and she immediately eased her posture. "Hephaestion, several buildings in New Dis are."

"Your home? The bed frame I've been sleeping on?"

"No, no, nothing Yitz and I would ever own."

Timidly, the disheveled curtain pulled aside to reveal a visibly terrified Adam. "There has been a misunderstanding. How may we sort—"

Hephaestion cleared his throat loudly and attempted regaining his composure, then turned to Adam sternly. "You understand that the trees you cut down for your shop were once people, condemned to live as trees as punishment for suicide, yes?"

"Well, certainly. The forest below is dangerous, and the loggers can charge inordinate sums for their lumber. It is a luxurious commodity, indeed."

Hephaestion sighed, defeated. "Then there is no misunderstanding. I'd rather just go naked." With that, he stepped around Boudica and walked out the front door.

Next to Adam appeared Yitz, his face red with embarrassment. Everyone eyed each other over, waiting for the prolonged silence to break.

Boudica opted to do so. "He's growing on me."

CHAPTER 11

Once clear from the audience, Hephaestion allowed himself to buckle. With his hands on his knees and head hung low, he thought of Thebes.

Thebes had burned for days.

When the polis had thrown out Alexander's puppet government, Thebes became a beacon of rebellion in Greece. The nations to the East would see this, believe that Alexander couldn't keep his own homeland in order, and rebel in turn.

Great and mighty Thebes had to be the place where all thoughts of rebellion would stop. Future generations had to witness that Alexander would not tolerate secession.

So they put Thebes to the torch. They sold its women and children into slavery, and put its men to the axe or the noose by the thousands. They decapitated fathers in front of their sons and forced boys to dig mass graves for their elders. Never had Alexander brought such ruin upon the conquered, and never would he again.

The uncharacteristic wrath had unnerved Hephaestion, who begged Alexander to show mercy, framing his pleas as politically motivated. "If you do not spare the people, Greece will call you tyrant!" he said, but Alexander's rage was savage and personal.

To avoid watching the slaughter of the surviving garrison, Hephaestion sought sanctuary in one of the many Theban temples in the center of the city. Shock troops had already cleared the area and declared the temple secure. He made his personal escort of thirty Companions wait outside so he could pray for the women and children of fallen Thebes in peace.

Each torch burned brightly, flickering among the columns and elegant blue statues. Moonlight pooled in through each archway as the night breeze carried in the wails of the distant condemned. Hephaestion slid off his cavalry helmet and rustled his hair with his gloved hands in an effort to keep himself awake. Rubbing his eyes vigorously, he saw only white, but when he opened them and looked about at the temple's interior steps, he wished them closed again. But his eyelids would not obey.

A mound of lily-white robes and pale bodies lay elegantly spilled before him. Hundreds of women, their small children all curled into their limp arms, were piled at his feet, all dead by drinking hemlock. Hephaestion's eyes lingered on the various vessels strewn about the marble floor.

They'd killed themselves to avoid being raped, murdered, or sold into slavery. Alexander's wrath was so significant that it led to this, and Hephaestion had organized much of the siege.

They'd committed suicide because they knew Hephaestion was coming.

Were any planks in the tailor shop from one of them? Did Adam have a bed frame made from a desperate mother? Did that decadent man shuffle his bare feet in the morning across heartbroken priestesses? Was a stool leg that propped up my weight one of the children that took the cup, knowing it for what it was?

Hephaestion vomited, suddenly ashamed for every ounce of comfort he'd been provided by Yitz and Adina. Gripping his weak knees, he closed his eyes tight and tried to balance himself as the cobble street under him spun. He didn't need to breathe, but his lungs wouldn't stop pumping, and his throat gasped and drowned on his desperate saliva and sweat. Crippling fear clawed up his spine and into his chest, causing his heart to flutter in hopeless spasms.

What am I doing here?

He'd lost a majority of his gear, his allies and friends were beyond any kind of reach, and he stood naked in the street of a hostile city after having just thrown a tantrum that alienated the only kind people he had encountered—kind people who'd protected him when he needed it, kind people that kept him safe.

"You take the thing that keeps you going, and you keep it in your head," Boudica said firmly from somewhere behind him. "You do that."

Alexander. His thoughts drifted to Alexander.

Hephaestion lay entwined with Alexander in a bearskin by a fire in their tent. The snow had gently drifted from a windless sky, lazily blanketing the world outside, and the two men relished in being alone by their crackling hearth.

On this winter night in the east, somewhere near the friendly settlement of Samal, after they had made love, Alexander had started crying.

"Was I that good?" Hephaestion asked playfully, wiping his lover's tear.

"I had that dream again last night," Alexander whispered, almost terrified of being heard. He was speaking of Thebes. "I dreamt of all their faces. Thirty thousand people. Thirty. I've broken armies while commanding fewer Greeks. Thirty thousand sold. Mothers and children separated after their fathers had been killed."

Hephaestion knew that the sobbing would come soon. Regardless of the battle horrors Alexander had endured, nothing haunted him more significantly than the dreams of those faces.

Hephaestion stroked Alexander's hair and shushed his love. "You are a king—"

"I'm a monster," Alexander croaked.

"You are a *king*, and sometimes that's what a king must do. They were at least sold to other Greeks. You spared them the sword."

Alexander nodded and drifted to sleep.

Hephaestion had never told Alexander of the hundreds of bodies found in those temples, which he'd secretly burned in the streets. Alexander never knew of the Greeks so afraid of their king that they murdered themselves, and the children in their arms, to avoid facing him.

Hephaestion had washed up in Purgatory for his sins. His love had faced Minos and was trapped in the pit. Now, he clung to the image of

Alexander's face and the tenor of his voice, his legs regained their strength.

Knowing where the ground was again, Hephaestion gradually stood and pried his eyes open. Several well-groomed passersby stared at him agape, parasols no longer playfully spinning.

"Good. Now get out of the street," Boudica commanded.

Like a good soldier, Hephaestion obeyed. As he stood in front of her, he looked back to the door of Ancien Tailoring and muttered, "I haven't helped my cause any...."

"Probably not." Boudica grinned. "When I get caught up in how much I hate this place, I think of my girls when they were little. They get along far too well now, but when they were little, they would have the cutest arguments. I would eavesdrop for hours."

Hephaestion nodded, acknowledging Boudica's kindness.

Adina, Yitz, and Minu exited the tailor's.

Yitz approached Hephaestion first. "I'm sorry, Hephaestion." He sighed meekly. "I put you in a difficult position without thinking. We can get you something to wear from any vendor, but there are decency laws, and we can't have you running around naked."

"You sure?" Boudica mused from the periphery.

Minu said, "My home is not far from here. Everyone come to my house, and I'll sew something for our Lord here." Her eyes smiled as she made her command sound like a benevolent invitation. She took her spot next to Hephaestion and gently held his elbow, and the strength returned to his knees. "Besides, you ancient Greeks preferred being naked in the summer months, no?"

"We're comfortable with it," he replied as everyone resumed their travel formation. "But that was seasonal."

"It's always summer here in Hell. And don't worry about back there... at the shop. Didn't I warn you? They are unrepentantly *French*."

CHAPTER 12

Minu's home sat off a narrow alleyway through a crimson wrought iron gate. Its hinges announced their arrival with a tiny yet piercing squeal as they moved through and latched it closed behind them. Once inside, it felt as though Hephaestion had entered a completely different world. The floor of the foyer was comprised of tiny, intricately placed metal tiles displaying geometric shapes that spun and folded into themselves. As his eyes followed the labyrinthian patterns of vibrant blue and dull gold, he grew dizzy again.

He spotted no chairs for him to sit. In fact, no significant furniture existed except for huge scarlet and burgundy pillows piled into the corners and against the walls of the room. Each body-sized cushion was a work of art; threaded scenes embroidered on their fronts depicting ancient peoples and their various methods of worship.

"Be comfortable," Minu said. "Welcome to my home. Enjoy the pillows. I made them all myself." She swung her arms low but open in a sweeping gesture of presentation.

Without hesitating, Yitz selected a pillow with a man punching a demon on it. He sunk himself in with a sigh.

Boudica did the same, careful not to let her sword's scabbard snag on the stitching.

"This is lovely, Minu. Thank you for having us," Adina said as she walked among the pillows as though in an art gallery, admiring their roped tassels and silky textures.

"Come here, Lord Hephaestion," Minu beckoned while standing on a simple wooden stool. "Let me measure."

Whereas Adam the tailor doted and made a flamboyant production of such a task, Minu simply measured Hephaestion's shoulders, arms, and chest with her outstretched hands, finger to thumb.

"Give me some time," she said, spryly hopping down. "I'll be back soon."

At the end of the reception room stood imposing double doors. She vanished behind them, the tail of her niqab gliding through just as the doors swung shut behind her.

Hephaestion sighed, feeling exposed. The thought of burying himself in several of the pillows appealed to him, but he quickly chastised himself for desiring comfort. A cot was all he needed in Purgatory. How dare he receive more in New Dis!

He wanted to apologize to everyone for his embarrassing outburst. None of this had gone as planned. All of this had played out so much simpler in his head, a trek of survival through the rings of Hell. It was to take decades or even hundreds of years, but he would find Alexander and carry him out.

Yet here he stood, naked and unarmed, at the mercy of others.

The depth of his unpreparedness finally struck him, and his shoulders slumped under the sudden weight. To keep himself upright, he sat on Minu's tiny stool.

He took stock of what he still had and what had gone right. His segmented shield waited for him back at Adina and Yitz's home, functional and ready. Yitz had declared his greaves still viable, but in need of repair. Also, the Jesuits hadn't discovered him yet.

Then there were the unexpected allies. Adina was substantially powerful, as was Minu in her own way. Boudica might be as well, but fortunately, her power had yet to be required. As for Yitz, he was a shifty man, but a good soul. Adina seemed the sort to not tolerate a lesser man than what she deserved, so that vouched for his character considerably.

Despite having lost almost all of his gear, hew now had four powerful people looking out for him. Perhaps God's Grace stretched beyond Heaven, and occasionally touched rogue souls such as Hephaestion.

Could this providence be an endorsement?

"Thank you," Hephaestion said, his voice full and sincere.

All eyes drifted to him.

"All of this was simpler in my head. I was content to wander below, searching for him. I was an ass."

"Are you still going down? Is this a change of heart?" Adina asked cautiously, clearly thinking of her boy.

Hephaestion scoffed. "I didn't come this far on a whim. I'll get to him. I just realize what a desperate idiot I've been up to this point. I'll get to your boy, and after that I'll find Alex."

Boudica nodded. "You'll need steel, and —"

"Most of all, you'll need maps," Yitz interrupted, his eyes keen, with something in his gaze that made Hephaestion uneasy. "You and I will book a railcar to go to the Songhai enclave. Just us."

"With what money, husband?"

"With credit. I don't think we should wait on the first payment to arrive." Yitz was uncharacteristically commanding.

Boudica nodded in agreement. "The Africans have good steel. Songhai javelins are feats of balance and weight."

Adina chimed in. "The Japanese claim to have the best steel in all of New Dis. You can stop in their ward on the way there."

Boudica shook her head. "Japanese have a proven process in their forging, but their iron is little more than pig iron. You want Hellsteel from a Hellfire crucible, which means Persian steel. The Persians have their ward next to the Africans. Songhai will have access to that steel. I know." Boudica pulled at her short sword in its scabbard, exposing as little of the blade as possible. "They made me this gladius with their own Damascus steel while I was there."

Hephaestion stepped closer, leaning in to examine the blade, cast in a dull red with dark swirls, almost like it had frozen while still in a liquid state. Heat radiated from it.

"I won't take it out of its sheath here," Boudica said. "But I assure you, Lord Hephaestion, there is nothing sharper than this steel." She snapped the blade back into its resting place.

"Besides," added Yitz. "The Japanese in New Dis's enclave are all Christians. They've run out all their Buddhists and Shinto, and are run by the Jesuits now. You'll want to avoid them."

Hephaestion nodded. "All right, the Africans win it. Songhai, is it?"

"Yes, there you'll get the best maps. The Songhai are mathematicians, and many of them have descended here simply to measure and calculate Hell's rings. You'll need to speak to the Queen herself to get access to them, however."

Hephaestion had heard that Hell itself couldn't be mapped, so what aid could a map possibly be? He set his question aside, and opted to take the advice of wiser people.

Adina wandered over to Yitz and plunked down next to him, her head on his shoulder. "Will this mean you'll be leaving me alone for a few days then, husband? You certain you can trust me in such a town as this?"

"With two hundred years of credit to our names, you mean?"

"Mmm hmmm."

"Buy me something nice."

CHAPTER 13

Minu, a master at her craft, produced two lovely kameezes: one red with copper threading, and the other black with silver needlework. Both hung down below his knees, but high enough not to impede his stride. Each sleeve was elegantly cuffed and the red one boasted a high, regal collar.

"Something nice for you," Minu said. "I heard through the door that you're meeting a Queen." She watched Hephaestion spin slowly in his new garb. "You can fight in this. I picked dark colors to hide blood."

"I'm having a hard time figuring out if you looked better naked or not, Hephaestion." Boudica remarked from her pillow.

Hephaestion felt relieved walking back fully clothed to Adina and Yitz's apartment. He'd chosen to wear the red kameez first because it was Minu's favorite color and he figured it would please her. Despite the cloth being so finely thin, he felt warm to his core as he moved down the street, somehow feeling taller.

He examined the city streets with more confidence.

The people moving about had come from all time periods and regions. Many sported walking canes or decorative swords on their hips. Occasionally, a steam-powered trolley car would rumble by, parting the murmuring crowd. A man in a stovepipe rode by on a steel horse, its skeletal frame glowing from the blazing fire within its ribcage. He nodded politely, pipe in hand, at Adina.

Hephaestion took note that nearly everyone, no matter how well-dressed or imposing in station or stature, stepped aside for Boudica. Many nodded in respect, and several outright bowed specifically at Minu as Hephaestion's entourage passed.

"Are all of you well known?" he asked.

Minu tugged gently on Hephaestion's elbow. "Good deeds spread faster than bad news," she cooed.

As pleasant as this thought may be, he understood that this was no low profile he was maintaining. If the Jesuits caught word of the famed Hephaestion in New Dis, they would at least try to monitor him, and *that* would clearly be easy by the company he now traveled with.

Grateful to be back at the apartment, Hephaestion warmly thanked Boudica and Minu.

Minu bowed back, and Boudica returned a small, single nod.

Through the use of a courier, Yitz secured a lavish railcar for the journey to Songhai. "We aren't traveling in high luxury for the sake of opulence," he validated. "Extreme luxury and expense provides the best security available. I don't want us vulnerable on the rails."

A horseless carriage carved from volcanic glass came for them the next day. The spoked wheels were of polished red steel and the driver sat high on its rear, facing over the roof, a giant wheel gripped in his hands as though he were steering a schooner.

The valet, his powdered wig bouncing as he leapt off the carriage's side, snatched Yitz's handbag. With a stiff tug, he swung the door open on its metal hinges, inviting the two men to enter and make themselves comfortable among its cushions and hookah offerings.

The door glided closed behind them, encasing them both in momentary darkness until cords of light began to glow in a spiral pattern on the ceiling.

"An electrically lit horseless carriage," Yitz marvelled. "I don't even hear the street outside."

It swayed gently side-to-side, and Hephaestion tried not to enjoy his comfort too much.

Yitz eyed him over keenly. "What *is* it with you, anyhow?" he pried. "You'll be in the pits of fiery hell soon enough. You should take advantage of what fruits your violence has already yielded. Besides, you and I both know you aren't going down there to rescue Alexander."

Hephaestion was shocked, and felt as though he'd been slapped in the face.

Yitz took the hookah's hose into his hands and fiddled with the tip, wondering if someone cleaned it periodically.

"You'd better explain that accusation, Yitzhak," Hephaestion seethed.

"Don't start with me. I've got you figured out. You convinced all your buddies in Purgatory to let you go by telling them that you were going to rescue your man, when in your heart you know you'll fail. You just can't stand being without him so much, and you feel so guilty that he's down there and you're *not*, that you're punishing yourself. Know how I know that? Ask me how I know that."

"Is this your idea of being a friend?" Hephaestion snarled.

"Actually, yes. Now ask. Go on."

"How do you—"

"Well, thank you for asking! First off, every time you look comfortable, like when you sit in a cushioned carriage or when Minu puts a lovely garb spun of heavenly silk on you, joy crosses your face. For just a moment, mind you, but it's there. Then, the instant you realize you're having a moment of happiness, you punish yourself and reject the notion that you're pleased. In a room full of pillows, you sit on a tiny, uncomfortable stool. You're clearly punishing yourself and I've been observing it. New clothes? Never! Time for a tantrum!"

"I honestly don't think I should take your judg—"

"You damn well better take my judgments, and take them to heart. Do you know how often I've wanted to be down there, in the frozen wastes away from God's light, next to my son? I've wanted to cling to him for all eternity so badly. It's my fault he's down there. He saw my gambling and learned my vices, and I failed him as a father. How is it I was spared Hell and dumped on the rocks of Purgatory instead? It's unjust, and God made a mistake. I tell Him that in my prayers."

Both men swayed with the buggy's gentle motion. Yitz hazarded a puff from the hookah hose, and blew a smoke ring up toward the spiral light above. "You were a general of one of the bloodiest armies in Earth's history. You can't make sense why you were sent to Purgatory, instead of Hell with the man who committed every sin at your side. You're just like me in that regard and you hate yourself for it."

"I'm going down there to get Alexander out."

"On the surface, maybe you think that, and bless you for trying, but you will fail."

"Then why are you helping me?"

"I owe you. A fortune, it seems. And you might make it down there to tell our boy that he is still loved. But just drop the act with me, is all I'm saying... from one Purgatorian to another. You and I both landed on the same rocks, and spent years wandering the same cliffs." Yitz smiled, eyes crinkling at the memory of Adina standing high on the precipice, her tichel dancing in the salty breeze. He had stumbled into her arms, sobbing and apologizing for not being a good enough man for her. She'd bound him in wool, shushed him, and sang to him. It had been the best moment of his existence.

Perhaps Alexander would feel the same way if he saw Hephaestion standing in the distance, as well.

Yitz looked at Hephaestion, seeing a hint of doubt in the mighty warrior, and a pang of guilt hit. "Look, you will find Alexander. You will, and you'll either stay with him or spend eternity trying to rescue him. Who knows, but you can't hide from me the fact that you're going down there to be near him and the rescue is an afterthought. Like Adina left Heaven to find me. Good people, like you and her, lower themselves to those they love."

They spent the rest of the carriage ride in silence and smoke rings.

CHAPTER 14

The carriage's swaying gradually eased and the door swung open to reveal the valet bent in half, genuflecting, with Yitz's bag already at his feet. The carriage's two occupants stepped out into what appeared to be the interior of a gigantic tent adorned with hanging Chinese lanterns. At its center stood a sole passenger car of polished black steel, with brass ornamentation and a small staircase in position to help the men enter.

"Each railroad car is designed to look identical from the outside," the valet lisped. "But I assure you that once within, you will find opulent comfort *unbound*."

The three men walked along the rails toward the car and, following the valet's exaggerated gesture bidding them inside, Hephaestion and Yitz entered.

Every inch of the interior had been painted by a true master. The curved ceiling gave the car an open, domed sensation, and on each wall a mural depicted ships and sea life populating a chaotic ocean. The ceiling of the interior had been painted with stars in a vibrant night sky. Each star shimmered, a tiny electric light, their vibrancy emphasized due to the window shades having been drawn down.

The glory of it struck Hephaestion.

Yitz, on the other hand, appeared largely distracted, his nostrils swelling with the scent of a roasted meal at the dining table. "I smell honeyed ham!" he rejoiced, tossing his travel bag into an empty chair. "Wine?" He reached for two empty glasses.

"Yes, thank you," answered a voice deeper from within the car. A stark man sat in a wing-backed chair, his face angular and sharp, dressed in a

plain yet flawless cassok cloak. His still, un-breathing posture had masked his presence amid the distraction of the ornamentation and food.

He slowly stood, pale hands folded, his dark eyes evaluating them.

"This is our car," Yitz said flatly.

"Which is why I'm here. Yitzhak, is it? The man known for his wife instead of the other way around. And this tall and marvelous fellow must be Lord Hephaestion, champion of Alexander's Companions? It appears both of you men are defined by your greaters."

Hephaestion went rigid, and eyed a carving knife on the table a few feet away from him. He examined the furniture for possible barricades and cover in case this cloaked man had powers such as Adina.

Despite Hephaestion's alarm, Yitz appeared unfazed.

"As are you," Yitz said. "Aren't all Jesuits defined by the love of their lives as well? Christ?"

With good humor, the Jesuit nodded. "My name is Father Jose Acanth Franco, and please know that I am vowed to nonviolence in the name of Christ. I do apologize for appearing before you two gentlemen in this manner, but it's very urgent and I'm in desperate need of your attention." With that, he sat down at the head of the table, poured himself some wine, and rifled through the bread basket for a suitable loaf.

Yitz slid close to Hephaestion and gave him a reassuring pat on the shoulder. "Sit down and keep quiet," he whispered, barely moving his lips.

The two of them sat opposite each other, with their unexpected guest focused on the food he was piling on his plate. Hephaestion slipped a steak knife under the table.

"So, we all are men defined by our loves," Father Franco continued. "It's natural that love should move us to all ends. God intended as much for us. This is why I'm here, actually! This is why all Jesuits have descended to New Dis, to provide Christ's light: love."

"So we've heard," Yitz said, casually diving into the meal himself while tucking a napkin into his collar.

Father Franco nodded in approval. "Excellent. As you may know, the Japanese ward is already converted entirely, and the Jesuits have brought the light of Christ to several other wards and enclaves, converting many — Indians, Goths, and the like."

"Your mantra is, 'that we may be altogether of the same mind and conformity,' if I recall," Yitz offered, his mouth full and dropping crumbs onto his beard.

"Right you are! We are indeed soldiers of God, and I come under a banner of peace as one soldier to another." Father Franco smiled toward Hephaestion, who still sat motionless.

"And one Purgatorian to another," Yitz said with an unrestrained grin, mashed food in his teeth.

This statement seemed to give Father Franco some pause, but he continued after gathering himself. "Indeed. I was not steadfast enough in life to earn my place in Heaven, but as you both know, we all can still find salvation even in the darkest places in the afterlife. Which is why I come to you two gentlemen today. You've drawn some considerable attention to yourselves as of late. Major financial success through rigging the largest gambling event in New Dis is an impressive and astounding feat. I heard that even a member of the friars.... What is that order's name again?"

"Order of Mercy."

"Yes, the Order of Mercy, as quaint as it is, now has several talents of wealth in their coffers because of their involvement via a member named 'Albrecht.' A well-played gamble indeed, and all under the Peruvian's nose."

"You assume that Hephaestion and I had planned the wager?"

"Clearly, but no matter. This is the Peruvian's business, I suspect. I'm just remarking how flamboyant your fame has become." Father Franco motioned his hands open, presenting the rail car's interior to the men as if they hadn't seen it prior. "But we, soldiers of God, can't help but feel that all of this 'walking naked' in the streets is a distraction of sorts. Perhaps, the real intentions are to act out in plain view, until everyone eventually becomes numb to such flagrant behavior. Then the *real* plan is enacted."

Father Franco paused to savor a mushroom that had been soaked in bourbon.

Yitz sighed lightly. "Aside from our food and hospitality, what is it you want from us?" He shot Hephaestion a sideways glance.

Hephaestion took it as a signal to prepare to strike.

"It isn't what I want, per se," Father Franco responded, "but what Provost-General van der Meer wants. He needs reassurance that you will, on your souls, swear an oath that you will not descend into the pit — especially in some ill-conceived attempt to contact loved ones."

"What do you mean?" Yitz pried.

"Some people with enormous resources think that they have the privilege, or the right, to descend into the lower reaches in an effort to

aid or even abscond with their loved ones. It is a wrongful thing to do, and very much a crime against God and His judgment. No one but Christ may ever go down there. To do so is to interrupt the order of things, and the natural progression of sinful people's salvation."

"Yet many Buddhists do it. They spend years down there in campaigns providing warmth and prayer for the punished in the Malebolge."

"That practice is becoming more and more discouraged by Provost-General. We simply cannot permit it further."

"Those Buddhists are Heaven-bound," Yitz pointed out flatly. "Perhaps you do not like being humbled by the sight of *true* soldiers of God."

"I understand your resentment, and it's natural in one such as you to feel it, but the Provost-General and the Order of the Jesuits are looking to ascend all those we can. We wish to elevate all of humanity, damned or otherwise, to God's expected standards of us. We cannot allow our desires to get in the way. We cannot love one man or woman above all others. We all are subject to God's judgment and will. It is insulting to Heaven to toy with such a thing." When speaking his last sentence, Father Franco stared directly into Hephaestion's uneasy eyes. "So again, I delight in being able to report to the Provost-General that these two men, two men that have become the stuff of alley-way legend in New Dis, have no intention of violating God's Law."

Yitz slowly nodded, deep in thought. "I understand," he said. "Do you understand, Hephaestion?"

Unsure of what to do, Hephaestion readied his knife. Was Yitz giving him the signal to open the Jesuit's throat? Rip out the man's heart through his perfect, black cassock cloak right here on this table? Hephaestion knew well enough never to kill an emissary during parley, but in the city of New Dis the rules were well beyond him.

"Well," Yitz continued casually. "I think both Hephaestion and I would be delighted to offer such a promise, but sadly it would mean little. See, Hephaestion is a sodomite and I'm a Jew. Our word is nothing to you or your high priest."

"Provost-General. Provost-General van der Meer."

"That fellow. Yes. But we do thank you for coming and eating our food and drinking our wine."

"Perhaps I haven't made your situation clear to you?" Father Franco offered dangerously.

"I do apologize that when you return to your Pope-General that all you'll have to offer him is your full belly. But it is what it is."

Yitz stood, napkin still tucked under his chin like a stained, ruffled collar a French noble would wear. He strode to the back of the railcar and swung the door open. "We appear to have a stowaway!" he shouted to the Valet.

Within moments, valets armed with muskets filled the large tent.

Father Franco stood as graciously as able and, as he walked out with his head high, said, "I look forward to discussing this in the future with both of you."

After the door shut, Hephaestion watched through the windows as they escorted Father Franco beyond the tent flaps and out of sight — tall, rigid, and elegant.

Finally, he breathed. "I thought you wanted me to kill him."

Yitz waved a hand dismissively. "Nah. I've been wrangling Christians all my existence in one way or another, and he gave away far more than he should have. He's also low in the order, which means he has more ambition than brains. Men like him think that they will earn Heaven through victory. But... he made a good point with his threat regarding the Peruvian." He picked crumbs from his beard.

"How so? That the Peruvian might think you and I planned your wager?"

"Yes. Stranger things have happened."

"The Peruvian doesn't need to believe it. He just has to make his cohorts believe it. If he convinces everyone that you and I staged the whole thing—"

"He will cease payments... and worse. Yeah, that is occurring to me."

"Will Adina be safe while we're gone?"

"She's with her friends. I think she's safer with them than The Peruvian is in his tiny fortress, honestly. But not having the money will be difficult. Oh well. We'll see what happens. I've learned to let the game ride a bit before reacting."

Yitz plunked back down in his chair and motioned to the table. "You should eat. Like I was saying in the carriage, while we don't *need* food, it does make us stronger and more anchored to our bodies. If I were you, I'd take advantage of every chance you have to sleep, eat, and drink properly. If you are to make it to my boy, you'd better."

Hephaestion gave no argument, and as he took his first bite of baked squash, his tongue remembered the many feasts he used to have in the command tent with Alexander. They'd saved food like this for celebration, and often they both fumbled with a lute drunkenly. The

lute was carved from the helm of an Athenian trireme that was shattered during the second Persian War. One might think they would show more reverence for such a fine relic, but apparently the more drunken Alexander became, the more convinced he could play it with his toes.

The two men ate silently, Hephaestion lost in warm memory as Yitz's mental gears seemingly cranked away, no doubt regarding his potential situation with the Peruvian. The wine in their glasses began to ripple and the tassels dangling from the curtains jostled.

"Oh, I want to show you something!" Yitz bounded out of his chair and pulled the curtains up.

Through the windows, Hephaestion saw that the large tent had been partly peeled away, and in stomped two fiery mechanical beasts.

"What... what are those?" he gasped. "I've never seen...."

Both four-legged beasts looked as if they'd been forged from metal bones and plates, a fire bellowing inside their chests with flames licking through their steel ribs.

"They look like headless oxen!" he said.

In place of a head, a driver sat mounted between the machine's shoulders, operating levers and pedals to steer.

"Railroads back on Earth have bulls to pull the railcars into position," Yitz said. "Here, people built *these* things. Back on Earth, steam engines are strong, but in Hell and with Hell's fire, such engines here are limitless."

Large chains were linked to the bull's yokes by railhands, and with a lurch the two smoking beasts slowly glided Hephaestion and Yitz's railcar clear of the tent. Not even a drop of wine was spilt.

"Amazing!" Hephaestion marveled as his view expanded beyond the canopy of Chinese lanterns and into the rail yard. Similar bulls shifted and dragged hundreds of identical cars while large, black steam engines hissed into position. Each engine was different in that each had a giant chrome skull sculpted on the front of it that made a different expression. Some skulls looked playful while others looked stoic or cruel.

The bulls soon linked their car into another, and then another, and soon they formed an entire train and linked it into the back of an engine.

"I wonder what face our train is making?" Hephaestion mused.

"We can check once we arrive, but I strongly advise not leaving the car at any stop. And if anyone comes to the door, I suggest we do *not* answer it," Yitz warned.

Hephaestion nodded in agreement, and soon after a tall, white obelisk in the distance caught his attention. It stood high above the warrens of New Dis, and while the rising fog and smoke from the city obscured it somewhat, there was no avoiding its dominating, pale presence.

Hephaestion pointed to it. "What is that structure, there? It looks Egyptian."

"That's The Clock. Much older. Most people think it was built by the first humans to occupy the afterlife, and they wanted a way to figure out how long they'd been here. Under it is a series of smooth-carved caverns that pipe geothermal steam from fires below. You can't see from here, but each section of it rotates at a set rate. There are markings on the sides, so once you learn its system, you can tell how much time has passed since its construction."

"How much time, then?"

"It's been operating some 46,000 years. Granted, no one knows how long it took to build, and whoever built it isn't talking or around, it seems. Some say the engineers and workers that built it went into the caverns below it and incinerated themselves. It's rumored that whenever they reform, they just do it again and again."

"To feel oblivion?" Hephaestion asked.

"Seemingly. Perhaps it's the only way they can find true rest."

Pondering for a moment, Hephaestion continued. "So it's more a calendar than a clock?"

"Maybe. The way it's built, it goes up to one million years. Rather optimistic, if you ask me. God might be sick of our mewling souls and wipe us clean from the afterlife by then, and start fresh with some other type of life."

Hephaestion, having finally grasped that New Dis was a civilization all its own, wondered if it had a standing army or a set currency.

The two men sat at the table and chatted away as the train moved and reached its full speed, discussing the city in detail and all its intricacies. Hours passed, and it was such a pleasant and comfortable conversation that Hephaestion was reminded of his enjoyable centuries in Ulfric's care. Servants came to their car and cleared the table, provided more wine, and Yitz tried teaching an inebriated Hephaestion poker.

"This game is just lying," Hephaestion laughed. "You juss use ratios to your advantage and lie and win."

"You don't like it?" Yitz asked, his voice without a slur since he could hold his alcohol much better.

"No, I love it. Is political. We used to play a game of dice like this. Wooden or ivory or bone dice. Ish was a great game of lying."

"Just like life!" Yitz announced, glass raised.

"Just like life!" Hephaestion replied in same.

One more thing about New Dis interested Hephaestion. Yitz had explained that for the past fifteen hundred years, New Dis had been a dictatorship, after the old oligarchy fell into chaos. The new leader was a man named Sun Tzu.

"So, tell me more about thish Sun Tzu. He was an oriental general?"

"Ah, the mysterious Sun Tzu. Well, he moved in and took over during the Oligarchy Civil War. See, New Dis has no standing army because... who would invade Hell? So the whole thing had turned into a horrible brawl in the streets—buildings were burned, and hearts were gathered and jarred for ransom. It was just bad. This was before Adina and I arrived here.

"The story from some who remember is that Sun Tzu just started gathering crowds of random people and helping them form regiments and pike lines to defend their streets. Eventually, whole sections of the warrens became safe for business and shelter and sleep again. The various wards and enclaves of different nations calmed down, let go of the oligarchs they'd aligned themselves with, and everyone just started following his orders.

"He built a sizable militia, too—sent them after the oligarchs. Once he'd jarred the last of their hearts, he vanished. He still rules, though. Buildings all over New Dis are available for you to speak to his representatives, but no one knows where he lives or rules from. Some say he wanders the streets as a homeless man, or maybe he's even a shapeshifter. But when you hear about an assassination of a cruel baron, or a certain overly ambitious guild's hall burning to the ground, we all know he commanded it. His militia still keeps order."

"Would he stop the Jesuits if they got too strong?"

"Presumably, but whatever he considers 'too strong' is beyond anyone but God. I will say that some groups of people tend to find their taxes suddenly lax, or maybe their shop receives a sudden and mysterious boost in business. He's always pulling strings behind the scenes, keeping certain groups in balance while off-balancing others. He's a shrewd, shrewd presence that seems to have no interest in the glory of leadership."

"That... that wasn't my Alexander at all!" Hephaestion laughed.

"Oh?"

"Alex was great, in that he would honor the local custom and dress of every territory we entered. He embraced it, so each new territory was a whole new set of rituals and parties and weddings among the men with the local daughters. At every party, he was front and center, laughing and dancing and kissing people."

"Sounds like a bit of an untamed man."

"Oh he was, my Alex. He was... untamed." Hephaestion's smile faded. "And he'll run untamed again. Soon."

Yitz sighed heavily. "I want you to remember what I said in that stage coach, especially when you are down there."

"I will, and maybe there's more truth in it than I'd like to admit. But I won't forget your boy. I promise."

With that, Yitz folded out his bed from the wall, laden with sheets of silk and fine, threaded cotton, and soon fell into snoring.

Hephaestion blew out each oil lamp, dimmed the stars overhead with the dimmer on the wall, and sat in the wingback chair to watch the landscape roll by.

Much of the outer rim of Hell was a barren, red-rocked wasteland. Sometimes a distant light could be seen from a far-off compound or structure, but aside from the occasional opposite running train, the landscape was as vast and empty of life as the sky above.

CHAPTER 15

It was amazing to Hephaestion that he had traveled so far so quickly. He surmised that trains had changed the living world.

"Could you imagine the supply lines with these? The logistical advantages?" His head swam with possibility.

"I've heard that the current war on Earth uses trains, some even have cannons on them that fire when stationary to destroy cities." Yitz stretched from his rest. "We've gone about two hundred and forty leagues by now, so our stop is coming up soon."

Within an hour it did. The station itself stretched as long as the train, built of hard, baked clay. Upon closely inspecting the walls, Hephaestion could see the palm prints of those who molded its subtle lines and sloping angles. It reminded him of the structures of small hamlets that had welcomed the Companions on their trek east. Perhaps the Songhai people would welcome him in the same manner.

Hephaestion placed his own palm into a print of another in the wall. Would he have been a molder of walls if he hadn't been Alexander's companion? Certainly there would be no glory in it, but as Hephaestion appreciated the structure's tall windows and domed ceilings, he could see the pride in the craftsmanship.

"You're like a child," Yitz said. "Just have to touch everything."

"It makes it real."

"Well, the Queen we're about to meet is real. Don't touch *her*, for God's sake. We had to dedicate some serious money to one of her expeditions to earn this little meeting with her. If we fund her people going down there, we get to see some maps."

"Does that mean I'll have to travel with others?" Hephaestion asked.

"No, no... you just keep *not talking* and I'll handle the rest."

Two rickshaws, their canopies hung with blue patterned silks for privacy, stood waiting for them. Both runners were tall, black men of statuesque physique, their muscles oiled, and adorned with elegant gold bands around their wrists and necks. Each had short swords at their sides.

They bowed.

Yitz gave a wave and climbed in while Hephaestion made certain to return their bow in equal measure.

He felt not a single bump in the road through the seat cushions as the runners hauled their passengers without interruption. The crowds parted immediately upon hearing the tiny bells lining the canopy.

Through the silk veil, Hephaestion evaluated the people of Songhai and found them to be tall, with strong faces and magnificent color. Some wore vibrant clothing that covered them from head to foot with the most dizzying patterns, while others wore little but a belt and loincloth as they moved about, laughing and chatting. An emotive people, their hands pantomimed ideas and their feet always shuffled. There was less conservation of movement here, fewer cars, and not a guard in sight.

They rode under bridges of brick and through narrow streets of windows and dangling onlookers, until two enormous gates stood open before them. Throngs of people moved in and out, crowded shoulder to shoulder, but again the tiny chiming of the rickshaws' bells parted everyone. No one gawked or pointed or whispered, they simply moved undeterred from their conversations and activities.

Into a large courtyard they entered, surrounded by statues of great heroes and paragons standing tall for visitors to examine and honor. Passing under each one, Hephaestion wondered which were royalty from the Queen's lineage.

Soon they entered an antechamber of white stone and tiny flowing channels of water under their feet, cooling and ionizing the chamber's air. The runners lifted the veils, helped Hephaestion and Yitz to their feet, and led them toward a small alcove. In the center sat a round table, at which they were directed to sit. They squeezed in and sat across from each other, Yitz still clinging to his travel bag.

Both runners bowed and left, leaving Yitz somewhat dismayed. "So, we're in a tiny booth, and I have my toothbrush. I'm not sure what happens next. She might be busy so we may have to wait for—"

Suddenly, with the sound of grinding stone gears, the entrance to their alcove sealed up into a stone wall. They were trapped, and the sensation of moving took both of their stomachs. Yitz gripped his bag harder and Hephaestion clung to the table.

Soon the opposite wall of the alcove shifted away and the grinding noise stopped. They sat staring into a domed chamber lit by torches and magnifying mirrors along the walls. The room was built as a half-sphere, its perfect, curved walls depicting a mural of Purgatory. As the mural drew closer to the very top of the room, it faded to white and was illuminated by the gentle glow of dangling oil lamps.

Hephaestion stepped out of the alcove first, his feet landing on what looked like a tiny, tiled representation of a Chinese castle. The floor was covered with tiny buildings and streets, and to his left and right sat small cathedrals and towns and railroad yards and even miniature Zeppelins.

"Stay where you are, and I will guide you to me," announced a rich, womanly voice from the throne at the center of the room, a slim, angular chair. Its only distinguishing feature were the large black wings fashioned into its back, which reached high into the air. They cast a long shadow over the throne's occupant, obscuring her face.

Yitz stepped next to Hephaestion. "Well, here we go," he whispered.

"Currently," she began, "you are standing in the Han district. To one side are the Germans and the Gauls, and if you look on the other side, you'll see Indus. Take a moment to orient yourselves."

As she explained this, Hephaestion realized that the room's floor was a series of concentric rings, each one modeled after a level of Hell, and each slowly rotating against each other and at different speeds.

This was their map.

No wonder Hell can't be easily mapped. Each ring is in motion! Hell is an ever-changing clockwork landscape.

"Now step forward, both of you," she commanded.

The men obeyed, the next circle moving slowly toward their right.

"Currently you are standing in the mists. This ring is filled with those so sexually obsessed that all they craved was the baser sensations of the flesh. They had forsaken their humanity in pursuit of such, and are all reduced to ghostly vapors clinging to a cliff face that leads to New Dis."

Hephaestion and Yitz looked about their toes at the wailing faces subtly carved into the ring on which they stood.

"Forward once more, gentlemen," she urged.

The next ring moved much faster, and its white and jagged surface gave their feet difficulty.

"You stand on the gluttons, those who gathered or destroyed food. People who denied food as a weapon against rival tribes or cultures are found here."

Hephaestion knew this particular practice well. A besieged city might resort to cannibalism, or at the very least anyone within its walls that appeared well-fed soon found their throat slit and food stash stolen. When laying siege to a city, starvation was a far more effective weapon than any catapult.

"The next circle is the land of boulders," the Queen said, standing as she gracefully adjusted the golden shawl around her shoulders. Her skin was as black and perfect as polished onyx, so dark it exuded a purple hue as rich as her voice. "Those who hoard for no reason roll boulders toward the pit's edge, while those who were exceedingly wasteful roll them back. They do this endlessly as a representation of the uselessness of their life's pursuits — punishment for squandering oneself so successfully in life. Step forward again, but be careful. The next circle moves *fast*."

With one hand steadying Yitz, Hephaestion led the way.

"Next is the abandoned city of Dis, a place for the Hellbound long ago. Hell's free population became too great, so a great migration occurred, founding New Dis and establishing trade with Purgatory. But horrible things still haunt the vacant palaces of old Dis. Step forward again."

Looking ahead, Hephaestion saw that as they approached the throne, each circle seemed to be moving faster. Hephaestion and Yitz had to be spry.

"Here is the river of tears, filled with those who are wantonly wrathful without purpose, as well as those who are intently sullen in an effort to drag those around them down."

This time the Queen extended a hand gently toward the men, like a life-line soon to be in reach. They obeyed and took a leap forward. Both men jostled and clung to each other for balance as they rotated around her throne, her open hand following them.

"And now The Wood... saddest of all. Why people do not leave those trees in peace shames humanity. Please step gently on that ring, as we all have family there."

"We're trying, your highness!" Yitz blurted, one arm clinging to Hephaestion while the other spun outward for balance.

"Here is true horror and violence," she said. "These men and women are so bathed in the blood of the living that they boil in the blood of the damned in the fiery river of Phlegethon."

The circle they stood on was red with tiny bones painted all over it.

"Forward again, gentlemen, to the frauds! Fakers, falsifiers, and deceivers! Thieves of hearts and minds! Manipulators and sowers of discord!" she roared, as if the mere mention of such crimes raised her ire.

This circle was wider than the others, with dozens of smaller, shifting sections, like a puzzle that actively evaded solving.

As both men stumbled about for footing, she leaned out to them. "Take my hand, gentlemen, and step over the last and most heinous of all, the traitors. Do not pollute your heels with them!"

Hephaestion saw Yitz wince noticeably, and he understood at once. The man was thinking of his boy and what he must endure, perhaps even grateful that Hephaestion would be the one to see his boy in the throes of torment, because as a father, Yitz could not tolerate such a sight and remain whole.

The Queen's grip hoisted each man up to her throne's pedestal, and the two of them stood close enough to feel her hot breath barreling onto them. As tall and fearsome as Hephaestion, a hint of cruel joy danced in her eyes.

Suddenly every circle stopped its motion in an echoing 'clank' and everything fell still. "And, much like the Fallen One deep below, the throne is at the center," she continued. "You stand in the map room of Songhai, designed by Euclid himself. He has charted the rates and motions of each circle over the course of eight expeditions. It is the most accurate map of the Hells to exist." She bowed deeply. "I am Queen Nikaule Sungbon of the Songhai enclave, and I am at your service." Her clinking gold jewelry illuminated her angles, and her crisp pagne was cinched tight against her muscular frame.

Hephaestion returned the bow as best he knew how.

Yitz awkwardly followed suit.

"And you are Yitzhak Isserles, infamous gambler as of late and investor in Euclid's *ninth* expedition into Hell, yes? Your tall and comely companion is instantly recognizable to me, but I can't fathom why you'd keep such a famous associate secret. Why did you not make me privy that Lord Hephaestion of Macedonia himself was to grace my chamber? I would have prepared a feast." She offered her hand to Hephaestion.

He took it, and found her grip firm and steady. "Where do you recognize me from, my Queen?"

"Yours is a face carved in the mountains of much of the world. I remember being a little girl on Earth, and in a garden there stood a statue of you, perfect and bold. This was in Northeastern Africa."

"I'm embarrassed to say I am unfamiliar with that particular statue."

"Don't be, Supreme Champion of Macedonia. Greatness such as yourself cannot fathom its echo across the ages. Even today on Earth, they know your face." Queen Sungbon raised her eyebrows. "I was informed that you wanted to meet in order to procure maps of the coming expedition, yes? I must ask some probing questions before I part with the greatest treasure of Songhai."

"Of course," Yitz said.

She clapped her hands sharply, and servants emerged from the shadows with a long wooden table and three chairs. "Please be comfortable." She beckoned as she sat herself at the head.

Both men took their place.

"It is atypical for anyone to request access to our maps. While they are highly prized, to put it bluntly, most know better. Euclid's ninth expedition will be well conducted, I assure you. There is no reason for you to see any maps prior."

Yitz responded with his hands folded and back straight. "We have complete faith in your further handling of such explorations, Queen Sungbon. I apologize for any disrespect my request for your maps may have caused."

She nodded in acceptance of his apology. "Then it is settled. Let us talk about the transfer of funding, and we can hammer out the details regarding when the expedition will launch. We already have the team assembled."

Yitz swallowed hard. "I look forward to acquiring the money from my debtor to forward onto you."

She glared hard at Yitz, her nostrils flaring briefly. Her gaze turned toward Hephaestion, who sat calmly leaning back in his chair. "Am I to assume you do not have the funds *with* you? Even a promissory note?"

"No, my Queen," Hephaestion confessed.

Yitz jumped back in. "As I said prior, we have complete intention—"

"Intentions mean little to me, the Queen of Songhai, Mr. Isserles. Commitment through money, however, means quite a bit. I am also getting the sinking feeling that you only came for a glance at this room and perhaps my precious maps. Was this a limp attempt to get

something for nothing from Songhai?" She raised her voice without yelling, its richness filling every curve of the room.

Both men remained silent.

"I need a map," Hephaestion said flatly. "I might be able to find others elsewhere, but you clearly have the best."

"And what do you, pray tell, need my maps *for*, Lord Hephaestion?"

Yitz's foot jabbed into Hephaestion's shin from under the table, but he ignored it and answered the question. "I'm going into Hell myself on my own personal expedition. I cannot divulge any other details, but what I intend will not harm you or come back to haunt you in any manner. I'll leave here and you'll never see me again."

"So this is all personal?" she asked, eyes narrow.

Hephaestion nodded while Yitz sunk in his chair.

"This would explain the cable I received from a Father Jose Acanth Franco earlier today. He said that you two were planning something illicit and that, if I was involved in your expedition, I would be held culpable by law."

Yitz nodded in understanding. "Madam, we very much do intend to fully fund Euclid's next expedition that you sponsor. Please do not think for a moment our intentions are anything but genuine. Granted, it is true that we have additional intentions, but they are far from illicit."

"What are they?" she demanded, voice large again.

Shrugging with defeat toward Hephaestion, Yitz sat back and let him take over.

"I am going to do two things," Hephaestion began. "I am going to first find Yitz's son and deliver a message to him from his loving parents. Second, I am going to find Alexander."

"What do you intend to do with Alexander once you find him?" she pressed.

"You will never know, because I will never be returning to New Dis."

Drumming her fingers on her armrest, Queen Sungbon entered deep thought. "I do not appreciate being in this position," she said half to herself. "On the one hand, you have no money, so why would I even *cater* to you. On the other hand, I deeply desire a ninth expedition, and by the off chance you fulfill your financial commitment, I will have it."

Hephaestion went to speak but Yitz's hand instantly found his forearm and squeezed ferociously.

The gesture drew the Queen's attention, and she stared them both down. First her gaze pierced Yitz, but when it settled on Hephaestion's face, it softened.

For a moment, she had a flash of memory. Queen Sungbon was a little girl again at a handsome statue's feet, humming the songs of her grandmother while wiggling her toes in the Earth's soft grass.

She clapped her hands sharply once more. Men came again from the shadows, and the tallest one bent his ear to her lips. After receiving her whispered commands, he nodded to the rest of the men and everyone scattered as quickly as they had come.

"Gentlemen," the queen said, "I don't appreciate the Jesuits issuing veiled threats to me. I suspect whatever law they speak of is their own, which merely encourages me to violate it. Tell me exactly what it is you need, and the fewer details regarding your intentions, the better."

Hephaestion and Yitz initially asked only for maps, but it was clear that the Queen might be willing to provide more. With growing boldness, Hephaestion and Yitz requested kindling, rope, several flambeaux, and before the afternoon was done, Hephaestion found himself being fitted into a splint mail cuirass, with a short sword at his side and a javelin in his hands.

"Do I look more like your statue, my Queen?" Hephaestion asked.

She smiled. "No. Your statue was completely naked."

CHAPTER 16

Queen Sungbon offered Yitz and Hephaestion lodging for the night in the palace, and both men graciously accepted.

Soon Yitz found himself joyously lost in the pleasures of the bathhouse, a scrawny pale figure among taller and darker ones. Taking full advantage of the Queen's hospitality, he received massages and mud baths that eased his stresses and rejuvenated his humor.

The Queen cordially challenged Hephaestion to a game of chess, and guards led him to her personal chambers. The rooms were extensive but small and intimate, each adorned with paintings of animals, mountain ranges, or oceans.

"Earth changes so much," the Queen said. "We try and paint it as best we can remember. Future generations will have their *own* Earth to adore and remember. On these walls, you will see *our* Earth."

On the chess board before them, of regular size, each piece had been carved intricately from bone.

"This chess set was a gift from a man named Emmett Landis," she said. "He's an unusual man, and you will most likely make his acquaintance when you descend into the pit. He has a tower on the edge of the Suicide Wood, where he keeps watch to scare away lumberjacks and offer safe haven to traveling Buddhists. You need only show him that you have a map from Songhai in your possession and he will guard you ferociously."

"Thank you again for all of this," Hephaestion said.

"You are welcome." The Queen moved her pawn. "It's your move."

The two played in silence, their pieces spreading wide over the board. Each square soon became a dangerous trap with multiple pieces protecting each other in a battle of foresight and strategy. Ulfric had taught Hephaestion the rules to this game, and had even taught him several dirty maneuvers to lead to a quick and cheap victory. Hephaestion restrained himself though, instead wanting to draw the game out for the sake of his rare company.

"So, Alexander is in the blood-river of Phlegethon," she bluntly offered.

Hephaestion nodded. "I know."

"Despite having a map through the Hells, it would be extraordinary to locate a single man among the millions of murderous people that boil there."

"I know, but it can be walked — every league if need be."

She nodded in understanding before moving her bishop. "I would do the same for any of my sons."

Hephaestion finally took a leap to attempt a victory, moving his knight into position. "How many sons do you have?" He intended to distract his opponent with conversation.

"Six."

"Six? That's a lot of sons." He chuckled.

"I know it!" Her smile shone with fond memories.

"Did you have to hunt them down in the afterlife?"

"No, they were all Heaven-bound and came to me in Purgatory. They were *very* good boys," she beamed, her pride bolstered even further as she intercepted Hephaestion's knight and took it.

The game quickly cascaded into a war of attrition, pieces falling on either side rapidly.

"So many different cultures and nations claim to have invented chess," she mused. "The Chinese had a version they play with dice so that no outcome is certain. The Koreans had several different kinds of pawns."

"Do you know who actually *did* invent chess?"

"People living south of the Hindu Kush along the banks of the Indus River... but perhaps that is merely the people I choose to credit. Perhaps everyone reached the same idea of chess."

Silence reigned again as they exchanged killing blows against each other's chessboard minions.

The Queen finally broke the silence. "Some expeditions go missing when they descend near the River Phlegethon. Even some monks have

gone missing. Things are strange down there, and it certainly isn't our maps that are at fault. Mr. Landis writes us letters reporting that he sees smoke in the distance, and some sections of Suicide Wood is entirely stripped clean. You must be mindful of the pits of Hell."

"I will be."

"If you are caught with our map, you must swear to me its destruction. It cannot fall into the wrong hands, especially Jesuits. Most of all, them. They did not earn this knowledge and yet demand the privilege of it."

"I will be certain not to let them have it."

"The Jesuit Order has driven out the Shinto and Buddhists from the Japanese enclave, and many seek glory under their banner. The Jesuits promise the fastest path to Heaven through *them*. They are powerful and have alluring promises to those who are desperate."

"I understand."

"Do you? Do you know how many people in the afterlife would love you as a trophy? Or feel vindicated in peeling off your skin?" She took Hephaestion's queen with her own.

This gave Hephaestion pause.

"You have many enemies, Lord Hephaestion. All conquerors do."

"That life is over. I'm just a man looking for another man. That's all I am now."

Queen Sunghon placed a long-fingered hand on Hephaestion's arm. "Moving on isn't so simple, Lord Hephaestion. You certainly can understand that, for some, all they have is what they loved on Earth. And you and I both know you took *much* when you lived. You took much of what others loved."

Her pieces had surrounded his king, and he had no move to make.

CHAPTER 17

Their eyes wide with wonder, Yitz and Hephaestion's heads craned over the "map" of the Hells. As their car teetered and ricketed on the rails, both men took turns spinning and twisting the various dials and gears on the device.

"So, it isn't a map, per se, but more of an astrolabe?" Yitz said, befuddled while examining the Queen's gift, no larger than a dinner plate. "Makes sense, I suppose. How else would you map a moving landscape?"

Hephaestion was somewhat intimidated by the thing. "She said it will be far easier to use while in the pit itself. The Queen discussed it with me a bit over chess."

Several icons on the astrolabe seemed to indicate landmarks and particular environments, and he felt confident that if he deciphered the astrolabe correctly, it would guide him toward Alexander.

"Stunning marvel of engineering, this," Yitz said. "These markings here seem to indicate bridges and towers. If we can find something distinct like that, you are golden." His fingers combed over the object as thoroughly as his eyes did. "Strange worlds require strange maps."

The Queen's generosity hadn't ended with the astrolabe, either. Hephaestion now had proper armor, and he wore it over Minu's kamees for the sake of comfort and warmth. The armor, a combination of leather and small scales like those of a fish, was accompanied by boots that reinforced the ankle and heel. His shoulders, however, remained bare despite the protection to his chest and torso.

"Armoring the shoulder slows down the killing blow," Queen Sungbon had said to him while he was being fitted.

At Hephaestion's side hung a simple short sword of perfect weight and edge. The dark swirls in its surface indicated the finest steel that Persia had to offer. With a leather ergonomic grip, it would be a perfect thrusting weapon.

The javelin gave some concern, however. Hephaestion found it too light and flexible. When he lunged with it, the tip would bounce about, skewing his typically precise strikes.

"This is not a spear, but a hunter's tool. Lovely as it is, it would be better suited to slaying gazelle than men." He'd handled it in the train car for some time before, but practicing his thrust had only frustrated him.

"And the pistol?" Yitz asked.

The Queen's final gift, a pepperbox pistol, was a tiny firearm, each of its four barrels designed to fire at once. It sat in a holster high between his shoulder blades, its handle peeking from behind his neck so his right hand could reach back and grab it in emergencies. Hephaestion had never fired a gun before, and he found the weapon heavy and awkward.

He shook his head and sighed. "I honestly have no idea. As warfare changes on Earth, I suppose it does here too." He sank into a plush chair. "When we return to your home, I'll prepare and head out soon after. I'm eager to get underway. Please do not take offense."

Yitz perked up an eyebrow. "Why would I take offense?"

"You, Adina, Minu, and Boudica have been kind. I was never expecting that from the capital of Hell. Do not think me rude to leave your hospitality."

Yitz nodded in obvious appreciation.

Both men relaxed as the train ride continued in comfortable silence, Yitz napping with his feet on the dining table, Hephaestion gazing out the window into the dark, misty beyond of the distant abyss. As he fidgeted with the astrolabe his worries grew. In the pits below lurked beasts and monstrosities undreamt of by sane minds. He'd heard tell of places of freezing ice and searing, licking flames. Some sinners were shackled to their punishments, while others roamed free to punish their peers. Heartbreak, misery, and violence beyond Earthly measure waited below for him. Something as simple as slipping from a rock could lead to his heart being devoured or burnt to ash, and how many decades would it take to reform? How many centuries would this journey take? How mad must he be to do this? What insanity has possessed him?

Love, clearly. Soothing warmth crept into his face and brought him a smile. They would live in purgatory, he and Alexander. They would have a hut in Ulfric's stead and help other lost souls find peace. They would drink mead and wine and make love in the evenings.

Hephaestion's most secret wish of all came to mind: they would eventually work their way into Heaven together, holding hands, bathed in gentle beauty.

Such dreams and wishes filled Hephaestion until the train slowed to a gradual stop, having arrived at their station. The fire-bellied mechanical bulls pulled their railcar back into its tent in their smooth and practiced ritual.

Reluctant to wake Yitz just yet from his comfortable nap, Hephaestion continued to fumble with his mapping dial when he heard a slight *thump* on the ceiling of the train. Then a tiny *tink* came from the side below the window. The valets hadn't come to open the door, and he could see none through the windows.

Suddenly, all of the hanging Chinese lanterns above went out, bringing the railcar to complete darkness.

He dove to his knees and slithered along the floor to the light controls, and raised them just enough so the electric stars above gave off some light.

"Yitz!" he hissed. "Yitz, we're surrounded. Get up!"

Yitz only stirred and picked at his nose.

Hephaestion drew his short sword, and cursed himself for leaving his shield with Adina.

They came through the windows, three of them, clad in studded leather armor with red masks. They moved for Hephaestion with hooks and chains.

Yitz yelped and dove under the dinner table.

Hephaestion drove his blade upward into the groin of the nearest one, causing him to screech. With his free hand, Hephaestion gripped the man's throat and drove him back into his comrades, giving a twist of his blade to castrate his assailant. Injured and gushing, the man wailed in agony as his two comrades stepped around him, weapons ready. One hurled a hooked chain aimed at Hephaestion's head, but he deflected it with his short sword. The other pulled a cone-shaped pistol, but before he could fire, Yitz shoved a chair at him from his hiding place under the table, striking the gunman's hip and causing the blast from the weapon to hit the ceiling.

Sparks rained from the stars.

Hephaestion grabbed the loose chain and tugged *hard*, bringing its wielder in closer. With three rapid and expert swings, he slashed the attacker's throat and chest, which gushed open as Hephaestion kicked him to the side.

The gunman remained. He dropped his spent pistol and with a flexing gesture, blades sprung from both his arms like long bear claws. Roaring forward, he swiped wildly.

Hephaestion's armor took several of the blows he'd been unable to deflect, but soon the man had gained an advantage. Losing ground and being pressed into the wall, Hephaestion continued to parry what he could but just couldn't keep up, and one of his adversary's blades struck into his shoulder.

Just when a second swipe was about to dig into the opposite shoulder, a sharp metal point burst from his stomach stopping just short of Hephaestion's chest. Yitz grunted from behind the attacker, bent javelin in his hands, as he tried to steer the skewered enemy against the wall.

Without hesitation, Hephaestion sliced his sword upward into the man's underarm, severing his auxiliary artery.

With all of his meager weight, Yitz pinned the man downward, javelin still gripped firm in his hands. "That's *it*," he snarled. "I'm getting our money back for this damned rail car!"

Hephaestion, his shoulder bleeding and huffing for breath, sunk below the windows. "Stay low. This isn't over," he whispered, adjusting his grip on his sword.

Yitz nodded, grumbling as he failed to dig the spear out of the assassin's body. "These are boys of The Peruvian," he said as he spied the chained weapons. "Bastard is going to renegotiate his interest over my payment for this!"

Hephaestion took his pistol from behind his shoulders and handed it to Yitz. "Aim for the heart."

Yitz gripped the weapon in both hands, clutching it close while drawing back the hammer.

"I can only assume," a booming voice called out, "that since my men haven't dragged you out here to confess your crime, you managed to handle them!" The voice came from somewhere in the darkness outside the railcar, within the tent.

"Is that *him*? The Peruvian?" Hephaestion asked.

Yitz nodded, cleared his throat, and projected a voice much calmer and more confident that his demeanor implied. "Indeed we did. Do you have more?"

"Yitzhak, bravado is unlike you," the Peruvian called back. "And I have grenades. If I wanted you in pieces, I would have made it happen."

"My wife prefers just the one, thank you!" Yitz replied.

"She's not here to protect you. And don't think a man like me doesn't have his ways of dealing with the powerful, Heaven-bound or not. You *cheated* me."

"*What?*"

"I admit, I couldn't figure out how you did it, but that man in there was your surprise horse in the betting. You and Albrecht, thick as thieves."

"Where are you getting such bizarre ideas? Is this your attempt to renege from what you owe? Paying me doesn't hurt you any! You made a fortune off that wager!"

"Do you think me a *moron*? My entire reputation is in danger! The Jesuits have proof of you two being in league, and when that gets out before I handle the situation personally, no one will ever use me as a bookmaker again!"

"You and I both know the Jesuits *lie!* Ha! Just wait until everyone finds out you act on claims of proof without actually *seeing it*. You're just the next step in their takeover! Do you think they will permit any betting to continue once they've got everyone fighting amongst themselves? They're doing this because they want Hephaestion!" Yitz's calm, melting rapidly, gave way to anger. "But I'll tell you what *will* ruin your reputation: betraying the people you owe money to just so you can keep it to yourself! And using 'the Jesuits said so' as your pathetic excuse makes you a *puppy!*"

Only silence came from outside the railcar.

"Well?" Yitz demanded. "Are you going to see reason and talk with us, or do we all sit here until trumpets sound?"

The Chinese lanterns glowed again and the two men ventured a glance outside.

The Peruvian sat in a wooden folding chair in the tent, surrounded by a dozen men in red masks. His fingers paddled his trim beard as he stared at the railcar.

Hephaestion knew he couldn't possibly hold off such a large force.

"All right," the Peruvian said. "But let me see this man, the Hephaestion."

Hephaestion slowly rose to stand before the window.

"You're the man that clawed his way out of a glutton at Minos's feet, yes?" the Peruvian asked.

Hephaestion nodded.

"Why in the world would you do such a thing?"

"I am going into the pit to rescue someone."

"What?"

"You heard me."

"Who?"

"Alexander the Great."

With that, the Peruvian nearly fell out of his chair.

"Wait... Alexander? You're going into the pit to rescue Alexander? And does the Provost General know this?"

"He does, because they already threatened us and said they would have *you* come after us as well."

"Father Franco was in our railcar waiting to intimidate us!" Yitz interrupted, pistol still quivering in his hands. "Would it be amiss to guess that name rings a bell, sir?"

With a sudden and angry motion, the Peruvian stood and snapped his fingers, and his men snatched up his chair and folded it. "Leave my men there, if you please. I also suggest that you begin your journey into the depths sooner than later, sodomite." He spun on his heels, and his entourage followed the Peruvian as he moved toward the exit flap of the tent. "Oh," he suddenly called over his shoulder. "One more thing... The Order of Mercy hasn't seen your friend Albrecht since that fateful day of your fame and fortune. You might want to check on your friend. I *do* have to pay him as well, after all."

CHAPTER 18

Minu's home swelled with lamenting refugees from the Japanese enclave. Those who had refused to kiss the General Provost's cross had been exiled from the entire Japanese ward of New Dis, and many now wandered the wastes searching for refuges. Some had found Minu's home, having followed the rumors of her infinite tenderness, to New Dis's central ward.

When Hephaestion entered Minu's foyer, exhausted and bloodied with Yitz at his side, he witnessed the sobbing mass in their disposed shame—a tragically familiar sight for him. Regardless of race or creed, people suddenly finding themselves cast out of their nation always had the same bewildered look in their eyes.

"What in the Hell happened here?" Yitz called, running to Adina. His hands flew about her face and ribs to make sure she was uninjured.

"People in need, dear husband. They're starting to flood parts of the ward and Minu has taken in all those she can. We...." Adina stopped mid-sentence upon seeing Hephaestion's bleeding shoulder. "What happened?" she asked sternly, a cold fury brewing in her as she examined the shoulder wound, bound in a ripped table cloth from the posh railcar.

Her veneer of calm had apparently reached its end, and the air began to ionize around her.

"We were attacked," Hephaestion said. "The Peruvian was pitted against us by a Jesuit, a 'Father Franco,' and apparently that's not all. Albrecht is missing."

"That much I learned while you were gone—about Albrecht." She glanced around. "These people refused to swear allegiance to the Jesuit Order, so they were driven out of their homes by their neighbors that *did*. The General Provost put several members of his order in charge of the Japanese, and the Samurai are maintaining martial law there. I don't know how something like this could possibly happen! Wouldn't Sun Tzu have intervened?"

Yitz clutched his wife, the two embracing with the frantic relief of the other's safety. Afterward, Adina shifted back into crisis-management mode. "Go in the back with Minu, both of you. She's meeting with someone here on account of Albrecht missing. If you get a chance at all, try and see if anyone here needs some wine or maybe a sweet roll. They are proud people, but comfort wouldn't go amiss in these times."

Both men obeyed.

The double-doors, behind which Minu had previously stitched and sewn in secret, stood propped wide open. Wooden looms had been pushed against the wall and several tables had been set out into a makeshift dining area. People clamored everywhere, some wandering about offering kind words, a few crying on the floor while gently cradled by their loved ones.

A young Christian monk, bald with cobalt-blue eyes, sat across from Minu. He had a cup of tea in his hands and they whispered to each other as he sipped.

Minu's eyes flickered in Hephaestion's direction. She spied his injury immediately, rose to her feet, and guided him into her empty chair. "You have been attacked, and you look like you could use some tea. Abbot?"

Yitz, feeling anxious to learn about Albrecht, pulled up a chair and watched Abbot Gottbert as he tended Hephaestion's shoulder. The abbot appeared to be more boy than man, his physical age no more than late teens. Albrecht had gushed about him on occasion during his bouts of endless chatter. 'Gottbert is as tender as a lamb,' or, 'Gottbert died too young to properly sin.'

Looking at him, Yitz hoped that Abbot Gottbert was as marvelous as Albrecht had said. Despite being loath to admit such a thing out loud, Yitzhak was terrified for the well-being of his mouthy friend. He waited silently and patiently as the abbot's hands cupped Hephaestion's wounds.

Abbot Gottbert began to mumble a devout prayer under his breath as his eyes rolled back into his head and his eyelids fluttered.

Hephaestion sat still, seeming more curious than concerned.

The abbot pulled his hands away and revealed that Hephaestion's lacerations had completely healed — as if they never existed.

"How did you do that?" Yitz asked. "I've never seen that before."

"Christ's blood, the transaction it provided, allows for healing," the boy-abbot said in a gentle, tenor voice.

"I am not Christian," Hephaestion confessed.

"Christ died for humanity, not merely a *portion* of it. Through me, He provides his intentions to *you*." Abbot Gottbert smiled, his youthful eyes lighting up.

"Do you know where Albrecht is?" Yitz blurted, unable to contain his worry further.

"Actually, that's why I'm here. I was hoping you could tell us. We at the order are worried, and when the Peruvian delivered a large sum of money, it compounded the mystery. Hearing that he was last seen with you, we eventually wandered here." Gottbert paused and, after a moment of thought, sighed with defeat. "You do not know where he is, either?"

"No, the last I saw him he was distracting the Ushers as they were chasing after Hephaestion here." Yitz gestured. "If none of us have seen him, could he still be in the compound?"

"We thought it probable. Unsurprisingly, none of the Ushers answer their knocker and we can't seem to contact them otherwise." Abbot Gottbert, like any denizen of New Dis, knew that the Ushers were some of the first people in the afterlife. Each Usher, an ancient cave-dwelling human being of heartless disposition, had found purpose in fulfilling the condemnations of Minos. "We're still making efforts on other fronts, however."

"Please tell me you aren't *just praying* for him." Yitz moaned.

"Nonsense!" The abbot's politeness melted instantly into temporary indignation. "God grants *strength* through prayer, not *favors*. We've sent an appeal to Sun Tzu."

"Fine lot of good he's doing lately," Yitz mumbled.

"Can we go in there and get him?" Hephaestion asked.

"That would certainly lead to violence, and we at the Order of Mercy cannot allow such a thing. Besides, to do so would bring the ire of Sun Tzu directly because it would be seen as a major violation of Hell's operation." Gottbert spoke firmly, both palms in the air as if to bar the men from discussing it further. "Tragically, our hearts at our order will continue to be broken until his release. Perhaps the money the Peruvian sends can serve as ransom payment for Father Albrecht's safe return." The abbot turned his focus to Hephaestion. "Despite being morbidly fascinated by Minos's judgments, as well as the vices of gambling, Father Albrecht clearly saw you in your state of need and fulfilled our order's duty. He took mercy on you, and seemingly sacrificed his liberty in doing so. Please honor him."

With that, the abbot stood, bowed to both men, and went off to tend the needy.

Hephaestion and Yitz's eyes met, both clearly reaching the same conclusion. Someone was going to have to go into that mysterious compound and get Albrecht out.

"Boudica," Yitz whispered, eyes wide in epiphany. "She's got what we need."

Both men found their feet quickly, and began searching about for the tall woman. Her blue swirl-patterned tattoos made her stand out in the throng of people, and the two men hurried to her.

Yitz tugged at her elbow, catching her attention as a child would a busy parent. "We need your help!"

Gazing at Yitz and Hephaestion quizzically, she rested her knuckles on her hips. "What?"

"We need your help. We need your ripper," Yitz said.

Boudica's eyes went wide. "You two, outside. *Now.*"

With a gruff shove, she guided both men out through Minu's foyer and through the crimson front gate. "How stupid must you be to mention such a thing in Minu's home? You know how she feels about violence. Besides, they are illegal. Blabbing that I have one in front of a bunch of desperate people could bring Sun Tzu's men to my door. Why do you need one, anyhow?"

"What's a ripper?" Hephaestion interrupted.

Despite looking annoyed, Boudica began to explain the device's function. "So, we all regrow from our hearts, right? So if I chop off your arm or head a new one grows back within a couple of days or a week and you are up and about again. Well, I have a heart-ripper. It looks like

a bear-trap you grip with your fist. You punch it into someone's bare chest, jam the back of your elbow with your knee, and it chews out the person's heart. You grip the handle, give a yank, and there you go. A human's heart."

Hephaestion nodded in understanding.

"So, why do you two need one?"

Yitz cleared his throat and stood as tall as his frame would allow. "We're going to get into the Usher's compound, and Albrecht is a large man. We can't carry him out, but we certainly could carry out his heart."

"*You* aren't going in there," Hephaestion commanded. "I couldn't keep you safe, and Albrecht is where he is because of me."

"Albrecht is *my* friend!" Yitz shouted, spinning on his heels to Hephaestion, fists balled.

Instead of yelling back, Hephaestion only smiled disarmingly, placed his hands on Yitz's shoulders, and steadied the small man. "You're good with a spear, and you've got guts, but it's going to be much easier if I go in alone to get him out. I'll need you as a lookout on the street, and you'll help me escape. Odds are I won't be getting out as easily as I'm going to get in."

Yitz looked to Boudica and saw that she clearly agreed with Hephaestion.

"Before I offer my assistance," Minu said, appearing out of nowhere behind the three of them with a tea tray in her hands. "Let's all have some tea back inside."

CHAPTER 19

"I know a man," Minu said during tea, addressing Hephaestion, Yitz, and Boudica on the other side of the table. "He's far older than most, and was a part of the exodus from Old Dis. He walked the Earth before all Pharaohs."

"Where is he from?" Hephaestion asked.

"His people's land no longer exists. It was swallowed slowly by a mountain range, but he is Heaven-borne, always happy to chat. He calls himself Baron Bo. There are no peoples in New Dis he doesn't know. If there's anything to learn about the Ushers, he'll know it."

"He'll know about their compound?"

"If anyone does," Minu answered, glancing up from the table as another handful of refugees came through her front door. "I'll take you to where you can find him. His schedule is very reliable. I'll introduce you, and then I'll come back here. I'm needed."

With that, they stacked their teacups, told Adina they would return shortly, and then hurried down the street to a large intersection, where they caught a steam trolley.

It reminded Hephaestion of a tiny train; a steam engine rumbled in the back, black smoke curling from a stack in its center. The benches where cushioned and the handrails crafted from polished brass. A small man in a tuxedo operated it, and as each person entered, he tipped his top hat in greeting. Once everyone was seated, he yanked several levers and the trolley lurched forward with a jolting vibration, its tracks leading them past the building fronts in a blur.

Hephaestion closed his eyes to keep from feeling disoriented, his stomach crunching in his gut.

"You think *this* is something?" Boudica chided from the seat next to him. "You should ride in an *automobile*."

"Trains have already left me scarred." Hephaestion sighed. "I miss horses."

"You can buy a mechanical one, Hellfire fueled," Yitz said. "They respond to pressure on the sides just like a real horse, too."

Hephaestion cracked an eye open, spying his small companion. "Trust me, they are not just like a real horse."

"He's right, Yitz," Boudica said, her face taken by a grin. "They're not just like a real horse. A real horse bucks you off or kicks your head in!"

Hephaestion sighed. "I get what you both are saying. I truly do. But in combat, you don't need a vehicle, you need a *relationship*. That is the path to victory: relationships. It's why Alexander and I led so well."

Minu nodded in approval.

Boudica retorted, a playful tone still in her voice. "I can understand that, but I also can understand raw power and its application. And most of all, I understand that we are at our destination in ten minutes, instead of thirty."

The trolley rolled to a stop as a tiny brass bell dinged their arrival. With a tip of his hat, the operator received his payment from Minu, and soon they stood in front of a squat building, its front decorated with laughing faces sculpted in dyed-green mud. Despite being made of solid steel, the doors swung open easily with Minu leading the way.

Inside, the lights flickered dimly, crude brass oil lamps hanging low over tall hookahs of various colors and styles, each representing a different region and era. Some were long and made of delicate blown glass with poetry etched into their sides, while others were made of sturdy bronze and fat piping. Around each hookah puffed thinkers and artists and writers, misty vapors curling about their heads like clouds filled with aimless thought.

Minu led everyone, like a mother would her ducklings, through the plush leather couches filled with sleepy smokers to the far back corner. She gently pulled a beaded curtain aside, revealing an alcove with a single occupant: a dark-skinned man, impeccably dressed, with silver hair and a trimmed beard to match.

His crimson waistcoat displayed constellations embroidered in gold thread, and Hephaestion instantly recognized Minu's handwork. The man's features were broad and almost primal; his brow appeared as if carved from stone, and his fingers were thick beyond human

expectation. With legs crossed, he sucked casually on his hookah pipe, filling the air around him with lavender. After placing a bookmark, his eyes drifted lazily upward from his book as he shut it.

Once he recognized Minu, his posture changed from calm to excited. He sat up and scooted deeper into the alcove, then excitedly waved in all four of his guests.

"Please! Please, Minu, bring all of your friends in. So good to see you!"

Minu ushered in the others. Boudica and Hephaestion flanked the man, with Yitz on the end, briefly tangled in one of the coiled tendrils of the hookah.

"Sadly, I cannot stay. I am sorry, Bo. Could you answer some questions from my friends?" Minu implored.

"Certainly, madam! Always and forever. Can you not stay? I miss our chats!" His gentle, tenor voice brimmed with excitement.

"No. I have taken in displaced people."

"You are too kind, as always, madam. Is it Japan?"

"No such thing as too kind. And yes." With that, Minu bowed and took her leave.

Baron Bo's eyes followed her out, even through the beaded curtain, and he punctuated her departure with a longing sigh.

"I'm sorry she had to leave so quickly, but I am not sorry that she left such comely company. I am Baron Bo, but as friends of Minu's, please simply call me Bo. Please tell me how I may be of assistance. But first... your names!" He beamed.

"Boudica."

"Yitz."

"And I am Hephaestion."

He nodded at each person, his eye contact committing their name to memory. "A pleasure to meet you all. How may I serve?"

Boudica and Hephaestion looked at each other while Yitz took a drag from the hookah, its top bulb bubbling as he did so.

"We need to know about Minos's Ushers. Anything you can tell us would be appreciated." Hephaestion said.

Bo's eyes sharpened under his massive brow, evaluating Hephaestion. "Interesting..." he began dangerously. "Recently, the Ushers dragged an upstart before Minos's feet. The fellow minced them and wandered off afterward." Bo's eyes shifted to Yitz, now taking his third drag from the mouthpiece that he held in both his hands.

"Do they regenerate like everyone else?" Hephaestion asked.

"Certainly. They grow from the heart, but stories tell that they grow back meaner and more savage each time. Bigger, even. The bigger the Usher, the more he has died."

"Are they all male?" Boudica asked.

"Maybe, madam," Bo said, pondering the question. "No females have ever been seen, so that means they either are all male or they burn off parts of themselves to all appear alike. That, or the females don't leave their compound."

"What do we know about the compound?" Hephaestion inquired, subtly tugging on Yitz's hookah hose in an effort to slow down his friend's intake.

"Its location is no secret. It is four, maybe five leagues away from Minos's court. The Ushers take tunnels to get there. Even during the Egyptian riots, they never stopped dragging the damned before Minos."

"Do we know the inside at all?"

"No. What few people have been insane enough to go in, haven't been seen again. There are no windows, but look for drainage ditches along its side. I've heard if one is so inclined to get in, that would be how. The front door with the knocker is just décor, and some doubt even the Ushers themselves put it there. That door has never opened."

"So, there is zero hope of knowing what the inside looks like?"

"No records I know of. None in the civic archives, at least. Their home looks like a hill more than a building, so it could just be hollow or like rabbit warrens on the insides." The baron fussed with the lowest brass button of his waistcoat. "Maybe they change it up by moving everything every couple of centuries."

Hephaestion and Boudica ruminated on their strategic disadvantages while Yitz exhaled a smoke ring toward the ceiling. "Who are they?" Yitz asked, admiring his work as it expanded slowly into oblivion above them.

"The Ushers?" Baron Bo inquired.

Yitz nodded. "Yes. They had to come from somewhere. Are they Hellbound? Are they as old as they who built The Clock? Were they here before Minos?"

"I'm old, but not *that* old." Bo laughed. "The Ushers were here before language, so who knows. They aren't keen to speak to anyone, so no one will know unless that changes, but they seem to have found fulfillment in the afterlife through purpose. There are several stories that are retold regarding their origins. Some claim they're fallen angels, denied their wings, which explains their physical enormity. Others

think they're born of the aether, like Cerberus or Minos. I suspect they were the first sinners, the first humans conscious enough to sin and know shame, the first humans to suffer divine judgment. When they died and came below, Hell was empty and barren, and they clawed tunnels and found their place serving Minos as their God, without ever knowing any different."

"If we can find what they want, we can bargain with them," Yitz speculated.

"Unless they already have all they want," Boudica countered.

"Then we generate a new want!" Yitz snapped, frustrated.

"Either way," Hephaestion said, "if they are as ancient as you say, then their tactics and combat abilities are stale. They've been wrangling weary and naked souls. When they fought, they swung from the shoulder and used all their weight. They can be taken," he concluded. "One last question, Bo...."

The baron's eyebrows rose accommodatingly.

"If we go in, engage, and fight them, will there be long-term consequences?"

"Certainly. People do not like the Ushers being interfered with. People see them as a vital cog in the machine, a cog that does a job no one else wishes to do. Sun Tzu's guard will deliver justice upon interferers, if no one else does."

Yitz looked grim, the joy of his hookah evaporated. "No one should go in there alone, Heph," he said. "If Boudica or I get into trouble for doing it, I can bribe our way out of it with the guard or whomever. If you go in by yourself, and get snatched, it will be all the more difficult to get you out."

"I'm an outsider, not like you or Boudica. You two live here, whereas I'm just passing through," Hephaestion said with finality.

Baron Bo listened as he returned to his own hookah hose. "If you *do* go in," he mused, "accomplish whatever it is you wish, and actually see your way out, be certain to come back here to me. I'd love to hear all of it. Be it foolishness or insanity, it makes a good story, and nothing makes me more interesting to people than having a good story to tell."

CHAPTER 20

Hephaestion, Yitz, and Boudica stood across the street from the Ushers' crude compound in a tight huddle. Squinting into the distance, each examined the Ushers' hill with bafflement. It had no windows or markings, and if Boudica hadn't pointed it out directly to him, Hephaestion would have thought it merely landscape. It was clearly ancient, constructed long before the idea of architecture ever occurred to humanity. No roads or streetlamps ran near it, and the alleyway the three of them now hid in was shadowed by the nearest any building dared to be.

"There are drains at uneven intervals around the foot of the hill. See there?" Boudica pointed. "That's all I can see. Once inside, you'll be on your own."

Yitz opened his mouth to speak, but was quickly silenced by a ferocious glance from Boudica. He sighed in defeat, gathered himself, and said, "We also don't know how deep it goes, since it is forbidden to dig under it. That was the first thing that came up when I inquired around as to its structure."

Hephaestion knew that Yitz had called upon a few of his more tempered fellow gamblers, and had found them willing to share any information with him in order to get into his good graces. Being unfathomably wealthy had its perks, it seemed, especially among people on the civics counsel of New Dis.

Hephaestion's shield hung in two pieces on his back, his pistol rested in its holster between his shoulders, and his short sword hung in its sheath at his side. Adina, while he'd been in Songhai, had replaced

the leather straps of his greaves with thick silk ones, making them lighter and yet just as strong.

His heart was pounding, and a kinetic vibration resonated through his limbs, all preludes to a fight. Rescuing Albrecht was a must in Hephaestion's eyes, since he held himself responsible for the man's capture. The Christian had played a chief part in his rescue by Adina and Yitz. Despite Hephaestion's desperation to get into the pit and underway in his search for Alexander, he would not take Albrecht's sacrifice for granted.

He jumped up and down, delighted to find his armor surprisingly quiet. For a moment, he felt truly alive again. Up until each now, each fight had been thrust upon him. So far he'd been forced into defensive positions of frantic survival, but this was different. The Ushers no doubt felt safe and cozy in their dark little hill, leaving the elements of stealth and surprise to his advantage.

Boudica handed him a small, leather bag. "This is the ripper. You'll figure out how it works easy enough."

Hephaestion said, "What about both of you? What if you're spotted? Aren't you two going to go back home?"

"No," Boudica said flatly.

"Just be safe," Yitz added. "If something bad happens on your way out, we'll help however we can, but be safe. My boy still needs you to tell him his mother and father are thinking of him." Yitz then guffawed. "I can't help but find all of this worry amusing, honestly. I've seen you chew your way through people *twice* now." Yitz slapped Boudica's elbow, provoking a glare. "He'll be fine! Just remember, Heph, the Ushers have spent so many tens of thousands of years dragging their knuckles that their outsides now match their insides. All that ugly and muscle you see coming at you is exactly how they think and feel. I wouldn't consider them human. Don't talk or reason with them. Just do what you must, and get Albrecht out with as little risk as possible."

"And we're *sure* he's in here?" Hephaestion asked.

"No one saw him or any sign of a struggle after I parted from him," Yitz continued. "They probably dragged him back through their tunnel to the compound. Supposedly, they've done it before when someone pissed them off enough."

Hephaestion nodded, his hands quivering with adrenaline. There had been minimal preparation in this, and his anxiety was rising. Alexander had been the impulsive one, whereas Hephaestion always planned and organized of each and every motion on and off the

battlefield. Never would he send troops into enemy territory without properly scouting it first.

Despite this being a hasty venture, Hephaestion's confidence remained high. First off, he'd already fought three of the hulking Ushers, and they'd clearly been combat-ineffective. The beasts, unaccustomed to fighting against a worthy adversary, most likely relied on brute strength and intimidation against their naked, vulnerable prey.

Secondly, Hephaestion had the best possible support he could ever have asked for. He was wearing master-crafted gear from Ulfric and other artisans, but even more importantly, powerful people surrounded him, namely Yitz and Boudica.

If Yitz could find the courage to hoist a spear, surely everything would be fine — *should* be fine.

With a sudden flush of worry, Hephaestion mumbled, "Wish me luck." After tying the ripper's holding sack to his belt, he rolled his neck on his shoulders to loosen up. Starting at a trot, he ran forward, leaving his comrades behind. Within moments he picked up speed, exposed in the open, eyes wide and unfocused so he could perceive any possible motion from his periphery.

The hill loomed ahead darkly. As he got closer, he ran at full speed, with his arms pumping faster and his feet kicking higher.

When he spied the drainage ditch, he leapt down inside, landed with a grunt, and instantly saw the opening. Though only a few hands wide, it appeared long enough for him to roll into. Gripping his sword handle, he aligned the blade with his thigh, tumbled onto his side, and shoved himself through the muddy filth into the dark.

Falling free for a moment was disorienting, but he landed in ankle-deep sludge, the reek of which hit him so hard that he stumbled. With his arms out for balance, he found a muddy wall and clung to it. The running had caused him to pant, and with his eyes clamped shut, he soothed his body down. He whispered to his heart to ease its beating, his breathing stopped, and the rhythm of his pulsing body became minimal.

Sometimes it was difficult reminding his body that he didn't need air or food or sleep. Most in the afterlife never mastered such discipline, but Hephaestion knew he had to in order to persevere, especially in the pit.

He stood in a tunnel constructed of muddy stone. Despite its being thousands of years old, the stone pick marks that formed it still scoured its caked surfaces. Curved and long, the passageway stretched beyond

his sight in both directions, and at every few steps hung tiny chain lanterns filled with Hellfire embers, bathing everything in a dim red glow.

Straightening up, he slid the shield's two halves from his back and locked them together at the center. He pounded several fur-covered bolts into place with his knee, until the heart appeared whole at its center, the shield perfectly round and three hands in diameter. He felt safer as he slid it onto his left forearm.

It was not *merely* a shield, however; the grip for his left hand had a trigger on it connected to a small hand pump and piston. Priming the pump's handle, Hephaestion built the mechanism's pressure higher and higher, until he didn't have the strength to keep going, and with a final grunt, he locked the handle into place.

Ulfric had been proud of the design. "A shield with a built-in piston!" he'd declared upon its conception. "Just punch something while it is primed and pull the trigger, and you'll hit harder than even *I* do!" The tiny air-powered piston could crush through chains, locks, doors, and certainly armor and bone.

Now, which way to go in the tunnel?

He sniffed deeply and, though both directions seemed equally foul, one had the sweet tang of human rot, so that's the direction he chose.

He stalked forward, keeping his splashing to a minimum, and drew his sword. The tunnel bent in a constant curve to his left, ideal since his shield was on his left forearm, and he was grateful for the conditions of his entry. He hadn't been spotted as of yet, and with a shield, he could handle himself better against an enemy inside a tunnel than he could out in the open.

Another thought suddenly struck him, and a smile crept onto his face. The single largest advantage that he had was this: no one had ever tried it before. He might be the first person to see this specific tunnel, and the first one mad enough to enter it willingly and of sane mind. His enemy might not fathom his intrusion until he was already successful.

Alexander had said to him on the eve of facing the fully-mustered might of Persia, "Darius will be defeated, and we will be the ones to do it. Know why, Paty? Because no one has ever beaten Darius before, and he's got us outnumbered five to one. We aren't supposed to win, which is why we will!"

Alexander would love to be here, standing next to Hephaestion. The opportunity for glory and righteousness would have swollen Alex to the point of giddy delight.

The thought of Alexander's presence lingered in Hephaestion's mind as the tunnel gradually elevated, and the ankle-deep water become shallower, until his heels found solid rock. In the dim red light, he could see a large chamber ahead, domed and jagged in construction. The center of the chamber had a hole in the floor several yards across, and its depth was so significant Hephaestion couldn't gauge how far down it went. He surmised it to be an oubliette, which was a place of forgetting. If a person or a thing posed a significant problem, it was merely thrown down the hole.

As a blast of hot, stale air yawned from it, hundreds of frail arms stirred along the oubliette's wall. Hephaestion jerked back in alarm, sword extended, horrified to see that each disembodied hand pointed a finger at him. With his back flush against the low wall, he shuffled around the huge hole as the aimed fingers followed him, silently accusing him of his invasion.

Then they began clapping. Though ill-coordinated and clumsy, the clapping was deafening given the hundreds of arms that filled the circumference of the hole. Hephaestion scrambled frantically to locate an exit, and found one within seconds, but it was blocked by an Usher.

It snarled in alarm, both of its grasping hands reaching to crush his head, but he stabbed his sword right above its knee, twisted the blade, and made the thing stumble directly into his waiting shield-piston. With a popping hiss, he discharged the weapon into the man-thing's forehead, crushing its brain in its skull. Hephaestion grunted as he used his shield to leverage the Usher to the side, and he stepped through the exit while frantically priming his shield's pump again.

More roars and snarls echoed through the labyrinth of tunnels. The clapping oubliette was behind him, still applauding his presence as he gazed upon three different exits before him. He came to the horrifying conclusion that this place may have been built intentionally as a maze. Every dim Hell-ember burned the same dark red light, removing any distinction from his surroundings, and he no longer could tell what direction he was facing in relation to his entrance from the drainage ditch.

He randomly picked one tunnel and sprinted, fearful he'd bolt into another Usher or a pack of them. Worse yet, he could fall into another oubliette.

Clanging his sword against his shield, he echoed his position to all listening ears nearby. He had to disorient them, lead them on a chase, and thin their numbers.

Two came huffing from behind him. He fled, dodging through several curved twists and turns before he spun, crouched, and waited. The first Usher came around the corner, club high, and Hephaestion dug his shield into the jagged floor to make a ramp and trip it. He then used the forward momentum of the second assailant to drive his blade directly through its sternum and lower trachea. Blood erupted from its frothing mouth and the beast crashed into its comrade, pinning it down just as it was scrambling to stand. With two swift stabs and twists of his blade, Hephaestion silenced them both.

The Usher's were clearly physically superior, but decades of combat training with Ulfric had made each of Hephaestion's sword swings an organic and fluid motion, even when he wielded an unfamiliar blade.

He clanged his sword and shield again.

How many would there be? How long could he do this? Did most of them reside in Minos's court? Were the ones here just on rest? What kind of culture did these things have? Was the maze serving a greater purpose?

Too few answers.

When the cautious footfalls of another Usher whispered nearby, Hephaestion crept low and relocated around a nearby wall, keeping the two fallen Ushers in his sight. It approached from the shadows, shoulders low and a long-handled stone ax in its meaty paws. It kicked at one of its fallen fellows, nudging it gently. Then it grumbled some ancient curse of frustration.

With its back fully turned, Hephaestion scurried forward and punched his piston right into the back of its knee. It cried out briefly and fell, and before it could bellow for help, Hephaestion cut its throat deep to the spine.

The red lamplight that saturated everything suddenly grew brighter, and when he spun about, Hephaestion saw an Usher in full-plate armor and helm, with two Hellfire stones mounted on its shoulders in small cages. Instead of gauntlets over its hands, it simply carried metal balls covered with crooked spikes.

Hephaestion rapidly searched its segmented armor for striking points, but, as if it knew what he was thinking, it charged him to deny him his moment of strategy. The first fist hit his shield directly, pushing him back. Another swing came in at an upward angle, knocking him off balance and causing him to stumble over the flopped leg of a dead usher.

After hitting his shoulder into the wall, Hephaestion instinctively ducked. Chips of stone rained on him from above from the blow meant for his skull.

Shoving his shield between the man-thing's knees, he threw off its footing. The Usher flailed its arms and stomped about trying to step on him, but Hephaestion kept banging his shield into its knees, keeping it in a perpetual state of stumbling. With a quick motion, he drew his pepperbox pistol with his free hand, pressed it firmly into the monster's nearest underarm, and fired.

The loud report of the pistol reduced his hearing to a shrill ringing, but the weapon had done its job. Hanging by shreds of sinew and chainmail, the Usher's one arm dangled at its side. Dazed, it looked down in bewilderment. Hephaestion took the chance to shove his blade into the other underarm, grinding the point upward into the socket.

It roared in agony, both arms hanging useless and dripping. With a sudden lurch, it brought its head down to crush Hephaestion's face, but he'd readied his sword, and the thing instead impaled itself below the jaw and through its cranium, the helm lifting off of its skull and teetering on the blade's tip.

With a side-step and a yank of his weapon, Hephaestion let his enemy clang to the floor. He then listened without a breath—no more roars, no more footprints, and no more clapping. Satisfied that he'd handled all the Ushers in proximity, he gathered his pistol and primed his piston pump.

His search continued, and as time passed, he grew more and more anxious to find so much as a room or a holding cell. Finally catching an idea, he began crawling low to the ground, examining the stone floor. This structure was thousands of years old, and if he followed the most worn sections of the floor, he would see where they walked the most. After several winding hallways and declines, he reached his destination.

A torture chamber.

On the walls hung nearly a dozen shackled captives in various states of either decomposition or torment. The body nearest to him had been disembodied and fed its own innards. Next to that one hung just a torso, with skeletal arms and legs that had been devoured.

One body stood out and seemed fresher than the rest—a bald, chubby, pale man with no eyes. They'd been burned out, and the seared scar tissue had swollen and puffed to the point that he appeared to be wearing grotesque goggles. A metal clamp held his neck fast to the rock,

and his legs were bound with cord and wooden boards on either side. Nearby rested a mallet and dull wooden chisel.

Hephaestion had seen this torture before. Two wooden planks would hold the leg straight while the chisel's tip was slipped between each twist of cord. With every mallet strike, the bone would break in a precise place, and once completed, hundreds of fractures would have reduced the leg to a bag of bone dust.

A tiny wooden cross hung around the man's neck. This was Albrecht. Hephaestion took a knee in front of him and lifted the man's limp head, his broken jaw swinging loose from his face.

"Nod if you can hear me," Hephaestion said.

Albrecht nodded, weary beyond all measure.

"I'm getting you out of here, but it's going to hurt."

He began to cry, clinging to Hephaestion with gratitude.

"You saved me, so I'm saving you," Hephaestion whispered kindly, and started digging the heart-ripper out of its leather bag.

Albrecht began tugging at Hephaestion's armor frantically.

Is this an objection? Does Albrecht honestly expect me to carry him out?

No, he was pointing in the direction of the other prisoners.

Hephaestion sighed. "You want everyone out?"

Albrecht nodded sternly, his fingers finding his cross on his neck and ripping it free. He shoved it at Hephaestion, and then pulled his cloak open to expose his chest. Clearly, Albrecht had figured on his method of rescue.

The heart-ripper, a streamlined piece of complicated mechanical equipment, slid over Hephaestion's fingers and into his palm with ease. It was an engineering marvel of appalling cruelty. With a comforting hand on Albrecht's shoulder, Hephaestion said, "Are you ready?"

Albrecht nodded with resignation.

With a squeeze of the heart-ripper's handle, its blades along the knuckles unfurled like a blossom in the sun. As it drove into his chest, Albrecht's face flinched, but the man remained determined even as it gnawed out his whole heart. Hephaestion twisted and jerked while pumping the handle of the device's mechanism, then retracted it. Within the drenched blades sat the heart of a man, quivering with its last beat.

Wait. What am I going to carry all these hearts with?

He rolled his eyes, then tugged and yanked awkwardly at Albrecht's body. He disrobed the Christian and folded his cloak up into a makeshift satchel. Then he went about each other prisoner and gathered up their hearts with sucking *splorts*. Bloody and frustrated, he

grumbled, and when he tossed the cloak over his shoulder, he found keeping them from rolling out to be difficult.

He retraced his steps and eventually found the four dead Ushers. Then he did the opposite of what he'd done before—he followed the stone flooring that looked least traveled until he'd returned to the Oubliette. The disembodied arms and their attached hands again pointed accusatorily. Hephaestion returned their gesture with one of his own as he passed them by, his back to the wall and toes far away.

His boots soon found water again, and he traveled the drained filth until the opening from which he'd entered appeared above his head, teasing with crisp and fresh air.

First, the hearts. Shoving hard, he tossed them out onto the hill's surface. Next, he threw his shield out, then sheathed his sword in preparation for lifting himself to freedom.

"No," a barely human voice called. An Usher stood at the far end of the tunnel, halberd in hand, with a curved blade as long as a horse's leg. Its eyes had a furious intelligence the others hadn't, and Hephaestion knew he was outmatched. Its entire body was a crude tattooed canvas of wailing faces in a celebration of suffering. This was the alpha.

Hephaestion scrambled for the opening.

It roared and charged, blade down and steady. The water kicked about and splashed, barely slowing it down.

Hephaestion's fingers tore through the mud above seeking a proper grip, but it was too late. He wouldn't make it, so he dropped down and spun to his side to dodge the incoming blade.

The mountain of angry flesh slammed him against the tunnel's wall, but its halberd was too long to move effectively in the close quarters, and it clanged aimlessly about.

Hephaestion drew his sword and slashed at the beast frantically. Several slices drew spurting blood and seeping fat from its lower belly, and it quickly decided the best course of action was to break the halberd's handle in half. With only the blade in hand, it drove the tip into Hephaestion's chest with all of its weight bearing down.

The splintmail held, but Hephaestion felt his ribs buckle and crack. Stabbing at the alpha's forearms, he drew more blood and even exposed bone, but it meant little. Pain was nothing.

With one of its massive hands, it gripped Hephaestion's arm like an angry parent scolding a child. The alpha jerked upward, hoisting Hephaestion up to the tips of his toes. It reached way back, halberd blade in its other far hand, ready to slice Hephaestion's lower half off.

With a perfect jab, Hephaestion drove his sword directly into the alpha's eye.

It laughed.

Hephaestion twisted and dug the blade around.

"I only need the *one*," it snarled in its nameless language.

Hephaestion, seeing his own terrified reflection in the remaining, glaring eye, dropped his sword, swung both his heels up, and clamped his legs around the alpha's neck. The sudden shift in weight brought both fighters down, Hephaestion's legs still holding firm. The alpha hacked away at Hephaestion but his armored back deflected and absorbed almost all of the blows. His ribs took more beating, but he held firm and squeezed his thighs together with all the might he had.

The hacking slowed, and the halberd blade's repeated strikes became weaker and less frequent.

Apparently, the alpha had never learned *not* to breath. It lacked the discipline and skill to control its body, and Hephaestion watched with satisfaction as its eyes rolled back into its skull and its tongue flopped about purple and swollen.

The alpha went limp, and soon after so did Hephaestion. With burning in his chest and sharp pains delivered to his insides by floating ribs, he sheathed his sword once again and rested for a moment, hands on his knees.

"Well?" Yitz called from above through the hole. "What, you toss out everything you need before climbing out?"

Hephaestion tried not to laugh—broken ribs and laughter made for painful bedfellows.

Boudica crouched beside Yitz, and soon four arms were dangling down at Hephaestion.

With a fire in his sides, he reached up to them. Their fingers found a grip among his, and they pulled with all their might. With his boots scrambling in the slippery mess, Hephaestion managed to get his head and shoulders to freedom.

Yitz tugged at his arms while cursing in Yiddish, as Boudica gathered up several rogue hearts that had rolled free of Albrecht's robe.

Somewhere below, the water splashed, followed by what sounded like the grunt of a bear.

"Oy!" Yitz called. "Boudica! Do your thing!"

A rumbling snarl came from the dark below.

Hephaestion couldn't manage words, but his wide eyes and red face likely made it clear to his comrades that the alpha had gripped him by the legs.

Boudica dove past Yitz, head-first into the hole. The alpha first sounded delighted, offering an intrigued grunt, but an instant later a flash of light boomed below as if lighting had just struck, and Hephaestion was free.

He tumbled over Yitz, both men flopping clear of the smoldering hole. With ribs cracked and lungs wheezing, Hephaestion brought himself to an elbow so he could crawl back for Boudica, but... he sighed and relaxed, delighted to see there was no need.

Boudica climbed out under her own power. The woad-dyed patterns on her skin now beamed with an electric blue glow, the rising steam giving her an ethereal presence.

"We should get going," she ordered, scooping up the remaining loose hearts. She tied Albrecht's robes more securely, and handed the bloody satchel to Yitz. Next, with a single motion, she gripped Hephaestion by the wrists and tossed him over her shoulders like recently killed game.

With Yitz carrying hearts and the two shield halves, and Boudica carrying Hephaestion, they slipped away toward Minu's home.

CHAPTER 21

Gottbert eyed the pile of gore-caked hearts displayed at the center of Minu's sewing table. They'd been delivered to him in Minu's home, bundled in Albrecht's robes, and a small crowd had gathered to witness the result of the bold rescue.

Shintos peered over each other's shoulders, murmuring to each other in disbelief that someone actually stormed the Usher's compound, while Adina and Boudica leaned in close to examine them.

"While I'm grateful that these tormented souls will now be in our care, I am saddened at your employment of violence to rescue them," Gottbert said grimly as his glowing hands sealed the lacerations along Hephaestion's bare back.

Exhausted and battered, the Grecian sat slumped forward with his forehead resting on his folded hands as the monk healed him. Occasionally, Hephaestion would yelp as one of his ribs found their proper place with a muffled snap.

Yitz, who looked on while Minu returned to tending her needy guests, said, "Do we know which is which? Which one is Albrecht?" He was trying to determine a means to appraise the hearts. "Does one seem more talkative than the others, somehow? Is one a bit chubby and pale, much like its host?"

"No. And no, they spilled on the way back... several times," Hephaestion mumbled. Each breath hurt and crackled in his bruised lungs, but to *not* breath was just as painful.

"We will take them all into our care," Gottbert said. "Even if a monster or two is among them, they deserve mercy as our order

dictates. We will pray over them, and sing them back to full health."

Yitz rolled his eyes. "Your chant will drone any rejuvenation right out of them!"

Adina slapped her husband's shoulder. *Hard.*

"Be nice to me!" Yitz implored, feigning injury. "I looked like a bloody Father Christmas carrying these things back!"

"Ours chants promote growth and good humors, but we would welcome you and your violin, if you wish. We don't often get to listen to a proper stringed musician."

Yitz was taken aback by the sudden and generous invite from the typically judgmental Gottbert. Before he could graciously accept, however, Adina chimed in.

"You invite my husband, and you *still* won't be listening to a proper musician!"

With a frown, Yitz tried to salvage his dignity. "My violin is rusty, and I haven't played with the New Dis orchestra in many, many years."

"We would be pleased to have you, Yitzhak. Proper or no, Albrecht would be very happy for it, as would all of these individuals. They'd be grateful for any attention or music. Lord knows what torments they suffered at the hands of the merciless." Gottbert turned to Hephaestion and lifted his weary head to force eye contact with him. "I cannot actually thank you for rescuing these people, you understand," he said, his youthful eyes stoic but piercing.

Hephaestion nodded and replied, "You're welcome," and put his forehead back down.

"Well, enough of that," Boudica chimed in. "We need Heph to get some rest. I've booked passage on a dirigible for him and me to cross the pit. I've been cooking a plan to get him down into Hell without being noticed. It was Gottbert's idea, really."

"I've arranged a contact with you by wire," Gottbert continued. "Several Buddhist monks will be waiting for you at the airship's arriving dock on the other side of the pit. They're preparing for another prayer expedition into the depths, and they'll provide you safe escort as far as the Suicide Wood. As for leaving New Dis undetected, they have robes for you."

"Once those hoods are up, you'll all look exactly alike," Boudica said. "We'll figure out a way to disguise your javelin as a walking stick or something. They don't carry weapons into the pit, so it will be a challenge."

"How do they survive without weapons?" Hephaestion asked.

"Even the very worst of Hell won't raise a hand against a gathering of Heaven-bound Buddhist monks. The men you'll be traveling with exude such grace that it stays any violent hand."

Hephaestion was glad for it, and his gratitude for his heavenly company increased even further than before. He'd briefly encountered those of Heavenly tenderness and power while in Purgatory, but never did he expect so many good and kind people to come to his aid so immediately. Gottbert, Adina, Boudica, Minu, and of course, Yitz, had all rescued him from his foolish zealousness.

He stood with arms out, wincing through his injuries, and hugged Boudica, yanking her to him. "Thank you."

Taken aback, but only for a moment, Boudica returned the gesture. Both held each other, hands clapping on each other's back, for a long moment.

Hephaestion pulled away, smiled, and nodded to his fellow warrior while patting her shoulder, and then moved over to Adina. It took the small woman a moment to realize that she was in for a hug next. Trying to form a polite protest, Adina fumbled her words as Hephaestion moved in quickly and wrapped his arms around her, sinking her tiny frame into him.

"There, there, you're... welcome?" she said, muffled, while patting his back accommodatingly.

Next was Gottbert, who already had his arms open in delighted anticipation. "May all arms be open to you always," the young priest said, kissing Hephaestion on both cheeks. "And may you always open your arms to others."

Everyone then turned to Yitz.

"I'm not a hugger. I'm a Jew," Yitz clarified.

This did not deter Hephaestion from scooping him up, Yitz's arms dangling at his sides. "I'll miss you, my reluctant savior. I hope you find adventure without me."

Yitz straightened his waistcoat once his feet found the floor again. "Well, actually I was thinking of joining you and Boudica on the airship, and seeing you off with the monks. It's only right that I see you to the end of your road here."

Whether it took years or decades or centuries, Hephaestion would accomplish what he intended, and he would see to it that his promise was upheld. Yitz and Adina's boy would know he was loved. After all, Hephaestion had been eager to be on his way, but the moment he heard that Albrecht was in trouble, his priorities changed.

Yitz cleared his throat and handed Hephaestion several documents bound in a leather bundle. "I'll give this to you now, Heph. These are illustrations and details regarding our boy. During your trip, we'll read over them together."

"Of course," Hephaestion said, untying the bindings on it and thumbing through them. The top sheet or parchment was a composite drawing of their son. He had the hardness of his mother's eyes but the wily smirk of his father. "I'll find him."

Gentle as a breeze, Minu's hand brushed against Hephaestion's elbow. He didn't know if hugging her would be acceptable, but he instantly had his answer when she rested the side of her head on his arm in a child-like motion of adoration.

"You are the *good* kind of broken man, Hephaestion," she whispered. "When you are whole, find us again."

CHAPTER 22

Hephaestion had taken a day for rest, and after another round of goodbyes, Boudica arrived with her car out front of Minu's home. Yitz had told Hephaestion that he'd rarely been in such a vehicle, and he stood on the curb with his bags packed excitedly humming like an impatient child.

"I'll let you sit up front," Yitz said graciously to Hephaestion.

Boudica knew how to drive, and the car was hers, a small and noisy machine without a top. When she spun the crank in the front, it coughed, gurgled, and growled to life with Hellfire under its bonnet. The red glow also acted as a forward light, its intensity focused with polished flanking steel sheets. As they drove to the dirigible docking towers, the illuminated road before them flickered with red light.

"I love driving," she said in a rare moment of unrestrained joy, as she, Yitz and Hephaestion loudly jittered their way through the cobbled streets, slowing for the various crowds and wagons rolling by. "When I walked the Earth, we had nothing like this. Our machines were made of wood and weighted stone, held together by nails and rope. I am so excited to see what trickles down to us next."

"It's just not a *horse*," Hephaestion said, returning to his initial complaint. "Nothing feels like a horse. Nothing is more powerful, and the horse keeps you warm at night and gives you shade during the day. This car is impressive in its own way, but I could roll it over with my arms and then it is helpless. It would have no place off the road, or on a battlefield."

"True," she said, "but the 'car' has a big brother: a *tank*. It's giant and weighs many, many stone. They roll like a metal avalanche, crush trees under them, and at the top sits a *cannon*."

Hephaestion's eyebrows rose, impressed. He liked Boudica. She seemed to be on his wavelength, and despite being anchored to Heaven, she had a rough edge about her that was approachable.

"How did you die?" he asked without thinking.

"I killed myself."

This stunned Hephaestion. "How are you not a tree?"

"Not everyone who kills themselves is committing suicide. Suicide is giving up on your humanity, and permanently destroying the world that surrounds you. I fought to the last, Hephaestion. I watched tens of thousands of my people executed in front of me. When the enemy came to me, they meant to take me as a prize to return to their mad emperor. They wanted my people beaten by breaking me, so I ended my life before they could."

"Do your people not have a ward here in New Dis, or an enclave in Purgatory?"

"Here and there. When I first died, and landed in Purgatory as you did, I sought out every one of those tens of thousands of souls to beg their forgiveness. They stood against Rome in service of my will, and by following me, they all died. I understand what you're doing, Hephaestion. I do. And you'll do it, just as I did."

"Do what, be free from Purgatory?"

"No. Well, maybe. But you'll settle your old life. You'll move on."

Hephaestion's hand settled on the small leather pouch containing the heart-ripper. He would cease Alexander's suffering, rescue his soul, and sing his body back into being with the ancient hymns of Macedonia. He would sleep next to his love's heart, hum to it, and breathe loving life back into its beating chambers. And they would be whole like Minu said, and move on together like Boudica.

Soon after, Boudica slowed the car and brought it to a jolting halt by tugging on the handbrake. Before them stood a large field of metal towers constructed of beams and rivets, and at the very tops of some of them drifted giant balloon-like constructs.

"I... I've never imagined anything like that. Are those airships?" Hephaestion said, standing in his seat.

"Indeed they are! Can a horse do that?" Yitz chirped from the back seat.

"Ha! No! And we're going on one?"

"Across the pit, it's the fastest way. It saves at least two days in travel time and it's safer than anything. I imagine you've had enough of trains," Boudica said as she climbed out of the driver's seat and began unpacking her travel pack.

Hephaestion did the same, gathering his sword, his javelin, and the halves of his shield. Inside his shoulder sack was the astrolabe map, all the documentation Adina and Yitz had provided, and a decanter and some basic provisions for the journey.

"It looks like a long climb," Hephaestion remarked as he surmised the towers to each be as tall as a mountain.

"It's no climb at all." Yitz smiled and beckoned him forward.

Hephaestion had never been in an elevator before. It was like a cage, and they were packed in with numerous other passengers of various races and cultures. Each nodded to each other politely, but when it came time to pack into the elevator, there was zero room for personal space.

With a metal grind and a sudden jolt, the elevator ascended. As it rapidly accelerated, Hephaestion felt his stomach go queasy and he held onto Boudica's shoulder for balance.

She laughed at his awkwardness, steadying him with a hand to his back. As they rose, the shouts and hisses and other sounds of the street fell away to a windy quiet. The dirigibles were like nothing he'd ever seen before, and he surmised that they floated by some unearthly magic born of the afterlife. Each was basically a small craft, some of metal and others of wood, tethered to a large air bladder that held them perilously high above the rooftops of New Dis.

"Are they safe?" Hephaestion blurted in a sudden panic.

All eyes locked onto him.

"Just like any ship," Yitz said, "they are as safe as its crew. I booked us a cabin on a reliable one."

Boudica pulled Hephaestion to her and pointed out the most ragged, battered ship of the bunch, a large monstrosity with a giant, steel bladder. The ship that dangled underneath it looked like a frigate liberated of its masts and plucked directly from the water. The rudder even dangled loose from its stern.

"It looks like *shit*," Hephaestion blurted, causing the elevator to erupt into laughter. The surrounding crowd wriggled their hands free to pat him on the back reassuringly as several voices gave playful cheers.

The elevator arrived and the front gate slid open with a screeching metal grind. Everyone piled out, still grinning and giggling at Hephaestion's sudden onset of honesty. Embarrassed, he gathered his things and followed Boudica and Yitz to their gangway, while the rest of the crowd splintered off to their various airships and destinations.

He gripped the railing tightly, and did his best not to look down, but he couldn't help himself. The view of the central ward of New Dis

was magnificent, and the white clock loomed in the distance, but he couldn't possibly enjoy it while in such a panic. Both his hands clung onto the railing, and he crouched lower and lower as he walked, his shoulder sack dragging along the grated walkway.

"Are you afraid of heights?" Boudica asked from somewhere above him.

"I'm not sure. This would be my first experience with them, I suspect. I've been up mountains and on buildings, but I've usually been able to handle it. This is something new."

She tucked her hand under his arm and hoisted him up. "Hold onto me, Lord Hephaestion, general of the Macedonian Companions and co-ruler of Greece. We'll get you onto the ship, and you'll fly across the pit like a cloud. Honest."

He nodded anxiously.

The captain, who'd been close enough to watch the exchange, stood at the entrance of his ship's gangplank shaking Yitz's outstretched hand. A gruff looking man, he had a braided beard adorned with glass beads, a wide tricorne hat, and a sheathed cutlass at his side. Tucked into his leather belt were two revolvers, hammers cocked, flanking a polished silver buckle.

"Welcome aboard, sirs and madam!" he bellowed. "Come aboard the finest ship that ever was. We sailed the seas of the Earth, sailed the seas of the damned, and now we sail the sky! We've all the same crew, in death as in life, and we rebuilt our same ship plank by plank! I'm Captain Adam Alan, and the lovely lady you are about to board for a twenty-six hour journey is Mom!"

Boudica bowed her head slightly. "Thank you, Captain. Please forgive my friend here. He has never been up this high before. He also just rode in his first elevator." She gave Hephaestion a tiny shove forward to introduce himself.

"I've also never been in a car before today," Hephaestion grumbled, adjusting his satchel and looking the captain in the eye. Focusing on the man before him helped alleviate his anxiety.

"And you're going to end the day soaring through the air!" Captain Alan laughed.

"Is your ship really called... Mom?" Hephaestion asked cautiously.

"Yes! Yes it is. We love Mom. Mom loves us. Even bad men love their mothers. We take care of her and she rocks us to sleep. She belongs to all of us, and we belong to her. So, climb aboard Mom, find your cabin, and watch the dismal fires below pass you by!"

CHAPTER 23

Hephaestion enjoyed fond memories of sailing. He and Alexander toured through the Aegean Sea on the royal trireme many times, plotting out island locations for future hideaways or monuments. Sometimes they would get the entire forward deck to themselves at night, and sip wine while star gazing. Such evenings were some of Hephaestion's favorites.

"That's a penis," Alexander said, tracing his finger through the air at a constellation he'd just discovered.

The two men had splayed out their bedroll on the ship's deck, their feet propped up on bundled rope and their cloaks folded under their heads as pillows. Several bottles of wine surrounded them, one of which had been completely drained.

"Always penises with you." Hephaestion laughed lazily.

"I am what I am," Alexander confessed. "What do *you* see, Paty?"

"Stars."

"What, that's it? Just stars? You don't draw things with them like the scholars?"

"Whatever you want to see up there is what you see. Scholars want to see a tiger, and then we all have to pretend we see the tiger, too."

"As your king, I demand you see penises," Alexander regally pronounced.

"You subject me to yours often enough. And besides, I don't see any stars close enough to draw your snail to proper scale."

"I'll remind you of that next time I'm in the middle of doing that thing you like so much."

"You fucker."

"Only if you apologize to your king!" Alexander chided.

Both men laughed heartily, their joy echoing over the still water that lapped at the ship's hull.

"But seriously, you don't see a bear or a hunter?" Alexander inquired.

"I just see stars. Stars are beautiful enough on their own. Maybe I lack imagination. Maybe that's why you have the vision and I just keep the parts moving."

Alexander rolled onto his side, facing Hephaestion, and placed a hand on his lover's shoulder. "I hate it when you diminish your role in the world, Paty. I need you. Macedonia needs you. All of Greece, and all the world needs you."

With that, Alexander let the wine take hold. He nestled his head under Hephaestion's arm, bound himself in his cloak, and promptly fell asleep. It was always impressive to see how instantly Alexander could rest. No matter how traumatizing or thrilling the day, the man could sleep instantly anywhere. It was indicative of inner peace and a sign of completely knowing one's self.

Hephaestion wondered if he could attain such internal calm.

The boat rocked while the wind whispered. Hephaestion spent much of the night counting and organizing the stars into groups by brightness and size, while his arm fell asleep under Alexander's warmth.

It was a peaceful, warm time—one of many—and as Hephaestion reflected upon it while swaying in his cot suspended from the wall, he wondered exactly how safe Mom was as it dangled over the pit's depths.

Then Yitz began to snore.

CHAPTER 24

Three hammocks were anchored into the wall of their small cabin, one above the other, providing all the comfort the room had to offer.

"The intention is to make our passengers wander about and explore our marvelous ship!" Captain Alan explained. "It's why the cabins are so unwelcoming. Meander and get to know Mom! We also cut out the bottom of the hull and turned it into a viewing deck so you can see directly down into the pit. You used to be able to see a perfect red ring of the boiling river glowing through the murk. Go on down and have a look!"

Hephaestion turned green at the thought.

"Or don't," the captain cheerily said, clapping Hephaestion's shoulder. "Climb into a bunk, let Mom care for you, and be lulled to sleep. We shove off in just a few." With that, he had spun about, shot Boudica an inviting wink, and scampered down the narrow hallway to tend to the crew.

"As the shortest of us, I think I'll take the bottom hammock, if you don't mind," Yitz said, lazily rolling himself back into its sagging folds.

"I could use some rest, too, after my recent beating," Hephaestion confessed, fumbling awkwardly with the top bunk.

Boudica held it steady for him to climb in. "I won't let you lounge for long. You'll regret not seeing down into the pit directly. Not many get such a sight."

"Is that why you chose this airboat?" Hephaestion asked.

Yitz yawned an affirmative, and then continued. "I chose Mom and her crew because they've been together since they were young men, and that meant they couldn't be bribed or corrupted against each other. That

means none of them would report our goings or comings, and we wouldn't have to worry about one yanking out your heart and tossing it overboard."

Hephaestion's hammock swung gently as Boudica steadied herself against the cabin wall.

Yitz was already halfway asleep.

"Feels like we're underway," Boudica said. "I'm going up to the main deck to enjoy the view. You can find me easy enough, Hephaestion." She closed the door behind her, leaving the only light in the room to be a dim brass oil lamp mounted on the wall.

Hephaestion and Yitz lay still, swinging with Mom's gentle motion, watching the tiny flame flicker. Despite his frustration with himself and his peculiar terror of heights, Hephaestion was glad to be in a dark, warm place.

His mind wandered.

Would the monks be talkative? Would they chat with him and help him find not only Alexander, but also Yitz and Adina's boy? Would the journey take years, or decades, given that they intended to stop and pray for any souls they encountered? Was traveling with them worth it, or would he make better time striking out on his own.

He immediately chastised himself for his impatience. He would be doomed alone in Hell, and his fate would have already been sealed if not for the company and kindness of others. He just hoped the monks would be as charming and delightful as Boudica, Minu, Adina, Gottbert, and Yitz. Or even the boisterous Captain Adam Alan.

The movement of Mom swung Yitz's hammock such that his ripping snore echoed from corner to corner.

Hephaestion allowed Mom to rock him into a half-sleep too, as she sang to him a lullaby composed of creaking wooden planks and whistling wind.

He thought of Alexander, and in his half-dream state, he could move forward and backward through time, reliving being boys together or being men on the campaign trail. Alexander's hands grasped, his mouth kissed, and Hephaestion could smell him and feel his stubble on his neck as his lips nibbled. It was like each and every sensuous moment between the two men had been rolled into a giant ball of elation, and Hephaestion delighted in being inside of it.

Heartache came, as a sharpness struck him in his dream—a searing pain in his chest. Hephaestion was suddenly lying in his last few moments of Earthly life, ill beyond return, waiting to die and alone.

Where was Alexander? Hephaestion felt his flooded lungs losing strength, and his fever made everything hurt, and his whole body shiver. Why was Alexander not here? Where did he go?

Hephaestion kept calling Alexander's name, clutching for his lover's hands to hold, but everything was so slippery. With a feeble tossing, he woke fully from his dream, but the pain in his chest remained.

Because a blade was through it... stabbed downward and gripped by a black figure. The flickering oil lamp light danced on the steel piercing Hephaestion's chest.

A murderer was in the cabin and had already struck.

First instinct kicked in, and Hephaestion gripped the attacker's forearm to keep him from retracting the blade and stabbing again. Next Hephaestion drove his knee into the man's head, rolling the hammock completely over and dropping him right onto a snoring Yitz.

In muffled alarm, Yitz's arms and legs flailed in a tangle with Hephaestion, and both men tumbled to the floor while the assassin regained his senses.

The short blade remained lodged in Hephaestion's chest, but at least it was out of his attacker's hands. Then he heard the man draw another blade and regain his footing for another attempt.

Both blades were of Japanese make, and the assassin had the dress and posture of a warrior caste that Hephaestion had heard of: ninja.

Ninja aren't particularly effective against four-barreled, snub-nosed pistols in close quarters. He'd surmised as much after he used his own to blast the assassin's head apart.

The gunshot rang brutally in his ears, drowning out Yitz's shouts of alarm as Hephaestion dropped the pistol to assess his wound. His armor had taken most of the blade's bite, but his left pectoral muscle had been pierced by the weapon, and he waited patiently to see if his breathing was affected.

A swift kick knocked the door open, thumping it against the dead ninja.

"Thank the gods you're here—" Yitz's gratitude ceased when a second ninja appeared in the doorway.

The body of the first blocked the warrior's entry, and Hephaestion tore the blade from his chest, shoved Yitz aside, and sprung to his feet. With all of his weight and fury, he crashed through the door's wood, sending splintered pieces flying as he descended on his target while stabbing wildly.

The second ninja, small of build, hesitated for just an instant, unprepared for such rage from a wounded victim.

It was enough. Like a bear, Hephaestion slashed into him with his nails and blade, tearing the man open at the throat, face, and stomach. Then, leaning back on his knees, he looked up and down the hallway for a third attacker, but saw only a slumped dead sailor.

"Boudica!" Yitz wailed, stumbling into the hallway. "Boudica, we need help! We're under attack!"

The wood about them groaned, and the world had a slight hue of blue to it when she approached from below deck. The woad-dyed patterns painted on Boudica's skin hummed and resonated with electrical power, and as she approached, the hair on Hephaestion's neck stood straight up.

"What's this?" she asked, sparks leaping between her teeth.

"Ninja."

"I see that. You had two of them come after you?"

"Yes!"

"Let's get topside and see the captain." With that, Boudica and Yitz stooped down and lifted Hephaestion by the elbow.

With his left arm tucked in close and his right hand over the wound, he limped along with her help.

"Sorry I missed it," she said. "I've never fought a ninja before, and they've got an impressive reputation."

"Airships are now on the same list as trains for me, by the way," Hephaestion told Yitz.

The three made it to the top of the ship's deck without incident. The sky was clouded and obscured by an ominous glow of light from far below. Hephaestion didn't dare approach the railing. The deck was radically different than the Bonny Sweetheart's, being significantly smaller and almost entirely made of wood. Only the beams and propellers that flanked either side of the ship contained steel.

They thumped slowly under the control of Captain Alan, who called out to Hephaestion from behind the wheel. "Hey!" he barked. "I've never seen a man bleed from airsickness. What happened?"

"You've got stowaways!" Yitz called back. "All black clothing and Japanese! Ninja! Be careful!"

Captain Alan allowed himself a brief moment to throw a fit, muttering curses and slander that no mortal ears but his could decipher. Then his eyes went keen and he commanded his first officer to sound the call on his boatswain's pipe. With a sharp tweet, the deck flooded

with sailors, and Hephaestion saw that several were carrying their fallen comrade.

"Captain! Ninja!" one yelled, dragging one of Hephaestion's would-be assassins by the legs.

"All right, all right!" the Captain commanded, cutlass high above his head. "Form two-man teams and scrub this ship up and down for any oriental barnacles! I want any remaining stowaways on this deck, kneeling before me, *now*!"

The crew scattered, pistols and curved short swords drawn.

Boudica leaned Hephaestion against the rigging to peek into his armor. "You'll be fine," she concluded. "You're lucky for the armor. Blade that sharp would have gone right through to the other side."

Captain Alan strode over to the two dead ninja, their blood still seeping out onto Mom's deck. He scowled at them, rolled the headless one over onto his front, and tugged down the neck of his gi.

"Looks like they skinned themselves recently," the captain observed out loud. "At least down their backs, where they normally have their tattoos."

"The shinto usually tattoo their heritage on their backs. This one seems to have forsaken all of that," Yitz said.

"Because they're assassins?" Boudica speculated. "To hide their identity?"

"Or because they converted to another religion other than Shinto," Hephaestion added, getting a clearer picture of the situation. "Captain, how could they have possibly gotten on board?"

"I don't see how. There just isn't much to climb aboard with while we're docked. Maybe under the gangplank, or along the rigging like rats, but surely they would have been seen!"

Within a few minutes, several sailors ran onto the deck from below.

"We've got another one, but he's squirrely! We're trying to catch him." Just as they spoke, a third black figure leapt from the shadows and fired off a flare into the murky clouds off the port side.

Captain Alan had both pistols out and gunned the ninja down before he could make another move. "Festering bastards! We've been made. Boys, back on deck!"

The whistle sounded again and the sailors assembled around their captain.

"One of those rats fired a flare, which means another ship is out there and coming for us. They'll board, take what they want, and send us to the depths right into Satan's maw!"

The men snarled and spit in rage, swords waving.

Hephaestion recognized Captain Alan's skillful methods of motivating his men. Despite being unrefined, it was oddly similar to Alexander's.

"Are we going to let that happen?" the captain called.

"*No!*" they shouted.

"Roll those three rats over the side. Get that filth off of Mom!"

"Look there!" a sailor called, pointing into the mists.

At first, it looked like the head of a dragon, jaws agape with white teeth flashing, three leagues out. Its unmoving eyes were fixed on Mom as it barreled toward them from a forward vector.

"Hard starboard!" the Captain shouted to the wheel.

As Mom began to swerve, the sailors took a knee for balance, while Hephaestion, Yitz, and Boudica clung to the rigging.

As the dragon came closer, now two leagues away, Hephaestion could see it was a dirigible designed to *look* like a dragon, wings folded back, suspended by two swollen cells filled with gas.

"Do we have cannons?" Boudica asked.

"No, too heavy!" Captain Alan pointed at several of his men. "Go get the girls, Bertha and Darla! Mount them up!"

Boudica's eyes got wide with an idea. "I'll get your shield and spear," she said to Hephaestion. "Stay put!" She darted below.

"Boys!" Captain Alan yelled, a tinge of joy entering his voice. "They mean to board us and then drop us! I know I promised you all Heaven one day by following me, but that will have to be postponed for the *naughtiness* I'm going to ask of you now!"

Cheers and whoops filled Mom's beams from her rambunctious crew. Men hauled two gatling guns onto the deck, each with boxes of ammunition belts and a hand crank.

As they began setting up the 'girls,' Captain Alan extended his spyglass. "Ha! They are shit sailors! That's what they get for rowing everywhere in the living seas. Lazy!" He collapsed his scope and turned to the crew. "Boys, they telegraphed their approach already, and will board on the port side for sure. Get the ladies aimed that way. Expect them to move fast, and to avoid damaging Mom until they've got what they want."

"What do they want, Captain?" one yelled.

"Yeah, what are we carrying?" asked another.

"Well, *him*, I suppose." Captain Alan pointed to Hephaestion.

Hephaestion's breath was snatched from his lungs as he slowly found the handle of his short sword with his prattling fingers. Would they try and bargain him away for their own safety?

The sailors crowded in close, eyeing Hephaestion over as if to ascertain his importance.

Yitz inched closer to Hephaestion's shoulder, wetting his lips as priming a weapon. If the crew decided to turn, Hephaestion hoped Yitz already had several bribes and threats prepared to set loose at them.

"He don't look like much," one said.

"Is he a ponce?"

"Pretty eyes, this one. They after the eyes?"

"Either way, he's ours."

"Yeah, we keep you below deck and safe until this is over."

Hephaestion spoke up. "I'd rather stay on deck, and kill more ninja, if it's all the same to you."

They roared in approval as the Japanese dragon ship now approached from only a league away.

Boudica returned to the deck bearing all of Hephaestion's gear and an additional trophy: a ninja's head dangling from her raised fist. "He was after your *map*." She handed him his satchel.

He slung it over his shoulder and adjusted the strap tight.

"My God, woman!" Captain Alan marveled. "If only you were a whore, we'd name a gun after you!"

Hephaestion, feeling the surge of adrenaline, and done nursing his injury, quickly banged his halved shield whole and fumbled with reloading his pistol.

A nearby sailor spied his trouble, and with surprising patience guided him through the process.

Having loaded the weapon, Hephaestion stood at his full height, rolled his shoulders back, and raised his shield. The javelin was still a disappointment to him, feeling far too light in his hand, but it was all he had by way of a spear.

Boudica stood by his left shoulder in the cover of his shield, her woad glowing again. "If we get me onto that ship," she whispered, "I can bring it down."

Hephaestion nodded to her. "Then we get you onto that ship."

Yitz wandered about aimlessly, trying to find a spot to hide on deck.

Captain Alan, knowing a rogue cannon could do more damage than good, set him to work by telling him to lean against one of the gun supports.

They now saw the whites of the dragon's eyes.

Like winged bats, they came: ninja on black gliders, swooping off the approaching ship and craning through the air under and over Mom. They tossed smoke bombs and flashbangs to disorient all those on deck.

"Hold your fire! Don't waste it!" the captain called through the din.

Grappling hooks with thick ropes launched from the dragon ship and nearly all of them found their mark along Mom's railing and deck. The sailors scrambled to wrench them loose or cut their tethers, but there were far too many.

"When they're level, sweep their deck!" Captain Alan commanded.

Several of the gliders landed, their ninja swinging wildly with steel blades as the sailors piled into them.

Mom's crew, comprised of brawlers and brigands, fought with every fiber of muscle they had, all the while spewing every blasphemy they knew.

The enemy ship's deck now came level, and an army of black-clad and steely warriors stood ready to attack Mom. Bertha and Darla erupted as their operators grinded their barrels and spewed molten mini-ball rounds into their enemies. It sounded like infinite volcanos were erupting overhead, the jolt of the rapid-fire weapon rattling teeth.

Regardless, the ninja swarmed. Leaping and climbing across ropes, they came without a yell or a shout. Even when one fell, he did so quietly, descending into the Hellscape below.

Hephaestion deflected numerous throwing stars and crossbow bolts, and soon noticed several sailors using him as periodic cover.

Boudica smirked in approval.

A ninja approached them from behind, and in an instant Boudica unsheathed her sword and sliced the attacker in two. Her blade seared with such heat that it stifled the air around it, and when she sheathed it again, everyone caught their breath back.

They'd managed to bring the first wave of ninja under control, but more were forming on the opposite deck for their follow-up assault. The ships were now close enough for a running leap, and Hephaestion felt dizzy at the thought of doing so, but he wouldn't let Boudica go alone.

"I'll be quick," she said, and stepped from behind Hephaestion's shield.

Before she could run, Hephaestion threw his javelin in a perfect and practiced motion. Like all honorable Greeks, Hephaestion had mastered the art of hurling a spear, but he had never hurled a spear like *this*.

Aiming low, he intended to strike the nearest ninja in front of him in the gut to make way for Boudica. The odd weight of the spear,

however, threw off Hephaestion's aim, and it went high—into and out of the head of his intended target, then into and out of the chest of the ninja *behind* him, and finally into the thigh of a third. The spear shaft had bounced about while knocking all three men into the pit.

Boudica ran and leapt, her way temporarily clear, and Hephaestion stepped back to do the same.

Having witnessed everything from under the barrel of a roaring crank-gun, Yitz realized he was about to be left behind. "No!" he yelled, the sound of his voice devoured by the loud din of battle. He leapt from under the gun and ran after Hephaestion.

With a running jump, Hephaestion leapt to the deck of the enemy ship.

With a running shriek, Yitz did the same.

Both tumbled onto the deck, Hephaestion drawing his sword while deflecting several blows with his shield, as Boudica gripped a nearby ninja with both hands and electrocuted a hole through him.

Yitz looked back, Mom's deck far more chaotic as the gun crews had engaged the enemy that was trying to silence their weapons. Despite that, he was now completely out of his element. For a man who prided himself on always thinking things through and sitting tight, he should have been ashamed of himself.

But he wasn't. Yitz saw Boudica's blade shave the head off an enemy, while Hephaestion struck another one down by slicing him behind the knee. Being married to Adina in the afterlife had taught Yitz a very important lesson: stay close to the most powerful people in the room. They're always targets, but they're the least likely to fall. Yitz was safer on the enemy ship next to Hephaestion and Boudica than he was on Mom.

Boudica spied Hephaestion and rolled her eyes in annoyance. Then she saw Yitz, and a brief guffaw escaped her as she cut a nearby support cable that held the dragon airship to its gas balloons above.

The ship buckled.

Three arrows entered Boudica's side, and she snarled and cut another cable. "Get back to Mom!" she shouted to the men.

Hephaestion dove and deflected several more arrows intended for her.

Yitz scrambled to keep up.

Hephaestion, digging his sword into a ninja's ribs, commanded her to, "Keep cutting!"

Yitz drew Hephaestion's pistol from between his shoulders and emptied it into a charging attacker.

Seeing no other choice, Boudica did as she was told, slicing through cable after cable. The ship detached from Mom and began to shimmy perilously downward on its port side. Ninja gripped anything they could to keep from falling, and Hephaestion dug his blade into the deck to steady himself on his knees. Yitz slipped entirely, gripping onto Hephaestion's leg for salvation.

With his shield down, several more arrows struck Boudica. One hit her throat, causing sparking blood to erupt through her teeth. She stumbled and fell onto her back, one hand gripping a severed cable and the other her sword.

A ninja with claws on his knees and hands scratched along the deck toward her, blades ready to strike as Hephaestion and Yitz looked on helplessly.

Looking up at to the gas balloons above, half their cables dangling, she pointed her sword and called down a bolt of searing lightning.

The light blinded Hephaestion.

CHAPTER 25

Alexander stood high in the saddle of Bucephalus as he eyed the front line ahead, just out of arrow's reach. Hephaestion had been giving orders all morning, making sure the phalanx were in position and the archers within range of the enemy's light infantry.

They'd already taken down Darius's war chariots, rolling weapons of bladed death, just after dawn's break with oil and fire arrows. It must have infuriated the emperor, because now he marched on Alexander and Hephaestion with all 200,000 of his troops in one unorganized lump sum. Neither side held reserves, no holding back for either front, and Alexander and Hephaestion's men were outnumbered four to one. The enemy was so numerous that a storm of dust and shouts had taken over the sky, and the dirt shifted as the world rumbled under the advance.

Just minutes ago, the forward troops had made contact with the enemy. As shields had clashed in the distance, Hephaestion gave the order for all archers to fire at will into the enemy ranks.

"Start the smoke, Paty," Alexander called.

Hephaestion raised his arm high and opened and closed his fist three times. Smoke began encircling the front line. It would be hard on the forward ranks of hoplite, but it was vital for Alexander's ruse.

"The cavalry is back far enough to pull out and flank," Hephaestion said.

Alexander placed his metal, wide-brimmed helmet on, and replied with a smirk of eager joy. "We ride into them from the west, and we pile in until we see Darius's banner. We *take* that banner. He'll either be there, or fleeing the field. What say you, Paty?"

"It's that or we die." Hephaestion nodded.

Alexander was often joyful in battle, smirking and winking and singing loudly, but Hephaestion was all business and pure focus. He didn't have the natural talents for tactics and maneuvers that Alexander did, so he had to work hard to keep up. It had never been a source of resentment for Hephaestion, but standing in the shadow of a giant tactician had always been a gentle reminder that Alexander was the great one, not him. Any bitterness ever generated by that revelation was drained away each time Alexander rested his head on Hephaestion's shoulder.

Both men tugged their horses' reins and peeled away from the command group, leaving others in charge of the line. Alexander galloped through the cavalry lines pumping his sword in the air, Hephaestion behind him and to the side. The Companions, almost 8,000 strong, silently raised their own swords, pumping vigorously and daring not to shout the courage in their hearts for fear of giving away their plan to the enemy beyond the smoked concealment.

Per usual, Alexander insisted on leading the charge. He would often ask Hephaestion to stay behind to keep the troops focused, but not this time. This was Darius. Alexander wanted nothing more than to have Hephaestion at his side when he pulled the emperor of Persia from his royal chariot.

The men leaned down on their horses, shields on their backs and lances across their saddles pointing forward. Following suit, the cavalry folded in behind them, forming an enormous arrow. With the help of the wind, the smoke screen covered their flanking maneuver, and when the Companions finally broke concealment, it was too late for the enemy. Startled Persian foot soldiers pointed and shouted, some turning to flee into the ranks for safety. They didn't have their pikes or shields at the ready, though, and Alexander and his horsemen swopped into the gathered enemy like a punch to a giant's ribs.

The crunch of bone and wooden shield rang as the horses did their terrible work. Hooves stomped and legs kicked as broken men folded unnaturally on the trampled ground. Like a dust storm, Alexander's Companions grinded into the Persian ranks.

"There!" he shouted, pointing with his lance for all the cavalry to see.

Ahead flew the magnificent scarlet and gold Persian banner of Darius.

Hephaestion kicked at his horse as he ferociously jabbed each enemy in his path with his lance, and pushed on with the wedge of cavalry behind him. Fixing his attention on the plumed helmet of his lover, Hephaestion continued to fight and charge and stab and stomp.

The royal guardsmen, swathed in purple and gold, stormed into Alexander with scimitars swinging. Bucephalus took several of the blades to his hooves and ribs, but nothing would slow down the steed's charge when Alexander rode upon him.

The Persian troops began folding in, wedging themselves into close quarters with the Companions to bring them down. Alexander had ridden too far ahead, and Hephaestion could barely make him out among the blades and kicked-up dust. Soon he could barely see or make sense of his surroundings.

Chaos ensued—flashing, blinding, screeching chaos—and a woman's pair of strong hands reached through it all and scooped him up.

CHAPTER 26

"Time to move," a woman's voice rasped from the darkness that enveloped Hephaestion. Her voice came out crackled, broken, and wet, yet somehow familiar.

With effort, Hephaestion opened his eyes. Smoke billowed and fire hissed all around him. A charred figure loomed before him, burnt beyond recognition with its lips, hair, and eyelids completely gone, but.... The blue glow of her woad still resonated. *Boudica.*

Affixed to her face was a grim grin, her teeth and eyes the only color in her face. "You were spared the fire, but impaled. We've crashed, and from the surrounding cold I think we're somewhere in the Glutton's circle." The heat from her cooked body steamed in the frigid air. "I dug out the beam from your chest, and you've taken a day or two to heal up. How do you feel?"

"Like I died."

"There's nothing like it. Can you walk? Your leg was crushed and I set it, so let's test it out."

Grunting, Hephaestion rolled over onto his knees, slowly rocked back onto his heels, and looked about at the smoldering wreckage, which stretched for at least a league. Flesh and wood smoked and sizzled all around; a plank here and an arm there. The dragon-ship must have crashed and tumbled into pieces on impact, scattering detritus as far as the eye can see.

"Is Yitz all right?" Hephaestion asked, prior events becoming clearer.

"Currently, he is fine. He's scavenging the wreckage. He didn't even lose his yarmulke in the crash. When Adina finds out he didn't

arrive on the other side of New Dis, she'll be so worried that she'll kill him on sight."

Hephaestion grinned, finding comfort in Yitz's courage. If Yitz could find the spine to dive into such uncertainty, then Hephaestion could follow his example.

"Did Mom make it?" he asked, suddenly worried.

"Last I saw she was floating away safely as we went down. Whoever was steering the enemy airship did a solid job, though. That or we were lucky they managed to crash this high up in the pit. Also...." Boudica held Hephaestion's satchel up. "Your things made it through just fine. Yitz found them while digging around. Make no mistake, Hephaestion, someone has been looking out for you." Boudica punctuated her sentence with a finger pointed up toward the void above.

He moved first one foot, then the other, and stood with a groan. He felt his joints pop and his back ease into place. "My shield?"

"Right here, but I couldn't find your sword, and that amazing spear of yours is most likely lost forever."

Hephaestion nodded in acceptance. "You should head up," he continued. "I can't risk being attacked again by a force this large. Descending is now or never for me."

"Without the monks as protection?"

"It will have to be the case. Returning to New Dis will just make me vulnerable to a thousand more dangers, especially if the Jesuits or anyone else is willing to launch an attack of this scale. Now is my chance to slip away."

"Yitz and I will climb our way out, then," Boudica said, pointing toward the red cliffs in the distance, covered by swirling mists. "I suspect whoever deployed this ship will come looking for it soon. Best you not be here when they find it."

"Any other survivors?" Hephaestion asked.

"Not that I allowed," she replied flatly.

A thought casually wandered into Hephaestion's mind. "Lightning? That is your power granted by Heaven?"

"No, I grant my own power, as does Adina and Minu. We all grant ourselves our power."

"What is Minu's power?"

"Altering the perceptions of the people around her. She can dull your pain or help you forget you ever met her. By far, she is the most powerful of the three of us."

"And your sword... is it lightning that makes it so hot?"

"No." Boudica's eyes rolled to the side of her charred skull as she formed the explanation in her head, drool dribbling from the corners of her mouth. "My girls knew I wouldn't let go of my anger easily—my rage—so they helped me forge all my hate into this sword. I hammered it in, and just like anger, I keep it sheathed. That is, until I need it and it serves me, then I draw it."

The two evaluated the smoldering landscape of wreckage for a time, lost in their individual thoughts.

Abruptly, Boudica turned to Hephaestion. "Perhaps it is not merely providence that you and I have met, Hephaestion. Maybe it isn't just *your* journey that is occurring here. I said earlier to you, in the car, that you will need to let go of some things...." Using her bony, blackened fingers, she unfastened her sword's sheath from her belt and held it out to him. "I will take my own advice. Use it when you need it. And trust me, you *will*. You're in Hell, now. *Hell*. There are no more kind souls to be found down here."

Hephaestion took the sword from her, hot to the touch. "Thank yo—"

"Don't," she interrupted. "Don't thank me for giving you my burden."

Hephaestion followed Boudica's gaze, scanning the ruin of the dragon ship, and spied Yitz clumsily stumbling through charred rigging wearing a tattered black cloak he'd scrounged. It was thick and layered, its inside made of thin chainmail meant to provide protection without compromising stealth.

It looked heavy to Hephaestion. "Yitz, you won't be able to climb up the cliff face with all that extra weight. I myself would have a hard time of it."

"I'm not climbing back," Yitz said, straightening himself up resolutely.

"If you stay here, the only rescue party you'll meet will make an end of you."

"I'm going with you," he said, gaze locked on Hephaestion.

Boudica and Hephaestion glanced at each other in disbelief.

"I'm going into *Hell*, Yitz," Hephaestion emphasized, "in case that wasn't clear."

"Where my boy is. This is my chance to see him. I'm already part way there, anyhow. We'll find him together. Besides, you're no good on your own, Samson. I find myself constantly coming to your rescue." Yitz stepped closer and tossed Hephaestion's spent pistol to him.

Hephaestion caught it. "You're a good man, and surprisingly handy with a spear or powder weapon, but you won't make it."

"Are you afraid I'll slow you down?" Yitz said, his brow wrinkling as his eyebrows dipped and converged.

Boudica apparently felt it wisest to remain silent.

"Partly, yes," Hephaestion said flatly. "There are obstacles in the pit for which I've trained decades. You haven't."

"I got through a flaming wreck smashing into the pit of Hell better than either one of you!"

Hephaestion sighed. Yitz was no soldier or tracker, but the man had an indistinguishable quality of survival about him. An irrational resistance rose in Hephaestion, and he spent a silent moment exploring it. A part of him longed for the quiet solitude of the coming descent. New Dis had unsettled him in some ways, and Yitz tagging along would be like the city itself was latched around his neck.

Most of all, Hephaestion didn't want anyone with him for when he rescued Alexander. Hephaestion wanted to do this alone, receive all of the praise and credit, and reinforce in a single sweeping gesture that he was the most dedicated soul Alexander had ever known—Yitz peering over his shoulder would diminish that.

As he formed a firm denial with his lips, and darkly considered the removal of Yitz's heart for Boudica's care, something occurred to him so suddenly that it halted the air in his lungs: Hephaestion was about to deny a father seeing his son.

Defeated, he hung his head, shaming himself with his selfishness; delivering violence onto Yitz was actually an option he was willing to consider.

"All right," Boudica said, perceiving Hephaestion's acquiescence. "I'll return home and tell Adina where you both are. I hope she doesn't melt me on the spot." Her voice had the connotation of bewilderment. "Stay together. Do what you must." With that, she turned toward the distant cliff face and called over her shoulder, "No matter how ready you think or feel you are, you *aren't*."

She trudged on, her arms wrapped around her leather-cooked frame as she strode beyond the warming fires of the dragon-ship's wreckage, toward her high climb to New Dis far above.

The opposite direction awaited Hephaestion and Yitz, and a pallid fog hung over everything ahead of them. Hephaestion, silent, bound the hot sword to his hip, braced his arm with his shield, and limped into the unknown with Yitz bundled up at his side.

CHAPTER 27

Hephaestion had experienced brutal winters. He'd once seen the moisture in the trees freeze to the point of exploding, frozen shards of wooden shrapnel imbedding in men and horses as they marched by.

The winters of Earth, of course, held the promise of spring, and no matter how many noses and ears were lost to the frostbite, everyone knew they would see the birds again and hear the rivers and creeks once more.

This, however, was not Earth. The ice lay brackish with frozen waste and feces, and the air hung still, without so much as a flake of snow or crackle of ice. There were no landmarks to guide him, and his bearing had purely been gauged by having the cliff face behind him when he started his journey.

Through the milky, frigid mirk, Hephaestion examined Yitz and, as expected, his companion's knack for survival was on display. The cloak he'd salvaged from the wreck was so large that he'd bundled about his body and head nearly twice. Its long sleeves drooped past his hands, and to keep his fingers warm he gripped them shut from the inside.

As for Hephaestion's own warmth, he clutched Boudica's sheathed sword tightly to his chest, and its heat radiated through his fingers and into his arms. The temptation to draw it and bask in its heat constantly nipped at him, much like the biting cold, but he would never dare do such a thing. He knew the real danger here, and it wasn't the cruel frost.

It was the bloody paw print on the black ice in front of them.

"Oh no," Yitz whispered to himself. "I'd heard tales...."

Hephaestion knelt down to get a better look. As large as the print of an elephant but with claws that had chipped up the ice with its long

stride, the print sat among others heading counter of the circle's rotation. The best way to avoid the monster would be to stay where it had recently been, so he pulled his astrolabe from his satchel and laid it flat on the ice to get his bearings.

"We can get through if we keep quiet," he said. "My research told me that if we don't act like food, we won't be treated like food. It has plenty of gluttons to keep itself busy with anyhow."

"Is it just the one hound?" Yitz asked, his gaze lost to the mirk all around them as he nervously looked about.

"I'm not sure. I've heard there couldn't possibly be only one with the number of gluttons here. Maybe they spawn in proportion to the number of sinners," Hephaestion mused as he tinkered with the astrolabe.

Still perplexed by the device, he fiddled with its dials, hoping to find a landmark to align it to. Miraculously, it did it itself. Soon one of the rings began moving, followed by the others, causing Hephaestion's hands to spring away from the thing. He held in his gasp of surprise as the astrolabe sprung to life, spinning and rotating with some unseen power. Was it magnetic? Did the momentum of the ring's movement somehow fuel it?

"Heh, figures," Yitz remarked as though half expecting the astrolabe's apparent magic. "That Euclid is a master of motion and magnetics. That little dial knows where we are better than we do."

The rings shifted smoothly and silently, the center ones spinning far faster than the outer ones. Hephaestion was delighted as he watched tiny etched landmarks spinning past each other, knowing that if he could just find one before him, he'd be oriented.

The question of where to go now entered his head. They could go in the direction of where the beast's tracks had come in order to avoid it, but that would make them lose their current bearing. They'd no longer be going dead straight from the crashed dragon-ship. Alternatively, they could keep heading in the direction he'd intended, hoping to avoid any further signs of the roving monster but not missing the next ring.

Hephaestion gathered the astrolabe, stood up and, holding Boudica's blade close, trudged forward in his initial direction. "We'd best keep quiet," he whispered to Yitz.

Step after step, they lost track of time, and the white blanket of nothingness before them gradually became hypnotic. The ice had little fluctuation, making the landscape fairly easy to travel over but dull and compelling.

Hours upon hours must have past. Hephaestion occasionally flexed his face muscles to keep it from freezing, and the crinkling sound from his skin seemed to fill all the misty space around them.

Yitz remained silent, wrapped in his dark cloak.

Finally they came to something different, something small — a rib. A single human rib lay frozen with icy strings of meat still on it.

With a dull mind, Yitz followed dribbles of blood to see that it was part of a larger carcass, gnawed, minced, and devoured beyond recognition. It still steamed, but barely.

Hephaestion's brain was too numb to dissuade him.

There were paw prints about.

Hephaestion held still, kept his breath minimal, and scanned the horizonless world about him while Yitz merely stood there, transfixed.

They heard sobbing, more than one soul. Blubbering and whimpering came from various directions, and as they rose from their frigid hypnosis, they realized they were surrounded, just beyond eyesight, by dozens of the weeping damned.

Something snarled, growled, and then a violent wet 'crack' echoed like a fowl's cooked leg being torn from its body. The beast was near, and Hephaestion had no spear.

Yitz dove to the ground futilely, his dark cloak preventing him from hiding.

In Hephaestion's research over the decades, he'd encountered conflicting reports regarding the three-headed hound known as Cerberus of the frozen gluttonous wastes. Some said only one roamed, while others said hundreds of monsters prowled about. Many speculated that if more than one beast existed, they would be territorial, and spend their eternity devouring the damned and shitting them out to reform for another inevitable devouring. Some gluttons supposedly tried to dig into the ice or bury themselves in the meat and feces that they could find, but in the end, everyone was devoured — the beast would sooner or later find its quarry.

No matter the truth behind the beast's numbers, its size had not been exaggerated. A spear would have been ideal against it, using its lunging weight against itself, but now his best hope was to slip by as it noisily gobbled a poor soul just beyond eyesight.

Crouched low, Hephaestion tugged at Yitz's robes and, with a finger to his mouth, commanded him to be silent and follow him closely. Moving with as much stealth as his shivering frame would allow, Hephaestion continued in his intended direction with Yitz slinking behind.

Cerberus's feeding took place just off to their left, but Hephaestion dared not change course for fear of losing their bearing.

Slinking ahead, he saw a large shape, slumped on the ice, head down. As Hephaestion moved closer, he judged it to be an enormous woman, her shoulders quivering from either the cold or silent sobbing; he couldn't tell which. With lengthy side-steps, he gave the woman a wide berth.

Soon he saw another, and another—men and women with their heads down. Some cradled their faces in their hands while others lay on their sides. Despite the oppressive cold, none of them huddled together for warmth. Each man and woman appeared as a fleshy, frosted mountain on a flat sea of ice, isolated in their misery.

One looked up, a man with hair twisted and frozen, his beard covered in the icicles of his tears. Yitz made eye contact, and the glutton pointed at him with accusation in his glare.

"*Stop!*" the sinner rasped.

Yitz halted.

Hephaestion's fingers curled around his sword's handle.

"You will listen to my confession, or I call the hound!"

Hephaestion pondered charging the man and taking his head off, but even as he weighed his options in a panic, Yitz calmly snuck on his knees toward the man, with his palms open and forward in a non-threatening gesture.

"You have my ears," Yitz said, his voice full.

A massive, grizzled shadow stirred in the cold veil beyond, and a glowing pair of blue eyes fixed in their direction.

"Come here or I scream, and the thing eats us all!"

Yitz got as close as he dared, just out of arm's length. The man's skin was frozen black in patches and his fingernails had fallen off long ago.

The creature's menacing eyes in the distance still gazed in their direction, and now Hephaestion could see the shadows of the other two heads gnawing the fat out of the quivering prey beneath its massive paw.

Yitz's attention remained on the glutton. "I will listen," he calmly offered.

"I await my turn again," the glutton said, "to be eaten as my punishment." His language sounded round and rich with vowels as it sprung off of his tongue. No matter the region, wealth almost always has its own discernable lilt. "You recognize me?"

Yitz shook his head.

"I was famous once, royal in blood and well-known in my region, but I belong here." His eyes flitted over his shoulder toward the beast.

The heads seemed to be in some disagreement, snapping and snarling at each other, trying to finish their current meal before moving on to the next.

"I ate while my vassals starved," the glutton continued. "I ate in front of their children, and laughed when I could count their ribs. Their cheekbones cast shadows. I *belong* here!" he confessed, both hands reaching out.

Hephaestion suppressed his reaction to draw his sword as the man pawed at Yitz's cloak.

"Forgive me!" the glutton rasped. "Forgive me!"

Yitz took the man's hands in his own. "Of course, I forgive you." He tenderly kissed the man's filthy hands. "And please forgive me," Yitz asked in return. "Forgive my son."

Through his weeping, the glutton gave the hints of a tormented smile. "I forgive all the world."

Hephaestion was shocked, and his knuckles eased. He stared into the sinner's eyes in disbelief as the glutton gripped Yitz's arms to steady himself and wobble to his knees, his large bulk rising off the ice. "It eats me *standing* this time."

Now two glowing pairs of eyes were fixed on *all* of them, and two of the three heads growled. The beast's fur twitched with endless hunger and bloodlust as its paws stamped in anticipation. It inched closer to them, its features becoming more apparent through the wintery veil.

"Run!" the glutton shouted, turning to face the looming shadow, its rows of teeth bare.

Hephaestion turned, gripped Yitz's elbow, and sprinted with all the speed of a marathon runner as he heard the monster lunge and tear into the man behind them, his screech of horror ending suddenly.

As far as their bodies would allow them, they ran. Their lungs froze, their noses bled from the cold air, and their arms and legs burned inside from the effort, but they ran. Gradually, their legs became delinquent, first Yitz's and then Hephaestion's, and they slowed to a trot. Controlling his breath as best he could, Hephaestion crouched down again, forehead against Boudica's sheathed sword, and listened.

Yitz stood, hands on his lower back, stretching backward, focusing his attention toward the distance from where they'd come.

"Don't ever talk to people down here," Hephaestion spat in frustration, doing a poor job of keeping his voice low.

"Like Gil? Don't talk to my boy? Or Alexander? We shouldn't talk to him, either?"

"That's different! Don't be absurd!" Hephaestion snarled. "This is exactly why I didn't want—"

"The glutton you popped out of... what was his name?" Yitz demanded.

"What?"

"His name! The man who's body you used like a motley costume. What was his name? What bargain did you strike with him?" Yitz's eyes glared with a hard edge to them that Hephaestion hadn't seen prior. After a moment of silence between them, Yitz continued. "As I figured, you fished out a soul, used him to your will, and disposed of him *on the floor at Minos's feet* when done. You didn't know his story. You didn't *care*. Only your Alexander mattered, not that man." Yitz pointed behind them. "Or the one you used getting past the docks. Or my Gil. Or Adina. Or me. Just *Alexander*." Hephaestion found meeting Yitz's furious gaze a challenge while his fuming continued. "If Albrecht treated people as resources the way *you* do, what would he have gained from *using* you instead of *saving* you?"

Silence reigned, with no whimpers or sobs or growls in the distance—just Yitz's heaving breath.

"Putz," Yitz said with disdain. "I speak to and listen to whom I wish. Now make yourself useful and lead us out of here."

Unable to think of anything worth saying, Hephaestion continued leading the way. As they moved forward in continued silence, his thoughts returned to the glutton. How long had it been since he'd encountered an undammed soul? Why wouldn't all of the gluttons hold each other for warmth? Couldn't they all talk among themselves and forgive each other as well? They all just sat there, waiting for their turn to be devoured. Was the beast's belly the only warmth they'd ever know?

And what of Yitz? He seemed far too prudent to yield to compassion, and yet he had just kissed the hands of a filthy sinner. How accurate was he in his evaluation of Hephaestion's selfishness? How many people over thousands of years had passed by Alexander in the boiling river and ignored him, much like Hephaestion would have ignored any glutton?

Glancing over his shoulder, Hephaestion looked Yitz over with not only a new respect, but a hint of discomfort. He'd not expected the man to be so perceptive.

CHAPTER 28

Never in his existence had Hephaestion encountered so much 'same' before. Was he still standing? Could his legs stop moving forward even if he wanted them to? Had his shield actually gotten heavier? Was his sword no longer producing heat? Had he gone completely deaf?

The endless white mirk floated all around him, and beyond several steps in any direction there was nothing. Sometimes Yitz would be on his right, and as Hephaestion blinked in and out of walking consciousness, Yitz would suddenly appear on his left.

Hell finally began to sink in for Hephaestion. *This* was it. This was what Hell *was* — an empty place with no stimuli or warmth or hope for change. It didn't need to be violent or cruel to torment. It could be a dreamlike state you're barely aware of but unconnected to.

He wanted to scream, whistle, talk to Yitz, or even sigh aloud to fill the void up with *something*, but he didn't dare. Footfall after footfall is all he focused on, and it could have been days that he'd traveled.

Is Yitz feeling the same?

Not sure if his eyes were playing tricks, he came upon several shadows before him. They moved about, clearly the outlines of men, as they dragged and wrestled with something large, perhaps an animal of some kind.

Hunters?

They clubbed at the creature until it stopped moving, and then, like a pack of hyenas, they fell to their hands and knees and began chewing into it.

"Women taste better. We should find a woman," one said in an ancient, nameless language.

"Stop complaining," said another. "Rub the fat on you. Keep warm."

Hephaestion's legs hadn't entirely stopped moving forward, and as he came closer in a daze, the sword dangling from his grip, he got a better look at the men.

There were five of them, each dressed in red steel armor and tattered leather, with clubs and crude metal cudgels hanging at their sides. One had a musket on his back, a bayonet bobbing on its end as his teeth tugged at the tough muscle of their meal.

Between them lay an open, steaming glutton, eyes staring dead into the pale void above.

"Give me the eyes," one demanded. He shoved another cannibal aside and began digging at the dead man's skull with his fingers.

As Hephaestion's slow mind processed it all, Yitz spoke from somewhere behind him.

"Stop," Yitz said, barely a whisper.

But they'd heard it, and their collective gaze landed on him, then Hephaestion. Weighing them both over, they clearly coveted their gear.

"Stop! They suffer enough." Yitz found his full voice, his lips cracking and bleeding with the effort of speaking.

Instantly, one of the five sprung to his feet, cudgel over his head, and rushed toward Hephaestion. Still, everything moved slowly somehow. The blow was coming down toward his skull to cave it in, and the attacker displayed nothing but glee in his blood-smeared face. They would take everything—Boudica's blade, the astrolabe, Yitz's heart. Everything.

It arced downward, the attacker's muscles surging with the might of many devoured dead.

Almost casually, Hephaestion spun on his heels and turned himself about in a full circle to the side, and the blow swung by harmlessly, the attacker rushing past. Hephaestion freed Boudica's sword from its sheath, and the blade burst forth with heat and fury as he drove it through both of the man's arms above the elbow. It glided through his biceps, and his dismembered arms flopped onto the black ice like flailing fish. The man ran a few paces farther, staggered, and fell with a groan at Yitz's feet.

The remaining four leapt up instantly. Hephaestion pointed the blade at them and knelt low, waving it in a semicircle in front of him in

a challenging gesture. He invited them to attack, but by doing so he discreetly melted the ice before him with the blade's searing power.

They spread out, blood freezing to their armor and chins. The one with the musket unshouldered his weapon and held it like a spear. Each of the other three had their bludgeoning tools at the ready, gripped with both hands.

They all came at once. The one from the front, his club high, ran in and instantly lost his footing on the freshly melted ice.

Hephaestion brought his blade up into the man's ribs and cut through his chest and out the opposite man's clavicle. The men's four halves flopped onto the ice and slid into the feet of the musketeer, who began frantically loading his weapon, his eyes wide at the sight of two of his comrades sliced in half.

The other two bludgeoners assailed Hephaestion before he could recover from his prior swing, and their weapons crashed into his shoulder and back. The shield took most of one blow, but his arm went numb from the other hit, and Hephaestion struggled to move out from between the men.

Yitz noted the musketeer's half-frozen fingers fumbling with a powder horn, and charged him. The two men collapsed into the ice, grunting and wrestling over control of the firearm.

Hephaestion deflected what he could while coming under a flurry of blows from the two cannibals. Unsure of how to recover his guard, especially in his weakened state, he called to Yitz.

"Run!" he yelled.

Then it came. A shift in the air made both of Hephaestion's attackers pause, and a moment later each of their heads vanished into a pair of jaws. The beast, which had come out of nowhere, lifted them up from behind. Cerberus's center head roared icy breath onto Hephaestion as the other two heads shook their prey back and forth rapidly, snapping their spines.

The blast of cold was almost crippling, and it might have shattered Hephaestion where he stood if not for Boudica's unsheathed blade. The beast's center head tore an arm off one of the bodies, the blood freezing to red powder the moment it hit the air.

Yitz gave up on the firearm, leaving the other man to flee into the cold. He scrambled to Hephaestion and helped him to his feet, and both men ran. They had no idea in what direction they were headed.

Hephaestion dared not sheath his sword, but he knew the beast would be able to follow them by its light. As he frantically tried to think

of a plan of defense, he heard its paws pounding the ice behind them as all three of its heads snarled and panted in unison.

Yitz couldn't keep up, and was falling behind. His cloak's hood had unraveled from his head, and when Hephaestion glanced back, he could see the fear in Yitz's expression.

As the thought of Adina never seeing her husband again flashed through Hephaestion's mind, he spun, dug his boot heel into the ice, and ran back in the opposite direction toward Cerberus. Six eyes glowed blue and three mouths gaped open. He charged it, blade high in his left hand as his right drew his pistol. At the very last instant, just as its jaws were scooping down to snatch him up, he fired into its center mouth while digging his blade into the side of its right head. Allowing his boots to slip, he slid under the monster and glided past its underbelly, dragging his blade through its gut, aided by the creature's forward momentum.

Black, reeking blood splashed out of it like tar, ice crackling and hissing from the sudden heat. Several links of intestines peeked out of the long wound, threatening to dislodge. All three heads howled a shattering discord of agony and rage.

Now behind the beast, Hephaestion stabbed into its hind leg, hamstringing it.

Gnashing its teeth in fury, it spun about but collapsed, buckling from its wounds and no longer able to sustain its weight.

With a final discouraging swipe, Hephaestion took off the lower jaw of the nearest head.

Cerberus retched and clawed about the ground, clearly giving up the fight, tussling in vain to keep alive.

Hephaestion backed away, clear of its flailing claws and snapping heads, the victor. There was no need to wipe the blade clean since its sizzling heat cooked off the gore, leaving a pungent odor behind after he sheathed it.

"Thanks, Samson," Yitz said, still catching his breath. "I figured you'd let it eat me and save yourself the headache." He chuckled. "We used to joke on Earth that you don't need to outrun the bear; just outrun your friend."

"Adina would murder me."

"At the very least she wouldn't break out the good tea whenever you'd visit." Yitz grinned. "Who were those goys?"

"No idea, but they had armor from a smithy. They looked like soldiers of some kind. I don't recall much on cannibal tribes in this ring."

"And they weren't dressed for the cold. Shame I couldn't get the musket from that one."

Both men, now recovered, left the quivering carcass of Cerberus behind

Not long after that, the endless mire of white began to wither in front of them. A light, yellow and crisp, shone before them, and they quickened their pace in anticipation.

They came to what seemed like a wall of dust, which swirled before them and obscuring their vision. Yitz approached first as Hephaestion took out the astrolabe, but Hephaestion immediately followed and set it on the black ice just before the wall. The freezing air eased, and the wall stretched endlessly in both directions, beyond sight, as if the dust storm had been contained by an invisible barrier right in front of his nose.

He reached a hand out, and as his fingers passed through it, they prickled with sudden warmth. This was the end of the glutton's circle. The rings began rotating, and he could tell that the circle before him was moving fairly quickly and toward their right.

Hephaestion packed the astrolabe up, secured his satchel, reloaded his pistol as Mom's sailor had taught him, and then Yitz and Hephaestion jumped through.

CHAPTER 29

The first thing to strike Hephaestion, aside from the wave of dry heat that made him gag, was the ground. It spun far faster than he'd expected, sweeping his footing out from under him and careening him onto his side, his shield clanging. He hadn't been prepared for the differential between the two spinning terrains.

Yitz, given that he carried less weight and stood considerably shorter, managed to maintain his footing.

"Oy," Yitz said, sucking in the new air. "Makes your skin burn."

Permitting himself a moment, Hephaestion remained on his back blinking at the barrier they just entered through. It appeared like glass, an endless and indistinct dark and cold world on the other side, from whence they'd come.

Yitz offered his hand to help Hephaestion up. Hephaestion took it, and Yitz's face turned red as he helped the warrior stand.

The two stood shoulder to shoulder and took in their new surroundings. They were up high, at the top of a long ridge that curved in both directions until their vision failed from the distance and the dust. Ahead lay a long slope downward, the ground cracked and dry, leading off into a pale brown cloud several leagues away.

It reminded Hephaestion of the Afghan campaign. Clouds and dust storms would rise from the desert floor and consume the war train, horses kicking and men shouting to each other to find their bearings in the stinging wind. Such a place was particularly horrible, because from the sands below, attackers would emerge from concealment and slaughter entire divisions before running away into the gloom.

Everything here was more open, however, and looking directly up far above, a singular light sat dim at the center of the sky. He'd been told that even in some spots of Hell, Heaven's light can still be seen. Like a tiny moon, pale but present, it presided over the dry circle of boulders.

He could see no creatures or other significant features, but a quick glance at the astrolabe showed they were on one of *many* long descending slopes that would eventually lead to the city of old Dis somewhere beyond the twirling veil.

Hephaestion had done enough research to know that traveling across this circle would be fairly simple and far less dangerous than the previous. So, taking the chance to rest his quivering legs, he sat and opened his satchel, and thumbed through the documentation on Adina and Yitz's boy.

With a tired groan, Yitz sat next to him and folded his hands.

Hephaestion cleared his throat. "We should be all right here for a bit. Let's talk about Gil..." Having seen Yitz almost eaten by Cerberus, Hephaestion felt he had to understand everything he could about Gil. If something happened to Yitz, which remained likely, and he was lost to the denizens of Hell, Hephaestion would be on his own to find Gil and deliver the message.

His name was Gil Maqabim Isserles, and he had leeched so much money and land from his synagogue that it eventually collapsed the township. Most of the paperwork contained interviews with people Gil knew in life, as well as those who had visited the lowest circle of Hell.

"We didn't know any of what he was doing," Yitz said. "He kept it all hidden from us. He had moved to another town when he married, a nice girl that was sweet but not too bright. Adina was never too keen on her, but I liked her well enough. Turns out she had no idea, either."

"Were you shocked when you learned Gil was in Hell?"

"At first, we just thought he was living a long life. Adina and I combed the shores of Purgatory. We even built a small hovel there, and it was like we were young again, waiting for a child to come while living simple and poor. He just never came. Then we began asking around, focusing on all the souls who recognized our language. It didn't take long to learn about what had happened to the town, and what he had done. Then his wife came, and we learned everything."

"You've gathered a huge amount of intel on him." Hephaestion thumbed through the sheets of parchment, enough warmth returning to his fingers so he could feel once more. "It's impressive. It must have taken years."

"Truth is it's my fault. The boy takes after me. I was always gambling and toying with such vices, grabbing for what I wanted the quick way. He inherited my low character, but he also inherited Adina's brains, which means he could do the wrong I did, but do it smarter and sharper. I would have been in Hell myself if I was more proficient with sin...."

Yitz's voice trailed off as he seemed to drift into some memories of his Earthly life, and perhaps that of his son.

"It's my fault Adina doesn't have her boy, and she's never held it against me. Not for a moment." Yitz smirked. "Woman would nail me to the cross for eying a pretty lady on the street, but forgives me without a word my crimes against God and home."

"It's clear to me that you've changed since your time on Earth, assuming you were as bad as you say," Hephaestion consoled.

Yitz gave his best shrug.

Hephaestion continued looking over the material. It was suspected Gil was frozen in the ice, up to his neck or face, as is customary in the Lake Cocytus, somewhere near the seat of Lucifer. To use faith as a tool to steal and betray was the chiefest of crimes, and worthy of elbow room with Little Horn himself. Such a place was farthest from Heaven's light, and it has been said to be so cold a man can freeze solid instantly, his lungs shattering into chunks the moment he breathes in.

Regarding the sketch of Gil, Hephaestion admired that the young man had the best features of both his parents, and it was clear that his good looks and charisma helped him drain an entire town to death. In the corner of the sketch, Yitz's name appeared scribbled in a frantic pen stroke.

"You drew this?" Hephaestion asked, impressed.

"I also painted one, a larger one, for Adina. We have it in the bedroom."

With wonder, Hephaestion's eyes followed each expressive line. *Can a father remember his son's face perfectly for hundreds of years? Did Adina help him recall each detail, each curve of the brow and each crinkle of the smiling eyes?* Hephaestion didn't envision Yitz as an artist, but he also never envisioned him as a violinist either, yet Gottbert sincerely invited him to perform as a healing measure for those in need.

"Are you as good with the violin as you are with art?"

"Well, that is a funny story. Adina always had a thing for the violin. Our romantic life took a rapid dive in the afterlife, and when we moved to New Dis I figured drastic measures were in order."

Hephaestion laughed. "So you learned something new? Perish the thought!"

"She always loved the sound of the violin. There was an old man who would play in our village during our courtship. I was always a bit jealous by how she looked at him when he played."

"So... did the violin work?" Hephaestion asked with mischief in his tone.

"Dear boy, when you hear me fiddling, do *not* knock on our door."

Both men shared a belly laugh, its warmth making Hephaestion feel completely thawed. *Yitz learned to play the violin in his afterlife? What else does he know how to do now that he didn't know then?* Hephaestion had spent hundreds of years combing the rocky cliffs of Purgatory for Alexander, pulling head after head out of the water by their hair to see if his love had arrived yet. Could he have also learned the violin in that time?

When Ulfric had taken him in, he became part of Ulfric's mission to help others ascend. For centuries, Hephaestion assisted Ulfric in helping people make sense of their lives, their choices, and their deaths. When not training with sword and shield and spear, Hephaestion aided Ulfric in the simple daily matters of running a ranch filled with the sullen and lost.

He never learned to play a flute, or read another language, or build a machine. Thousands of souls glided through Ulfric's camp like rich silt pouring down from a mountain by river, but Hephaestion had remained as static as a jagged rock in the water's center. He was as unchanging as the many statues of him that Alexander had commissioned.

Hephaestion had waited in Purgatory, waited forever, for Alexander to come. But he didn't, and Hephaestion could wait no longer. When World War I broke out, and the gates of Hell were flooded to nearly breaking, he made his move. Placing demands on everyone around him, especially Ulfric, they commissioned The Bonny Sweetheart.

And here he was, sitting on the lip of a giant, sloping chasm, closer than ever to his goal.

But he felt farther away than before.

Adequately rested, Hephaestion packed up and proceeded to stand, stretching his thawed legs. "Are you good to go? That cloak will come in use again, so definitely hang onto it."

Yitz obeyed, bundling it and tying its sleeves together adeptly, turning it into a bandoleer satchel. His arms now free, Yitz strolled ahead as if on a lazy afternoon, his gaze drifting about side to side as he took in the world around him.

Hephaestion followed, and both men walked the steep decline downward. Minu's marvelous kameez was thin enough to allow Hephaestion's body to breathe under his armor while still being soft enough to avoid chaffing, making his descent easy. The view was so enormous in scope that he had to look at his feet on occasion to make sure he wouldn't simply walk off the edge of the precipice and tumble several leagues into the obscured chasms below.

Time passed, and Hephaestion gradually heard a low rumbling, dull and filled with voices and shouts. Its cause was obscured by approaching dust clouds.

As they descended, they saw what they'd expected. In this circle suffered those who'd wasted their lives, and the time and efforts of others, in fruitless and empty pursuits. Here they continued their efforts infinitely.

The slope turned into a stone bridge and carried them over a pit as deep as a ship's mast, crammed with the naked condemned. The wretches grunted, heaved and frantically avoided each other, kicking up a constant cloud of dust as they each rolled a giant marble ball before them.

Each ball was almost ten hands in diameter, and so perfectly smooth and weighted that they could easily spin it upon the polished ground with little more than a shove of the hand. Every soul had one, either white or black depending on the direction they were rolling the ball, and each pit was a flurry of conflict as the giant marble spheres smacked and bounced off of each other.

People shouted and cursed at each other, shoving and pushing, the black marble spheres heading toward the back part of the pit toward the Glutton's circle, while the white marble spheres rolled in the same direction as Hephaestion and Yitz.

The rumbling produced from each sphere colliding with one another was a deafening din. Hephaestion felt it through his boots and into his knees from below. He craned his head over the side, looking into their desperate and determined faces. Some would snap cruel glances at others while cursing the inconvenience they suffered. Others merely toiled with their own sphere. Some intentionally smacked theirs into another's, trying to slow them down.

"Reminds me of life," Yitz said dully.

One woman, slender with deep eyes, gazed up at them. Her sphere slowed, and her lips formed a call for help. She seemed afraid to speak, however, but was unwilling to return to her sphere.

Yitz raised a hand in sympathetic greeting.

Before she could return the gesture, another marble ball smacked into hers, crushing her hand between it and her own. She howled in pain, cradling the injury. Another sphere plowed into her from behind, collapsing her hips, and soon the wave of incessant motion trampled her underfoot.

A white marble ball, now streaked with a red smear, slipped about its owner's hands complicating their task as it rolled by where she once stood.

"They could all just stop, all at once," Hephaestion said through his teeth. "They could all stop and move their spheres in an orderly fashion to avoid the grinding and conflict. Perhaps they could use each ball to build a means to climb out, even! Why don't they?"

"If one person is set on barreling through the crowd heartlessly, the rest were validated in doing the same," Yitz observed. "And people are people. Each obsesses over their burden the same way I obsess over Gil, or you Alexander."

"And so they keep it up in perpetuity, endlessly trampling in the land of woe?"

Yitz shrugged. "We just don't learn."

Whereas the previous circle of Hell provided the utter absence of motion and change, this circle offered nothing *but*—all motion and noise and frustration toward a futile and meaningless goal. Once each marble sphere traveled many leagues to the far end of the pit, it would change color—black to white or white to black—and then the journey would begin anew in the opposite direction. Each sphere handler appeared convinced that accomplishing this would gradually earn their way out. Each seemed convinced that everyone else was working against them.

Hephaestion wondered if the woman, foolish enough to stop and look up, was the closest to moving on. Without looking down again, he continued across the bridge with Yitz close behind.

League after league unfolded, and they finally came to a stone wall that rotated slowly toward their left. It stood almost a quarter league tall. From either age or disrepair, several cracks and holes in it passed by as it moved, some breaks large enough for Hephaestion to peek through. He caught glimpses of empty cobbled streets and storehouses, and knew they'd arrived at the abandoned city of Dis.

Yitz nodded that he was ready to leap.

Finally, through a large chunk of missing wall, they stepped in without looking back.

CHAPTER 30

The cacophony of boulders and hectic motion vanished the instant they entered the old city. Shafts of light stabbed through holes in the ceiling and a gray layer of ash covered everything. The roof had collapsed long ago, most of its damage sustained by time and neglect.

It was hard to step forward without making noise. The detritus consisted of broken ceiling tiles, sticks of burned furniture, and mounds of incinerated materials that had hardened over the centuries.

With ash drifting like snowflakes through the piercing light, Hephaestion figured that moving forward wouldn't be stealthy, so he relinquished and walked ahead at a normal pace, gripping brick piles and twisted metal frames to steady himself.

Yitz followed suit, his smaller footprints falling in Hephaestion's.

To a silent and dead city, they must have been extraordinarily loud, but something in Hephaestion just did not care. The made thie rway cautiously to the exit and, once outside of the building, stood on the street's cobblestone. They appeared to be in a town square, complete with a dormant fountain at the center mounted by a statue of a winged angel, sword to the heavens.

Each building facing the square stood tall and proud, the signs out front depicting their purpose through pictograms. An architect's guild appeared, several inns, a cobbler, and even a slave market depicted by two chained fists crossed.

"Not bad," Yitz said in approval, until his eyes landed on the slaver's sign. "Well, maybe a *bit* bad."

While researching, Hephaestion came upon information regarding Dis's ancient slave trade. Sometimes, those who ascended free of their confines in the lower circles of Hell would wander into Dis, bare and vulnerable, only to be snatched up and sold as slaves. Greece had always had slaves, and when Alexander stabbed into Persia, he'd been stunned to discover the Zoroastrians had abolished slavery long ago, having considered it an affront to humanity. While both Hephaestion and Alexander were delighted to keep those local Persian customs intact, every time they tried to implement the end of slavery in Greece, they were met with severe resistance and sometimes violence.

Some of the men on the campaign soured to Alexander's adoration of Persian customs, citing him as being transformed by the conquered and forgetting his superior Grecian roots.

It had been Hephaestion's duty to sequester those men away from the active combat battalions, and even execute them if he deemed their malcontent severe enough. He'd given the order personally for the immediate execution of several men, including Parmenion.

Parmenion, a bold general with a bolder laugh, always made eye contact when he bowed to his superiors. His son, Philotas, had attempted to assassinate Alexander, deeming the conqueror too Persian to lead a Greek army.

Hephaestion had ended the ambitious boy personally, but pleaded for the life of Parmenion. "He's the father. He's been nothing but loyal and noble! At least talk to him. He's hundreds of leagues away — "

"Commanding a large garrison on our supply chain, Paty!" Alexander yelled. "I hate it. I *hate* it. But we can't risk it! The moment he finds out you killed his boy — "

"For *treason*."

" — for treason, which his father may very well be in coordination with, he'll break our line!"

"Assuming he even *would*, it would be a disruption at best. His garrison isn't that large and our reserve would shore up inst — "

"You aren't thinking large enough, Paty. The troops shoring up such a supply line would mean we can't advance east this autumn. We might not lose territory, but we won't gain it, which might as well be the *same thing*."

Hephaestion and Alexander glared at each other. Alexander yielded first, giving a mournful sigh.

Taking the opening to lecture, Hephaestion said, "You're condemning a man to death half a world away because of something his

son did. You won't even give Parmenion a chance to defend himself regarding his boy's actions."

"No, I won't. The campaign east can survive a dead general to the far west. It can't survive a disruption in the supply line. Order men by racing camel to Parmenion. Kill him quickly and as painlessly as possible before he receives news of his son's treachery and death," Alexander commanded, eyes forward and into the distance. The matter for him was settled.

Hephaestion had sent slaves to do it. They assassinated Parmenion with daggers as he ate dinner. Later Hephaestion learned that Alexander had subsequently put the slaves to death. Soon after, Alexander declared the only slaves permissible within the forward campaign divisions to be those working off a debt or crime.

Slavery was always sour to Hephaestion. One human owning another human felt wrong to him, especially here in Dis—to ascend from the pit of Hell, to settle within one's soul their sins and folly and evil, only to be snatched up by your fellow man soon after. Yitz and Albrecht could have made a slave of Hephaestion if they had chosen to. While the people of Dis had climbed to the rim of the pit to settle a new city, it appeared to Hephaestion that their geographical location wasn't the only thing to have elevated.

As they followed the street deeper into the city, mounds of bones littered the corners of rooms and alleyways. It was clear by the occasional decorative pile of skulls that not only had Dis experienced a mass exodus; it may also have suffered a purging.

The various scorch marks and rusted, broken blades lay as withered reminders of the violent end of the city, and Hephaestion regarded them curiously as he stepped over each one. Did Thebes look like this for decades after it was razed? Centuries?

This was Hell, and this city, which might have been beautiful and full of promise, laid empty and spilled open. No one cared anymore about putting anything back. Hell was dead not only to the world, but to itself.

Feeling like a ghost haunting the skeleton of an unwelcoming civilization, Hephaestion proceeded deeper into Dis, his eyes wide.

Yitz looked entirely different, as if fighting to suppress the urge to whistle a tune.

CHAPTER 31

Yitz watched as Hephaestion drifted about like a ghost, his steps conscious as he peeked into every window and craned his head around every corner.

Yitz hung back, unable to stifle his impulse to explore. Whatever dangers lurked in whatever corners, they simply did not distract him from being curious.

Dis hadn't possessed the rich mishmash of culture and technology that New Dis did. It had been more conservative and less flamboyant. Every few buildings seemed to be places of either worship or torture, and on occasion Yitz would find altars dedicated to both. But it all still fascinated him, and he resolved to return to Baron Bo and share all that he'd seen.

They found little of value, as the bones of the city had been picked clean over the centuries, but Yitz still stepped into any interesting door that drew his attention. While Hephaestion scouted the intersection up ahead, Yitz walked into an apothecary.

Empty vials littered the floor, prompting him to tiptoe about like a goose. Stepping gingerly, he walked to the store's counter, set down his bundled cloak, and grunted with a stretch.

Slowly, he opened the cabinets in search of anything useful. Sometimes, one could find gunpowder or perhaps even a length of hemp rope. Despite Yitz having worn his most comfortable shoes, he had nothing aside from the cloak that could aid him in the journey.

He reached up and pulled the rusted, half-degenerated padlock from a high cabinet door with ease. Upon opening it, a round jar rolled

out, and would have shattered on the counter if not for his quick reflexes. Cradling it in his arms, Yitz quickly deduced that it contained a heart, given its size and weight. Someone had jarred a heart and locked it away for possibly thousands of years in that cabinet.

He placed it down gently next to his cloak.

Yitz then got on his knees up on the counter to get a better look into the opened cabinet's recesses, and saw that it was filled with jars, eight in all—eight souls deemed unworthy of consciousness and condemned to a cold, black hell within Hell.

He took all the jars down and gathered them in a clump on the counter. Each lid was fixed tight with some kind of glue-like resin, and he hadn't the strength to budge the lids.

Together they were too heavy for him to carry, and his cloak would most likely spill open, at any rate. Still, he wasn't about to leave them here. They could be people waiting to be smuggled somewhere, or perhaps slaves that were sold more conveniently this way. Perhaps they were prisoners, or innocent people. Regardless, he would not allow this to continue. What if Gil had been captured in such a manner and forgotten, lost for all time while Adina and he waited?

He unfolded the cloak and rolled a single jar inside of it. Exhaling, and recognizing his own foolishness, he hoisted the cloak up over his shoulder and swung it down with all his might. The cloth muffled much of the noise, keeping the echo to a minimum.

He reached in and rummaged through the shards of jar until he found the heart, dry and pruned like a raisin, then pulled it out and set it on the counter.

"What are you doing?" Hephaestion chastised in alarm from the doorway.

Yitz ignored him and did the same for another heart. "Freeing hearts."

"But why?"

"Explaining why is like explaining that water is wet."

Hephaestion ran into the room, hands out toward Yitz for him to stop. "I heard something fly overhead, and you are making *noise!*"

"Then help me do this quieter, because it *is* going to happen."

Hephaestion rested a hand on Yitz's shoulder. "We can't save everyone. It's like war down here. We have to keep moving and stay focused on what matters: Gil and Alexander."

Yitz sighed while rolling one of the jars in his hands. "We can't save everyone, but I can save this one."

"All right, well, how many are there?"

"I counted eight. Two are already free."

"At least break them under the counter. Wrap them up and I'll use my shield piston. That should make less noise, at least."

Soon all eight hearts sat in a row on the counter, pathetic and shriveled. A concern rose in Yitz's head that perhaps one would regenerate faster than the others, and devour or burn the other hearts. After wrestling with the thought for a bit, he arrived at the simple decision to leave the hearts together for the simplest reason he could think of: they were in Hell, but at least they wouldn't be alone.

"Why oh why would you two go and do something like that?" a man's voice whispered from upstairs through the floorboards.

Hephaestion drew his sword, the heat illuminating the hearts in sanguine light.

"And what exactly are you going to do with that sword?" the voice taunted, its British English crisp with that familiar wealthy lilt.

Hephaestion said nothing, only listened while zeroing in on the voice's location above.

Yitz slowly ducked behind the counter, eyes peering above it like a child at the store.

A floorboard above creaked, then another at the far side of the room. Hephaestion was tempted to draw his pistol and blind-fire into the ceiling, but the loud noise and waste of ammunition deterred him.

Minutes passed without further sound. Had they been stalked this entire time? How many were there? And why would a stalker give away their presence by speaking?

Unless they're curious, or so confident in being able to destroy an enemy, they don't care about subtlety.

"Or maybe you're completely insane," Hephaestion said out loud, sheathing his sword.

"Don't be dismissive," the voice quipped. It spoke in a smooth tone with a hint of graciousness, such as one would expect of noblemen and holders of high civil station.

Hephaestion opted to say nothing further, and motioned for Yitz to follow. Acting casual and ignoring their observer might be the best way to draw the man out. Only then could he accurately ascertain the threat.

With the satchel over Hephaestion's shoulder and the cloak bundled in Yitz's arms, they exited back out onto the street and continued on their way. Hephaestion rested one hand on his sword hilt as he strode casually among the bones and smashed window frames of the gray, ashen Dis.

On the roof, above and behind to their left, a tile shifted. Clearly their stalker could see the pistol mounted on Hephaestion's back, so he was most likely keeping his distance.

At the next junction, Hephaestion walked to the center of the square and stood at the derelict fountain, while Yitz kept his back against the nearby wall. Yitz scanned the rooftops all about, and spotted a lone figure standing tall half a league away. He was slender, wearing some kind of armor, and he slowly raised a finger and pointed farther down the street toward a courtyard.

Before Yitz could call for Hephaestion, the figure vanished. He ran to Hephaestion at the fountain, unnerved. It was filled with the tattered remains of clothing and toys, all apparently burned as fuel.

"I saw him... on the roof," said Yitz.

"So did I. What language did he speak?"

"English, a newer version—only a hundred years old or so."

Hephaestion nodded thoughtfully.

"Do you know anything about him?" Yitz pressed.

"Nothing. Could just be a vagrant, or someone like us looking for somebody."

"Well, he pointed toward a courtyard farther ahead. Want to check it out?"

"Absolutely not," Hephaestion said firmly. "We aren't here to explore, just get through. You are a good person, that's clear, but we can't go saving every heart. If we were with the Buddhists or with another escort, maybe, but you need to follow me and do what I do without endangering yourself needlessly."

"I understand, Samson."

"Whoever tried to knock Mom out of the sky may not have given up yet. We need to *move*."

"Okay. You got it. You're the boss." Yitz nodded his acquiescence.

They proceeded quickly, and Yitz's interest waned regarding the contents of each building. After the second juncture, he spied the wall of the courtyard the rooftop figure had pointed at.

"Let's look at the astrolabe again," Yitz whispered craftily. "I think we got turned around a bit."

"What? How?"

"At the fountain."

"No, we should be fine. I went straight ahead after that."

"Are you sure?" Yitz asked in a voice deigned to seed doubt, a skill he had mastered from Adina.

Hephaestion thought a moment, as if cycling back through his each and every step. He was clearly flustered.

Yitz tugged on his sleeve. "Here, take it out here by this wall, out of the street."

Hephaestion followed while unslinging his satchel, a sour expression on his face. He pulled the astrolabe out, and they both watched it spin and whir with life.

With a stray eye, Yitz examined the wall next to them. It was too solidly built to have any holes for him to spy through, yet as he ran his hand against it as if to balance himself, he found that it was surprisingly free of dust or ash.

"Hmm..." he allowed himself.

"What now?" Hephaestion asked, annoyed but still focused on the circular map.

"No dust. This wall is clean, as is... look! This part of the street is clean."

Both men looked around. It was as if a single gust of wind had recently passed through, pushing the years of grime away into the corners and crevices.

Then they both heard a voice from the other side of the wall. It was instantly familiar: Father Jose Acanth Franco.

"You pull perimeter guard," Franco commanded. "You and you, protect me. The rest of you fan out. He's alone, so you can manage it."

As silently as able, Hephaestion packed up his satchel and astrolabe. While he was crouched down doing so, Yitz slid his pistol free. With a wide-eyed glare, Hephaestion made it clear to Yitz not to fire, and Yitz attempted to reassure him by patting his shoulder.

Pressing themselves against the wall, they slinked forward until they reached the courtyard's entrance archway. Yitz was closer, and he dipped his head in for a moment to peek.

He'd never seen anything like it before — clearly a flying machine of some kind, with multiple fan blades propped high above its chassis. It had long, dragon-like wings with articulated flaps, and the front of its cone-shaped nose was painted to look like a snarling dragon. It could clearly carry ten men, and several crew members walked about it, tinkering with its flaps and engine.

Franco paced back and forth next to the thing's tail, his fingers pointing at each of his personal compliment of armored Samurai as he issued orders in a dismissive tone.

With a sharp eye, Yitz could still detect a faint hint of resentment in each Samurai's expressionless face as they stood at attention of their white Jesuit master. After being addressed, each samurai pulled down a protective facemask, increasing their ferocious appearance tenfold.

Yitz pulled his head back, grabbed Hephaestion, and switched spots with him.

Hephaestion only risked a fraction of a second to look, and pulled back, the blood drained from his face and his chest heaving. As their previous discussions had made clear, the big man had heard much of the samurai and their rich culture and warfare tactics. Hephaestion no doubt assumed that, if they were surrounded by the samurai, they would be slashed to ribbons. These weren't thugs or brutes; these were disciplined warriors, and most likely eager to prove their zeal for their new masters. Swordcraft had been their lives, and was now their afterlives. They were believers, energized converts, and clearly on his trail.

Hephaestion mouthed the word "samurai" to Yitz, and began gesturing for them to head back where they had come from, back along the wall and into the nearest building.

"They only saw me," Hephaestion whispered, unbuckling his shield's halves from his back. "If they spot me, I can draw them off. You take the map and keep it safe," he said while kneeing his shield into one piece.

"*Dumkopf,*" Yitz fired back. "We can just sneak by. Don't give me this thing."

"And if they spot *us* they'll see *you*." Hephaestion primed his shield piston. "I promised the astrolabe would be safe. And you don't want them finding the materials on Gil, either. They would have leverage over the wealthiest man in New Dis!"

Yitz rolled his eyes, knowing that discussing anything in their current situation would just exacerbate the problem. He scooped up the satchel and adjusted it to his back.

"Let's just backtrack and find a place to hide," Yitz implored, bundling up his cloak in his arms.

A brick shifted outside.

Hephaestion silently nodded, and Yitz led the way through the building's back door. He glanced down both directions of the alley, and it looked clear. He went first, crouched low but walking briskly as Hephaestion followed. A cobblestone shifted under Yitz's feet, however, and instead of stopping he sped up. To his dismay, many stones were loose here, probably due to flooding that had happened when the city was abandoned.

A shadow loomed in the alley over both of them, and from its size, Yitz guessed it to be someone on a nearby roof. The shadow held a bow, arrow drawing back.

Hephaestion dove forward and raised his shield over his head and tackled Yitz, covering them both to protect them against the projectile.

But it never came.

A moment later, the samurai crashed into the cobblestones behind them, bow skittering across the ground from the impact. Yitz and Hephaestion looked up to see the mysterious figure they'd encountered before, pointing into the distance.

"Two more *that* way!" the man called down to Hephaestion and Yitz. "Run down *this* street here, fourth block left. Ballroom!" With that, the man disappeared behind several chimneys.

A samurai burst through the door into the alley, steel out, and Hephaestion drew his sword. Stone, mortar, and wood glowed faintly red as he charged his enemy. The two clashed, the samurai's calm mastery of his weapon instantly apparent as he deflected each blow. Sparks showered over his mask as Hephaestion advanced.

Two more samurai appeared down the opposite alley. Swords out, they charged with their weapons low and forward.

Yitz gripped Hephaestion's pistol with both his hands, and fired when they were close enough not to miss.

One of them fell face-first, his body's full weight driving his head into the street. The other changed direction and moved for Hephaestion, knowing Yitz's pistol to have been spent, and seeing the Grecian as the more dangerous target. Within a breath, the samurai was behind Hephaestion, blade poised to run him through the back as he battled with the first samurai.

Yitz, thinking quickly and moving just as fast, tossed his cloak over the head of the flanking samurai, and tugged on the sleeves to throw off his balance.

The samurai spun about blindly, swinging aimlessly at where Yitz's head could have been.

A scream of agony echoed through the alleyway as Hephaestion's searing blade took off the first samurai's leg at the knee. He then turned, saw Yitz riding the other cloaked samurai like an angry bull, and drove his blade through the samurai's armor. The man's cloak burst into flame, and Yitz leapt off with a yelp. Hephaestion swiftly kicked the flaming injured samurai through the building's back door, and flames began to lick at its wooden beams.

"Run!" Hephaestion said, his hand at Yitz's back and pushing him forward.

The two men scampered around the nearest corner and, with all their might, hurried along the course the mysterious figure had told them to take.

Both men kept looking behind them, but saw no one immediately in pursuit. The building now raged in full flame, ages of dried dust having made it a tinderbox. Soon the building next to it followed suit, smoke belching into the air as though it had been trapped for centuries under each roof, waiting to get to Heaven.

They kept moving, shoulders against walls and heads low. Overhead, a humming sound erupted, and as it flew overhead they felt it thumping through the air. The small airship's shape was barely visible through the smoke, but the painted dragon teeth shone clearly.

They turned left after the fourth block and, as they turned down a small alleyway, saw a message scrawled in the ash on the wall. It was in broken Greek, but still serviceable enough to understand. It said 'ballroom visit' with an arrow below it pointing to their right.

Hephaestion led cautiously, his blade out and his finger on his shield's piston trigger.

Yitz held the empty pistol menacingly.

More arrows were drawn about on walls and other flat surfaces, the message occasionally repeated among them.

Soon they stood before a massive palace, its aged and decrepit opulence unequaled to anything Yitz had seen on Earth.

CHAPTER 32

"Seat of power of Dis," Yitz whispered.

No kidding, Hephaestion thought, and almost laughed.

They crept past a dead garden of decapitated statues, and ascended the stairs. The doors had long since been smashed in, the foyer's floors so bloodied that the tiles had been stained a uniform color. They proceeded deeper inside, where large tarnished mirrors and gilded ceilings ornately depicted angelic scenery. The room, as big as any Hephaestion had ever stood in, had two moldy chairs facing each other across a small fire on the floor at the ballroom's center. Flame flickered in the mirrors, the only thing now dancing in the once festive place.

Hephaestion sheathed his sword, its light ceasing and diminishing the room.

Someone had scrawled in ash between the two chairs the active word for 'wait' in Greek. It was a command, but the chairs and tiny fire seemed to want the command to be an inviting one.

With a sigh, Yitz sat gratefully into one of the plush chairs, which released a cloud of putrid gunk. Yitz waved his hand about while holding his cough in, then unbuckled the satchel and tossed it back to Hephaestion.

"You don't want to keep it?" he asked, sitting down more cautiously than his companion.

"No." Yitz coughed. "Looks better on you. Besides, you can outrun me. It's safer with you. Think we're safe here?"

"Enemy of my enemy—"

"Hardly means a friend, Heph."

"I know, but *not* an enemy might be just as good for now. Besides, we were getting close to the docks and we would have been exposed to Franco's air machine—a serious problem. Best if we hide and decide on another approach. And thank you, Yitz."

"You, sir, are always welcome. I would enjoy your gratitude even further if I knew what it was specifically for, however."

"That bit with the cloak was brilliant. And you're dangerous with that pistol."

Yitz shrugged. "Putz's work."

"Hardly."

The two men sat in silence, watching the flame between them flicker meekly. Hephaestion's mind drifted in and out of the present, flittering about his current predicament. How did the Jesuits get such radically advanced technology? He'd heard of ornithopters and other flying machines while sitting around Ulfric's mead hall, but to see one working so effectively was startling. It could land on presumably any stable surface, and clearly it could take off quickly when in danger. If only he had something like that, the entire decent to Alexander could take a few hours at most.

He suddenly remembered the river Styx, and winced at the thought. He figured this was as good a time as any, and decided to break the bad news to Yitz.

"What do you know about the river Styx, Yitz?" he inquired.

"Well, it's said to have so many tears in it that you forget how to think if you swim in it. You fall out of yourself. I heard that much."

"That's true, more or less," Hephaestion said.

"I also know that it's full of sinners—bitter souls. I heard the boats they use to cross the river have to be made with metal hulls to keep from being clawed apart."

"That's also true. Some boats actually generate electricity from the motion of the oarsmen, to shock anything nearby in the water."

"Each boat must have a lot of oarsmen," Yitz observed.

"Mmm-hmm."

"So, with just us two, how do we cross."

"Well, I'm glad you asked." Actually, Hephaestion *wasn't.* "I spent hundreds of years training my body not to convulse from drowning. I've practiced suffocation and drowning extensively."

"Everyone needs a hobby," Yitz said playfully.

"My intention is to crawl along the bottom of the river, hand over hand, until across."

Yitz's eyes went wide. "How far is that?"

"About seven leagues, at most."

"Wait, why not just go slowly across with a small boat?"

"The damned in Styx attack any boat they see. Period."

"Even a small one?"

"Even small ones."

"Are there no bridges?"

"All that are known have fallen or burned."

"Then how do *I* get across?"

"I'm glad you asked that, too."

"No, you clearly aren't."

"We're going to have to kill you."

Yitz stared blankly at Hephaestion. "I beg your pardon."

"You're going to have to be dead while I tow your body across the water."

"Oh, is that all?" Yitz asked calmly.

"Yes. For a moment, I thought you'd have a harder time with this. I'm glad to see—"

"*Of course I have a hard time with this!*" Yitz's voice boomed through the ballroom. "Some of us pride ourselves in not dying. Dying is one of my least favorite things to do!"

"But you'll be safe. With me!" Hephaestion argued.

"And dead."

"I didn't expect you to be here. This is technically your doing, Yitz."

"Did you actually just tell me it is *my fault* that you feel compelled to kill me? Unbelievable!"

"I can do it fairly painlessly."

"Oh? Well, now I'm clearly interested! What did you have in mind? Could you read off the menu for me?" Yitz's sarcasm flowed in full majesty now. "Is slitting my throat and keeping me kosher an option?"

Hephaestion couldn't help but smile. "Stabbing in the back of the head is instant. It will last for three days, but if we can find a dagger or sharp object, I can bind it into the back of your head," he explained clinically. "Since your healing would take much longer with an object obstructing it, we wouldn't have to deal with the risk of you recovering while we are submerged. Your heart would also work, since it takes weeks to restart."

"Well, we wouldn't want *that* now, would we?"

"No, we *wouldn't*. Because if you *did* spring back to life under Styx, you'd thrash about, and we'd be consumed by the damned over and over, every time we reformed, just to be shit out again!"

"Any other options?" Yitz bargained. "Like poison or something?"

"Poison? What poison?"

"Or wait until I'm asleep. Wait until then."

"Do you think you'll be able to sleep knowing I'm going to kill you? Honestly?"

"Good God, man! Work with me, here."

"Dying isn't really difficult. Everybody manages it, you know." Hephaestion suppressed a smile.

"Oh my God. You are a right *bastard*," Yitz snapped.

From the long shadows of the ballroom, their host gracefully emerged. Skinned down to the muscle, his body was an anatomy of the human form, clean and bloodless, as though great care had been taken in his skinning. Perhaps he skinned himself regularly, or had servants do it, but either way he strode with pride.

That wasn't the most striking thing about his appearance, though. Over his thighs, shoulders, forearms, and chest were bolted thin plates of red steel, most likely riveted into his skeleton. His face was also covered, a simple but artful metal mask affixed to his skull. It was of a cherub's face, forged with eye holes through which to see.

Walking forward without a hint of pain, the stalker sat down on the floor opposite Hephaestion and Yitz in a singular, elegant motion.

"Hello..." he purred, and crossed his legs in a fashion that made his battered stick of a chair appear as a throne. "I did not mean to overhear your heated discussion. I do thank you both for stopping by. I haven't had proper conversation in far, far too long."

"With this one here, you might *not* get any *proper* discussion," Yitz said, an angry finger pointed at Hephaestion's face.

"Well, either way, I appreciate your trust. It's not something I often come by these days," the skinned man confessed.

"Thank you for your assistance," Hephaestion said.

"And the place to rest," Yitz added. "Don't mind us and our bickering. Not to press your assistance further, but we were just debating how to cross the river. Any ideas on that? Preferably one that involves my *not* dying?"

"Actually, I was just hoping for conversation! Chat with me a bit, and I'll aid you in any way I can. Consider it a nice fireside chat," he said from under his cherub metal mask.

"Will the samurai find us here?"

"They landed in another part of the city, and I have employed means to lead them on a merry chase for some time. You two gentlemen will be safe in my care for the time being."

Judging the setting around him, Hephaestion surmised that the skinned, armored man viewed this as his personal court. He was the ruler here, Hephaestion and Yitz the guests. They had better act it.

He propped his shield against his thigh, and leaned back with an echoing creek of his chair.

Yitz crossed his legs, straightened his waistcoat, and tucked his thumb into his pocket.

Both sat, waiting patiently for prompting from the skinned man as he chuckled at the emptiness of the ballroom. "This town is *dead*," he said eventually.

"What brought *you* here?" Yitz asked, nodding politely in agreement.

"It reminds me of home," he said, a hint of melancholy peeking through his eloquence. "I miss the city life. Such a good warren for a fox to hide in."

"Are you a fox?" Hephaestion prodded.

"Oh yes, but far too good of one. I was never caught, even on Earth. I ate so many chickens and mice that Minos's pens nearly ran *dry* scribbling down my repertoire. A fox is a lonely creature on Earth, but here it occasionally gets the chance to sit by the fire and chat with fellow foxes."

"So I'm a fox, too?" Yitz asked, eyebrow raised.

"Certainly! Why else would the hounds be chasing you?"

"Hounds? The samurai?"

"To be more specific, yes, and led by that Jesuit fellow, judging from the robe and hat. They flew over the city, back and forth, for hours and hours until they finally landed in that courtyard. They had no interest in hiding from prying eyes. So confident. Just as sure as hounds. But don't worry!" The stalker cooed as though to a frightened child. "As a fellow fox, I postponed their hunt enough for you to easily make your way through the city down to the docks. Besides, they are merely hounds, loud and baying, scratching everywhere in circles — strong and dedicated, certainly, but no match for foxes like us." The cherub face turned back and forth between Yitz and Hephaestion. "So, I am here because it reminds me of home. Why are *you* here, friends? What brings one of God's chosen and a speaker of archaic Greek so well-equipped into the pit?"

"I'm here to find someone," Hephaestion said.

"Do tell!"

A thought struck Hephaestion, and he reached into his satchel and pulled out the paperwork. "This man here... there's a drawing of his face. He's down in the Malebolge on the frozen lake."

The man took the stack of documents from Hephaestion, his boney fingers gently gliding through them.

Yitz was clearly uncomfortable with such a wretched sinner thumbing through personal information. He glared at Hephaestion, but there was little else he could do without offending their host.

"Hmmm, such a petty crime when you think of it," the skinned man said. "Betraying the community and your religious institution simply for money. So many other, more interesting sins to commit. But surely he did not steal from a Grecian like yourself?"

"No, but his parents are dear to me, and I promised to tell the boy they loved him," Hephaestion said, apologizing with his eyes to Yitz.

It was impossible to read what went on behind the metal cherub's mask. The man's eyes unfocused, blinked, and then he handed Hephaestion back all of the documentation. "I hope you find him, then. I am sorry I can't be of help in that regard."

"You've done a lot to help already," Hephaestion said, placing everything back in his satchel.

"Enough seriousness, let's talk about the weather!" With that, the red man began spouting about how foggy his city used to be back on Earth. He spoke of icy snow and blistering summers and how the church bells used to rouse him every morning.

Yitz thrived with small, worthless conversation, and he was now in his element. The two men engaged delightedly, complaining about the complexities of finances and annoyances of the lesser peoples that pollute the city.

They both coerced Hephaestion to share about his time in Greece, and he told his host about the rushing waters pouring down from the Macedonian mountains in the spring, swelling the rivers and lakes with fish and silt.

The three talked of songs, instruments they were bad at playing, and the difficulties of their daily lives on Earth and how much they missed them.

Time passed, and Hephaestion wondered if all the pleasant conversation was to stall them to allow the Jesuit to catch up. If so, then why would this man have done so much to help in the first place? Do foxes toy with their prey?

"So, clearly you are ancient," the skinless man said to Hephaestion. "And clearly I must wonder where you have been for thousands of years. Many ascend to Heaven in far lesser time frames. Do you have residence in New Dis? Do you have no interest in Heaven?"

"I was in Purgatory."

"What an excellent place to waste your time, I hear. I've never seen it, but sounds dreadfully dull."

"There are good, kind people there. Very patient," Hephaestion replied, a little defensive.

"Did you stay there for thousands of years because of patient people?"

"No, I don't think I did."

The metal cherub's eyes bore into Hephaestion. "Well, you are here *now*, aren't you? Something significant must have pulled you from your perch."

"I got tired of waiting."

"For what?"

"For... someone. Someone to come to me."

"Come to you or come *for* you?"

Hephaestion shifted in his seat, sword handle against his forearm where he could feel it.

Yitz noticed the motion and, no doubt sensing Hephaestion readying himself to strike, said, "Is this how you speak to mice or chickens before you eat them?"

The red man roared with laughter. "Ha! Maybe my habits die hard, but no, Mr. Fox. The thought didn't cross my mind. I am sorry to pry so hard. My manners are all but lost. Sometimes I fear I will go feral in this mausoleum of a city. Truth is, you two simply speaking with me has been more of a help than you know. I am delighted to assure you safe passage through my city. Always. Do you intend to come back this way?"

"No, we'll crawl down the Devil's Spine to Purgatory."

"Ah, the fabled passage so many dream of. Well, if ever either of you do come back to my city, perhaps in a flying machine even, please stop by. I will always have a fire waiting for another chat. And perhaps you could take me for a ride!"

Hephaestion and Yitz allowed themselves a smile.

"Good," the man said. "Good." He stood slowly and took a knee before Hephaestion, then drew a long, curved line in the dust on the wooden ballroom floor. "Before you go, I owe you some simple advice. Please do not think me stingy, but your method for crossing is what I did. I held my breath, drifted into a trance-like state, and simply crawled along the bottom of Styx like a crab. It feels like ages ago."

Yitz's face looked bleak.

Hephaestion nodded in understanding, but felt sympathy for the man.

"I also wish to offer some advice. The boiling river..." the skinned host began.

"Phlegethon."

"Quite right, quite right. Phlegethon, home of those brutal and violent toward their fellow man, or woman, as the case may be. But as I was saying, that river... you need to be very careful in your approach to it. Keep your eyes open and don't speak to anyone you might see mulling about until you are certain they won't figure out who you are."

"And who am I?" Hephaestion asked suspiciously.

"Why, you are Hephaestion of Macedonia, of course."

Hephaestion was floored, and gazed at Yitz, who just grinned. *Am I really that transparent? Out of the millions of Greeks in the afterlife, how could a random denizen of Hell figure it out so easily?*

"How is it that everyone knows who I am? Thousands of years have passed!"

"Well, while there are many famous Greeks, few are as famous as *you*. Besides, your hounds were talking extensively about their fox once they had landed."

"So you knew the whole time?"

He nodded, his eyes crinkling with delight through his mask. "I didn't want to be rude, but I do think it important you take my advice."

"Beware our approach to the river," Yitz repeated.

"Indeed."

"And what of the hounds?" Hephaestion asked.

"I'll eventually let them pass. I'll let you reach the docks first and figure a way across the river, but then I'll permit them your scent again."

Hephaestion felt grateful at what help and information he had, but he still felt an uncomfortable wariness. "From one fox to another, thank you," he said.

The skinned man stood and bowed low with courtly flourish. "Speak of me well and speak of me often," he said. "Especially to the ladies."

CHAPTER 33

Like all good palaces, it had an escape tunnel, this one leading to the docks. Their polite host had shown them the way, bowing low as they left, his empty hand providing a flourish as though a phantom top hat were in its grasp.

Narrow and low, the tunnel ran directly to the main floor of the dockmaster's stone tower. The office had clearly suffered a fire, as all the documentation and wooden furniture had been reduced to dead cinder piled on the floor. Above them, a man-sized hatch opened through the blackened ceiling.

With Yitz boosting him, Hephaestion reached it and pulled himself up. He then reached back down and hoisted Yitz through. Once on the observation deck, they saw that the dockmaster's tower was a squat, wide structure no taller than the city's rooftops. Lying on their stomachs, hiding under its bronze roof, they combed the city with their gaze.

"A looking glass would have been a good idea, Hephaestion."

"They're heavy, and it would have most likely broken. Besides, not many areas are large enough or clear enough to warrant one."

He dug through his bag, pulled out the astrolabe, and placed it flat under the two men's noses. It spun about, orienting itself, and soon it emulated the rotation of the rings.

"I think we can cross here just fine," he said, pointing to the rocking shoreline below. "We'll move from cover to cover to avoid any prying eyes in the air. Once in the wood, we move several leagues clockwise until this tower here comes into view. The Queen told me to meet a man there named Landis."

Yitz nodded while reloading the pistol.

After slinking back down through the hatch, they ran out through the tower's doorless front exit to a bundle of bound tackle, where they could see the river.

Styx, cold and lifeless, its surface as smooth as untouched glass, washed away memory and worldly joy, leaving nothing but despair and bitterness. Hephaestion had heard some say it was once just a ravine, until the spiteful damned filled it with their selfish tears.

They sprinted forward again, and hid under a half-painted boat propped up on stone blocks. The cobble street had given way to pebbles, and in the distance stood wooden docks, clearly fashioned from the suicide wood. Triremes—longboats with dozens of oars on each side—sat perfectly still on the motionless river, their reflections pristine on the water. Styx had no direction or flow. Not even a ripple.

Some of the triremes had decayed to the point of sinking, their center mast and forward figurehead hinting at the sunken bulk under the river's glass-like surface. The boats themselves were long and wide, some of which held three rows of oars, and many of them had metal plating on their hull's exterior. Hephaestion's research had uncovered that many of the triremes' oar banks acted as electrical crank generators, and the combined electrical output of hundreds of oarsmen provided enough power to electrify the nearby water. The result was simple: if the damned condemned to the river Styx got too close, they would be shocked and deterred. This was necessary because, prior to such generators, the water-logged damned would swarm to any boat on the surface, capsize it, consume its occupants and drag everything below to their depths.

Just as the spiteful desired to drag others down in life, so they did now in eternal death.

Both men sprang from under their hiding spot and rushed to the stone root of the dock, where it reached away from the pebble shore and out over the water.

Yitz clung to a large post to hide his profile, its surface red with the oily blood that gave it a dull luster.

"I wish we could burn it. Burn it all," Hephaestion said, grimly looking at all the wood around them. "Burn it and give them some kind of release."

At the end of the dock, he looked out over the river in dismay. He saw no visible horizon, and couldn't judge the distance to the other side.

A distant thumping echoed over the river.

"The ornithopter," Yitz snarled as both men frantically scanned the sky. "This is how a rabbit feels."

"We have to move fast. We'll be safer under the river, but I have to enter extremely slowly, so I'll do it unde—"

A gunshot startled Hephaestion so much he nearly fell off the dock onto the pebble shoreline.

Yitz dropped to his knees, head back, pistol smoking as it slipped from his fingers. Blood soaked through his waistcoat over his heart. He had pressed the muzzle to his chest and unloaded it.

Slowly, Yitz folded onto his side, the last of his air slipping out of him in a postmortem sigh.

With an affectionate hand, Hephaestion closed Yitz's eyes. Perhaps he'd wanted to kill himself before he lost his nerve, or simply do it himself to retain some dignity. Either way, Hephaestion appreciated the gesture.

The flying machine grew closer, its echo now in every direction. Hephaestion rolled Yitz off the dock onto the shore, leapt down, and then dragged him under the wooden boards between the posts. Through the slits, he spied an ornithopter flying over the city main, its crew leaning out with spyglasses in all directions. Then he saw another, and another, and Hephaestion realized the sky was full of them, buzzing about like wasps, hovering and altering directions.

He pulled cord from his satchel and tied Yitz's arms tight to his sides, and bound his legs together. He didn't want his dead friend's limbs getting caught or brushing against anything dangerous.

Next, Hephaestion secured all of his gear and laid himself on top of Yitz as though his small comrade was a mattress. With extensions of rope, he tied himself to Yitz with some well practiced knots, and then rolled over with a grunt, Yitz's body following suit like a giant, long backpack.

After double-checking the knots, Hephaestion lay on his stomach in the gravel and, with the slowest of motions, dragged himself forward a centimeter at a time. Even causing a ripple from displaced stones could mean absolute danger.

He would have to go across the river along the bottom, crawling forward, as slowly as possible so as to not draw the attention of the drowned dead. Breaching the river's surface would be the most difficult part, and he moved so slowly he wasn't actually certain at times if he was even moving at all.

His fingers on his left hand were first. They entered the water, dipped in, found gravel, slowly grabbed hold, and pulled him just a bit forward. Then his right hand moved forward, deeper into the water. Next came his knees. It was achingly slow, and the weight of Yitz sometimes shifted, but he could *not* cause a ripple on the surface.

The disciplined art of not breathing is difficult, perhaps one of the greatest challenges to any soul. The man with armor bolted to his bones through his skinned flesh did it, and clearly was able and willing to do anything he wished. Hephaestion had to be like him, be a fox. He had to be not just *willing*, but capable of doing the impossible.

Hephaestion's chin touched the water, just barely. It was cool and oddly inviting without being frigid. His fingers continued to reach forward in turn, gripping the rock at the river's bottom, slowly dragging him in at a miniscule pace.

When the water finally hit his nostrils, he took his last breath, and continued.

It was agony at first. He had to wrestle with his lungs and hands and knees and feet, but they would obey. His body was his army, and this was his campaign, and he would lead it to victory across this river.

Clamping his eyes shut, he continued. The heavy armor, shield, sword, and Yitz kept him low in the water, and after he was finally submerged, he opened his eyes. What little light came from above sent shafts of light deep in the river, silhouetting the drifting bodies of the damned as they slowly spiraled about like asteroids, wisps of hair extending from their heads like paint strokes.

He moved on, his chest burning, trying to convince his instincts that air was only a comfort. The words 'air' and 'breathe' were soon banished from his mind forcefully, and he instead tried to think only of water. Hephaestion reminisced about the Aegean Sea and its many islands. Alexander and he had sailed by ship to where Troy once stood, and honored the graves of Achilles and Patroclus. On that night, after they made love in the sand under a bright summer moon, Alexander first called him Paty. Alex whispered it in his ear, and it made his spine tingle.

Somewhere, on the other side of this drifting, lonely, weightless tomb, his love waited.

He was deep now, the surface far above. His fingers clung to the bottom's mossy stones and he pulled himself forward, careful to avoid the occasional damned that would float nearby.

Leagues... leagues of silence and pressure built in his ears. The burning in his lungs would wane and wax depending on how much he

thought of it. He didn't know how long it would take him, but the singular light from above acted as an azimuth that guided him toward the far shore.

At some point, it struck Hephaestion how lonely he was. Throughout his afterlife, he'd nearly always had someone there — Ulfric, certainly, but even now, when in the pit of Hell, Yitz had been his company. Never would he have guessed such strength existed in someone so apparently frail, but how many times had the man saved the day? Could Hephaestion have even done this without Yitz at his side?

Onward he crept. Occasionally, he'd crawl by a sunken trireme or a boot from an oarsman. None of the dead clung to each other for comfort, or even seemed to know others were there. They remained completely dormant, content in their misery, only to be roused if someone dared disturb the surface above, reminding them that a world existed beyond the motionless, circular river that went nowhere.

It wasn't much, but Hephaestion could perceive an incline. He had lost track of time and distance, placing his mind in a trance as his body obeyed a simple pattern. Nonetheless, he'd drawn closer to the other side. Now he had to impose twice as much discipline on himself as before, fighting his eagerness to end the ordeal.

Left hand, fingers dug in, pull forward. Right hand, fingers dug in, pull forward. Over and over and over.

The incline increased significantly, until a glasslike barrier shimmered above his head. The gravel ascended to the surface in front of him.

He kept his wretchedly slow pace, his hair suddenly heavy from the water running out of it as he crowned. Next, his eyes were above water, fixed on trees in the distance — *away from the shore!* — red, mighty trees with trembling boughs and quivering leaves. They were gradually moving toward his right.

His nostrils rose free of Styx, and flared uncontrollably as air flew into his lungs, snorting and rippling the water's surface. Without taking a moment to chastise himself, Hephaestion sprung to his knees, his body weary from the weight of submergence and Yitz. He broke for the shore, knees kicking high and arms pumping wildly, and....

They came... bursting from the water like nightmares. Their clawing hands and pale, howling faces surrounded him like a swell of frenzied carp as they surged upward. Dozens of pale, bloated men and women clawed at the air, gargling and gasping in ferocious hunger.

Their white, dead eyes rolled about in their skulls, and that's when Hephaestion figured it out for certain: the damned in this river were blind. Not only did they drag anyone they could to their miserable depths, but they were completely blind — as blind in death as they had been in life.

As he fled for the trees, still knee-deep in the water, they clenched and clawed at Yitz. They had a firm grip, and were winning the tug of war. The ropes pulled tightly, straining his body and sending him into a coughing fit he couldn't control.

The bindings around Yitz's arms came loose, and Hephaestion knew he was about to lose him. So he drew his sword and spun his entire body around, Yitz's arms flopping about wildly, several of the damned still holding tight.

He drove his blade into them, its heat sizzling through their bodies, steam erupting from their mouths and nostrils. Flailing his weapon wildly, he sliced them down, the water now splashing chaotically as it reddened.

He couldn't turn now. He was surrounded, but letting them take Yitz... *that* he simply would not allow.

Out of the howling and screeching and gurgling, another noise roared, a new one that popped with a shrill staccato. Several of the damned jolted and shook where they stood, holes being blown into them. The automatic gun fire came from an ornithopter above.

It was the opening Hephaestion needed, even though he knew they were actually shooting at *him*, overeager to bring him down. he turned about and trudged through the shallow water as fast as he could for the tree line. Bullets impacted Yitz, his limp body acting as a meat shield, jolting with each impact.

Like a lumbering drunkard, Hephaestion bumbled onto the shore and into the trees. He'd crossed the river and made it into the wood, the ornithopter unloading its weapons futilely into the surrounding trees before banking and buzzing away in frustration.

CHAPTER 34

Once under cover, Hephaestion sliced Yitz's body free and slung him over his shoulders like a hunted deer. It was easier to run this way. He'd hoped to rest after getting clear of the river, but knowing that an entire flock of flying gunships now soared about made him anxious to relocate fast.

Immediately, he began stumbling. The ground was now exclusively roots, gnarled and tangled into each other from the red trees that stood straight and tall. Some were mightier than others, their canopies reaching almost beyond eyesight above and overshadowing all others. Most tragic of all were the saplings.

Where they children? People of minor impact on the world? Is the tree's size a gradient of either age or level of sin?

The wood was morose, and yet he could feel the presence of each soul. Perhaps Hell was a place where you were surrounded by thousands of others that felt as lost as you do, but where nobody spoke of it.

As he clumsily navigated the roots, ascending a large hill, Hephaestion grew almost eager to steady himself on any nearby tree he could reach. He didn't pry the bark or scratch the surface, but instead placed his heavy hand on each timber hide as he constantly balanced Yitz on his shoulders. Maybe, deep in the core of the tree or in its roots, it could feel the warmth of a human hand.

Supposedly, a human that committed suicide circumvented Minos entirely, and would crash from the living Earth directly into the ground in a spectacular and messy *crunch*. Some speculated that since the

person had judged themselves and killed themselves, there was no need for Minos. Being a tree is as far from human as possible. If a person ended their humanity, then so be it. Be a tree instead.

The mysterious logic escaped Hephaestion. He thought of Thebes again, and that temple filled with the dead. Boudica had given him a lot to think about when she said that to kill oneself isn't necessarily suicide, but Hephaestion still didn't know the boundaries of the system.

Worse still, those that had flocked to the temples in Thebes had died, one way or another, for tragic reasons, terrified.

Hephaestion tried to step even lighter than before, careful not to let his heel scrape on any roots.

A shout echoed among the trees, as someone called out to another. He couldn't make out the language or intentions, but he was not alone in the wood. Reluctant to drop Yitz, he crouched low to listen to any more calls, in order to get an idea of their source.

Several voices erupted.

"This one's good!"

"Got one here."

"Working...."

"Watch it...."

Each voice was of a different language, but they all seemed to be calling out in coordination. Were they searching for him? Why would they be so loud? The men sounded too gruff to be disciplined like the samurai.

Then he heard it—sawing... metal teeth chewing back and forth into wood. It came from one direction first, then another, and another. Soon the crackling of a tree's buckling trunk rang out. Shouts followed it as it fell and crashed down. They were loggers, the men who cut down and planked the suicides so that people could walk on them and sit on them and burn them. They carelessly tormented the tormented.

Hephaestion was *enraged*.

Creeping about the thick roots, he kept his combined shield fixed to his back. It didn't take long for him to see a felled tree, leaves and branches providing him ample concealment to approach.

With rue, Hephaestion thought of how he had chastised Yitz for lending his ear to the glutton, and for freeing the jarred hearts. The impulse to save as many of the trees as possible blossomed and his heart raced. As he crept closer, he saw that the men were unarmored and easy targets. He could cut half of them down before they could mount a defense or wield proper weapons.

But it would risk Yitz. It would risk everything. Furious with himself, he glared at the loggers now in plain view.

Drenched in dried blood, they shuffled about, each holding an end of a two-man crosscut saw. Fulfilling a motion they had done thousands of times, they aimed their saw's teeth against the bark of their next victim. One heaved and one pulled, and as the teeth tore into the wood, blood erupted instead of sap.

One day this would stop. Perhaps through Yitz's wealth or some other influence, Hephaestion would stop this. If even a single tree in this wood was from that temple, he would protect it. His only consolation was that a dozen loggers couldn't cut down trees very quickly.

As if to insult him, a new sound arose. After knocking several smaller trees down, their branches and trunks splitting with spurts of red, there came a *machine*, a long flatbed with treads on either side, climbing its way over the uneven ground of the wood. It was as long as a schooner, and on it lay a stack of felled and stripped tree trunks. Several tall pipes craned out of its sides, spewing black smoke into the air as the fire in its engine growled forward. It moved slowly, no more than a league an hour, and large mechanical claws hung from chains on both its sides to clamp and lift timber onto its back.

Several men walked flanking it. Others drove it and climbed around on it securing their bounty. Each member of its crew was covered in heavy armor that seemed as poorly cobbled together as the armor of the cannibals from the glutton's circle. What was their connection?

He sighed, resigned to stop pushing his luck, and instead chose to get Yitz to safety.

One of the armored men fell over and tumbled onto his back, as if an invisible force had hit him. Instantly, every single logger froze.

"Tower!" one yelled.

"Tower!" the others frantically replied, diving to the ground and trying to wedge themselves down into the roots.

A gunshot echoed through the trees.

Peeking over the canopy of the treetops was a tower, tall and looming in the distance, approaching from the previous circle. It must have been built in the river Styx, because it approached slowly behind him, from the same direction as the previous circle rotated.

The machine's driver went limp at the wheel, a telling gunshot echoing a few seconds after. That's why they all wore metal. They were

trying to increase their chances of survival from being sniped. The tower was Emmet Landis, the contact given to him by Queen Sungbon!

Hephaestion jumped to his feet and scrambled across the roots and gnarled knots toward the tower. Gunshot after gunshot echoed from the distance, shots occasionally zipping so close to Hephaestion that he heard the bullet 'snap' through the air past him.

Soon he came to the edge of the wood, the loggers still cowering in their places under their hulking metal armor. Hephaestion waved his free arm frantically, the other holding Yitz steady across his shoulders, flailing at the tower as it approached.

It stood at least a quarter league from the shore on a tiny island of stone. The tower's construction looked to be of pale soapstone blocks, thick and unyielding, with only several high windows. At its base was a steel door sealed tight, the water at its threshold.

From below Styx's surface, a metal walkway bubbled and rose up, the drowned damned screeching at its presence as they swarmed and clawed at it. Sparks hissed and flew, driving them away in mournful groans as it electrified them.

Once the damned were clear, the sparks ceased.

Hephaestion stepped forward, a boot cautiously touching the walkway's grate.

The metal door at the tower's base swung open, and a figure in a long coat and cowboy hat appeared.

Hephaestion raised his hand in relieved greeting, and immediately after experienced being shot in the head.

CHAPTER 35

When life flooded back into Hephaestion's lungs, the first thing he heard was someone pleasantly whistling. His eyes adjusted easily to the fluttering gas lamps, but his head raged with an ache he had never known. Keeping silent, he took in his surroundings.

Inside this low, circular room chiseled from ancient stone were walls crowded with small shelves, most containing a menagerie of tiny sculptures. Soldiers, horses, farm animals, buildings, and even a nativity with a manger adorned the room, all of them carved intricately from bone.

Hephaestion lay on a cot against the wall, and in the room's center under the primary gaslight, a man sat on a stool with his back facing him. His hair was dark and slicked back, his shoulders strong and rolling as he whistled a pleasant tune. Splayed out on some kind of stone slab before him laid Yitz, naked and still very much dead. Next to the man's elbow, a small glass jar sat half filled with smashed and mangled bullets.

With a wrench, the man pulled yet another round from Yitz's body. He examined it, pinched between his pliers, turning it over and over and whistling with admiration.

"Yer friend is a magnet," the man chirped with a spry and gruff voice. "As fer yeh, yeh done been shot in the head. Here...." A large hand dropped a twisted bullet fragment on Hephaestion's chest. "Keepsake!"

"Emmett... L-Land... Lan...." Hephaestion's tongue was lazy.

"Emmett Landis at yer service!"

"Queen...."

"Ah, yessir, that lovely lady, a true queen through an' through. She give yeh... this?" Emmett raised Hephaestion's astrolabe to the light.

"Why did you s-shoot me in the head?" Hephaestion asked angrily, his wits rapidly congealing.

"Oh, that's just how I greet everybody. I take no chances. Figured we'd talk after. If yeh'd been bad, I'd just toss you in the river with all them crazies. If yeh good, yeh git to wake up."

"Those loggers wear metal because of you?"

"Hells yeah, but enough with that. Rest up and we'll chat in a bit." Emmett refilled his tin cup of coffee, left Yitz's naked body on the stone slab, and limped to a small chair suspended from the ceiling of the round, stone room. Humming to himself, he fiddled with what looked like a telescope that extended from the wall. The optics appeared complicated, beyond Hephaestion's comprehension, with various scopes and eyepieces rotating into position for the chair's occupant to see through. He'd missed it when he first examined the room because of all the clutter on the shelves.

The ceiling offered a stark contrast to the pale walls and floor, covered in gears, gauges, and dials. Although Hephaestion couldn't discern the purpose of all the machinery dangling down, clearly the tower had been built around the mechanism.

Mounted on the sill of the singular window was the barrel of a long rifle, the butt of it designed to curve around the back of the operator's neck. As a weapon, it was far too large to carry, and too difficult to aim at close range, but Hephaestion could see that it would be a precise tool from a league or more away.

"I call it 'the middle finger of God." Emmett beamed. "Could light a cigarette from a mile out. Each cartridge is a work of artistic chemistry, refined with perfect patch and sculptin'."

The word 'sculptin' rang in Hephaestion's mind as he glanced again at the shelves along the wall. With his eyes now more responsive, he noted that some of the shelves depicted dioramas of battle scenes or monuments. One shelf, low and near Hephaestion's head, was filled with tiny white carved cows, some deformed or unfinished, revealing that Emmett had most likely been practicing the cow for a while just to perfect the form of the animal.

"Ah, admire all yeh like. Yessir, I am an artist! I'm workin' on a scene depictin' the siege of Ft. Sumter. I just need to keep workin' on them walls but I gotta wait until my tibia grow back!" Emmett knocked a knuckle against his wooden leg.

"Wait. You carve all of these things out of *your own bones*?"

"Boredom gits the best of yeh! Besides, an artist don't work with no junk."

As Hephaestion thought back on the chess set in Queen Sungbon's study, it became clear that Emmett Landis had made a long-standing habit of using himself as his artistic medium of choice.

"The little soldiers are all finger bones," Emmett said, raising his left hand sporting only two full fingers. "But the fort's walls need somethin' bigger. After yeh rest up, look around. Check out my stuffs." With that, the man stood from his suspended chair, coffee sloshing onto his stained plaid shirt, and wandered past Yitz to a floor hatch.

"He'll be up in a bit. I got the bullet from his heart first, but I wasn't keen on dressin' 'im, though, so that's on yeh." He descended a ladder to the floor below.

Hephaestion was safe, for now. Queen Sungbon had said that this man would protect him ferociously, and her word had proven ironclad thus far. The roar of his headache made keeping his eyes open difficult, but he was too excited at how near to Alexander he'd come. Too much thought and worry and consideration swam about his mind, and within a few minutes, he sat himself up, the cot creaking under his weight while his hands cradled his head. He couldn't see his boots anywhere, and wore only his kamees.

A few things just didn't make sense to him. Were the Jesuits really that threatened by him descending? Have they taken on the role of prison wardens, or did Sun Tzu assign it to them? Were the Buddhists, Euclid, and other explorers in equal danger?

His head roared, nearly forcing him to vomit up all of the nothing his stomach contained. Flopping back into his cot, he allowed himself rest.

With Alex in mind, Hephaestion rummaged through his memories. He could usually put himself into a moment, his love's face becoming more vivid, if he could just relive an event from their time together—a meeting, a dinner, a horse ride, or intimacy.

Their time together... less than thirty years. Hephaestion had been part of the afterlife for over two thousand years. Entire empires and civilizations had risen, crumbled, and been completely swept away by the wind in that time. Yet thirty years was all it took for Hephaestion—his first and only love of his life. They weren't given the chance they deserved. It had ended far too soon.

He drifted into a restful sleep, calm, knowing that soon Alexander and he would have all the time in the universe.

It must have been a restful sleep, for Hephaestion felt as if jolted awake the instant he'd fallen asleep, but Yitz now sat on the edge of his cot, fully clothed with a tin cup of coffee in his hand.

"You snore." Yitz smiled and took a sip.

"Alex had the same complaint," Hephaestion confessed, stretching.

"Adina makes me sleep on my side."

"Alex did, too."

From the suspended chair, Emmett pulled himself away from his optics. "Adina? Wait. I got a note. For yeh, I bet! Here you go, heeb!" Emmett ruffled through some papers and parchments on the floor, and produced an opened letter and a postcard.

Yitz took them cautiously as Hephaestion sat up to get a better view.

The postcard displayed a painting of New Dis with the words "Wish You Were Here" on one side, and blank space for writing on the other. Yitz then turned his attention to the letter.

"This letter is opened," Yitz scolded Emmett.

"Yeah, I know. I'm the one who opened it!"

"This is a private letter, cowgoy!"

"Nobody getting letters down here but me!" Emmett defended. "Sides, all in gibberish Jew-scratch anyhow."

Yitz had already tuned the man out, his distaste for Emmett having faded completely from his face before he had finished reading the first sentence of Adina's letter. His eyes devoured it, scanning side to side, searching each ink stroke for hidden meaning and expression through the curves of her words. She had touched this, and her hands had meticulously produced it.

Hephaestion saw that Yitz was reading the letter over again.

"It dirty? Wanna share?" Emmett asked curiously.

"Oh, my roguish gentile, it is indeed wonderful, but only for me."

Emmett frowned.

"Don't be getten' mail often. Comes in tiny spinnin' parachutes that Songhai launches once a cycle. They aim it, an' time it, so it lands right on the roof, here. Mathematical geniuses, them. Want more coffee?"

"Actually," Yitz said distantly, still lost in his letter. "I'd hate some."

"Suit yerself." Emmett smiled and set up two wooden folding chairs next to his own. "Come sit a spell, then. Hephaestion, nab some coffee while yeh at it."

Hephaestion had never had coffee before. It was black. Nothing a person ever drinks should be completely black.

"Smells awful," Hephaestion mumbled.

"Oh, don't worry. It is. Leave it for me if yeh rather. I'm almost out anyhow. Keep sendin' up them balloons with messages askin' for more coffee and bullets, and all I get is a letter for 'nother man. Thinkin' someone is shootin' my balloons down."

"It's possible. I've encountered some flying machines that were unfriendly," Hephaestion said, easing into his own chair. "So you just stay here and, as the tower rotates around the wood, you try to keep it clear of loggers?"

"Yep. Two birds with one stone. I snipe 'em out there while protectin' the trees for the Queen, and at the same time I house the monks when they pass on by. Strange fellas, them."

Yitz cried out in alarm. "Wait, what? The Monks come here? They cross the river?"

"Sure nuff."

"How?"

"I just raise the other bridge and jolt it."

Yitz glared at Hephaestion with all the ire he could muster, which was *substantial.*

"I got shot, too!" Hephaestion pleaded, holding the bullet from his head up between his fingers.

"Oh...." Yitz feigned sympathy. "You poor, wee little lamb." In one rapid motion, Yitz jumped to his feet and produced the jar half-filled with bullets for Hephaestion to admire. "These came from *me!*"

Emmett giggled with delight.

Hephaestion mimicked one of Yitz's shrugs.

"Hey, weren't yeh suppose' to be with 'em Buddhist boys, anyhow, Hephaestion? That was the last message I got."

"I was supposed to be with them, yes, but things didn't work out. What are they like, the Buddhists?"

"Bald," Emmett said, stroking the stubble on his chin while Yitz refilled his coffee and sat with the other two men. "They a good sort. One time they came here with a tard. Big, dumb oaf of a tard. I figured since souls cross to the afterworld, they have their spines straightened and their sight and hearing restored, so why was the tard still a tard? I asked 'em. I asked why God didn't un-tard the tard, and the Monk looks at me an' says, 'God only lays the crooked straight. There was nothin' wrong with this man to begin with." Emmett fell silent, letting the monk's quote resonate. "I don't understand that. I still don't. I don't get what use or place a tard has in the world. Which is why I'll never see Heaven."

The men sat in silence, pondering the gravity of the parable.

"So, you're Purgatorian?" Hephaestion finally asked.

"Heh, barely. Technicality, really."

"Do tell," Yitz said, working up the strength for another sip of coffee.

"So, I'm from America. A war broke out there between some rich folk to the south and some rich folk to the north. Poor folk like me got the honor and privilege to fight it for 'em. So, the side I'm on has lotsa slaves, tall, dark folk that work and sing and whatnot. So, I was given the job of watchin' the pickaninnies because the South was hurtin' in the war and it was pressin' the slaves into uniform and combat service. Let that sink in a moment. You get yer slaves to carry weapons and fight alongside you."

"That isn't strange. In Greece, we did the same thing."

"True, but in Greece, lotsa times you people treated yer slaves like *people*. In the South, we didn't so much. All cattle to us. Toys. The women especially. Men like me got a taste for dark ladies, and we never looked back. I been with many dark ladies, but few white. White ladies had to be willin' for ye. Dark ladies were just there for whatever you wanted. Anyhow, I was an awful man. Treatin' human beings like cattle and toys. Deservin' of Hell, I assure yeh. But the eve of a big battle, I walked around camp lookin' at all them dark faces sleepin' an worryin' and cryin' and knowin' they were to be sent in first against the enemy just to soak up damage an' shells an' such...." Emmett trailed off, lost in the moment, his eyes distant as he remembered the transformative moment. "So I let em go!" Emmett erupted, slapping Hephaestion's knee. He laughed so hoarsely, he nearly entered a coughing fit.

"You let them go? You set them all free the evening before the battle?"

"Yep! Told 'em where the line was of the enemy and sent 'em that way to defect, even! I knew if I just cut 'em loose, they'd be snatched up eventually, and hung after being whipped. So I told 'em to take their rifles and go to the other side! They done all defected!"

"Did they fight against you the next morning?"

"Naw. Hell, I didn't even see much of the next mornin'! They hung me as fast as they could tie a rope. I cursed their names and told 'em I'd be bangin' their mothers in Hell. As I was dyin', I knew I'd finally done somethin' right in my life. Unfair, really. Unfair that one good act git yeh out of the burning pitch below. All those poor grey backs are cookin' in the various Hells they done earned, but I'm here with coffee and guns!" Emmett's sentence lost coherence as his laughter bubbled out of him uncontrollably.

Hephaestion accommodated him with an amused smile.

Yitz did not.

"But yeah, I got a taste for dark ladies, pomegranate lips an' thick voices an' coarse hair.... I carved a chess set out of myself for our lovely and beauteous Queen Sungbon, a woman well beyond me, but lawd what a beaut. So why yeh two here? Yeh lookin' for a lad named Gil?"

Emmett rustled through the various documents on the floor, then snatched up Hephaestion's satchel and spilled its contents.

"Yes, and other things."

"Well, from what I read, he is farther below there, sonny jim. You wanna tread lightly. No angels be following you here. Weird things afoot. Lotsa smoke, for one. I'm seein' huge swaths of trees gone time to time, too. Odd folk, and the armor and metal is fairly new, too."

"How long have the loggers been so aggressive?"

"Yeh ask that question as though I have a concept of time!" Emmett laughed. "Do yeh really know how long ago you set foot in the pit? Don't yeh feel that time is just a 'thing' now that yeh don't really consider no more? For me, it's just this tower, this mounted rifle, my lever-action that ye've already been intimate with, and a few pistols. My purpose is to introduce hot lead into bad bodies."

Hephaestion nodded in understanding, succumbing to the impulse to rub his temples for the sake of easing his headache.

"Seriously, poncey boy. Go back to yer nap and rest up. Both of yeh. Rest while yeh can."

"Poncey boy?" Hephaestion asked.

"Yep. A ponce. I ain't judgin' or nothin', but I know a pole greaser when I see one. Not that greasin' poles is bad. I'm glad to have mine greased time to time, and I am grateful for it on such rare occasions. But yeh a ponce, and I didn't need no scope to spot that a mile away! Now get some sleep. Maybe I'll think of a way to make yeh less poncey as yeh descend after yer lad, Gil."

CHAPTER 36

Emmett whistled like a songbird for what seemed to be hours during an endless and steady fervor of crafting in the floors below Yitz and Hephaestion's cots. Occasionally, his whistling would degrade into a lyric or two of whatever song he was singing, usually about a lady or a card game, but he was always on pitch and springy with his tune.

He'd gathered up Hephaestion's armor and took it down a ladder through the trapdoor in the floor. The sound of clanking metal and rolling spools accompanied Emmett's piercing song as Hephaestion and Yitz rested. Nothing could keep Yitz from a deep sleep, it seemed, whereas Hephaestion was too anxious to drift again. Instead, he lay on his cot and counted the teeth in the ceiling's gears.

Soon after, Emmett came back up the ladder and poked at Hephaestion. "Hey, ye've got a Greek thing goin', what with the 'ponce' and 'shield' and all, but you need some America in yer corner. America's the newest nation there is, an' nobody does it better. See this?"

Emmett held up a large revolver of polished blue steel, clearly a well-machined and carefully-crafted firearm.

"This will fire even when wet. Not underwater, mind yeh, but just wet. Not like yer lady's pistol thar. This be a Navy Colt! God made all men, but Colt made 'em equal. An' this here Colt was made by his own hand in Purgatory! I got two of 'em, but figured if the Queen endorses yeh, so do I."

He handed it to Hephaestion, grip first.

"I'm not very good with guns," Hephaestion confessed.

"That is of concern, because guns are very good with *you*. But take it. It's single action, so hammer away at the trigger if trouble is in yer face. Here's extra rounds in a bandolier, too. I prayed over each an every one for hours so that Jesus may guide them right into the brainpans of any jailbird givin' a fuss."

"Thank you," Hephaestion said, amazed at how well his hand fit the bullgrip of the pistol. "This is a lot to give, but I won't turn it away. Thank you." He didn't say it, but he resolved to give the pistol to Yitz at first chance.

Emmett showed Hephaestion how the hammer worked and how to reload it. "Several hundred years of technological advance, right here!" he beamed. "Big difference from yer purse pistol. I got somethin' else for yeh." Scampering like an excited child, Emmett slid down the ladder again.

Hephaestion rose to his feet, stretched his legs, and looked out through the tower's window at the wood beyond. The trees marched slowly into the distance as the circle continued its endless spin. Serene and without wind, each bough reached out as still as a paint stroke.

"Seen anything since I got here? In the wood?" Hephaestion called down. "Including more loggers?"

"Nope! Oddly quiet. Even saw a few of those railless cars just sittin' in the wood, some still runnin', with nobody at the wheel. You done scared em!"

Hephaestion doubted that. His instinct told him he should be wary as he sat back down on the cot and began putting his boots on. He'd feel better with his boots.

His armor flopped up through the floor hatch, soon followed by Emmett's beaming grin. The cuirass didn't look any different than before, except for one distinct addition: it now had a left shoulder guard. A pauldron made of steel jawbones linked together would cover his shield-bearing shoulder.

"It's meant to deflect a blow in case you can't get your shield high fast enough. The steel ain't so tough, but it will help a bit. More meant to absorb a hit than to deflect it outright. Like it?"

In all, five jawbones linked from the collar of the cuirass and around the muscle of the upper arm. Hephaestion had seen designs like it among tribal warriors, but usually it was more ceremonial. Then again, those ancient decorations hadn't been dipped in molten steel.

"I... I assume those are all *your* jawbones?" Hephaestion asked hesitantly.

"Yessir! One of 'em I even lived through. Don't recall which. I was curious to see if my bottom teeth would grow back crooked each time, and what do you know...." Emmett pointed proudly at the lateral incisors. "They did. I be crooked no matter what, as God intended."

Hephaestion packed his satchel with Gil's documents, placed the heart-ripper in there as well, and cinched it shut. Fumbling around with the Colt, he couldn't figure out where to keep it on his person.

"I got a sash an' bullet bandoleer yeh can use. It adjusts fer over yer armor or without." Emmett rummaged through crates and under shelves.

The commotion finally woke Yitz, who sat up bleary-eyed.

Hephaestion caught his eye, motioning the pistol in an offering gesture to Yitz. With a shrug Yitz accepted and reached for it.

"Yep, here yeh go. Just wrap it over yer one shoulder an' stick it in yer —" Emmett froze, his eyes unfocused.

"In my what?" Yitz asked, only to be shushed violently by Emmett, his hand raised to demand silence.

"Hear *that*?" he then shouted, bouncing into his chair and squinting through the optics. His hands were a flurry as he toyed with the gears and dials in the ceiling, the entire tower rotating about on its tiny island. "I hear propellers... fans... of an airship. Weird echo...."

Both Yitz and Hephaestion slowly craned their heads upward to the ceiling.

"They comin' at me from above. Sunovabitch! They comin' straight down!" Emmett leapt from his chair, his wooden leg thumping on the floor, and craned his head out of the stone window.

He dove back in grimly. "Get ready, boys. Yeh gonna run when I tells yeh!"

Thumps came from the roof. Emmett pulled a lever on the floor and a choir of gears growled in unison from within the tower's guts.

Hephaestion checked his piston as Yitz threw on the leather bandoleer pistol holster. As Hephaestion frantically bound his armor on, Yitz checked the astrolabe and secured it in Hephaestion's satchel.

Several round black bombs rolled into the tower through the window, smoke spewing from them as Emmett cursed. He snatched each one up and rolled them back out.

"Dumbasses just gave yeh cover to slip away! Now git that shit on!" he roared as he pumped the lever of his Winchester.

The first ninja through the window had not expected a precise bullet to the head, and his body flopped back out. "Hey!" Emmett yelled out. "Hey, you played-out gallinippers! Don't be comin' one at a

time! That's borin'!" He spun toward Yitz and Hephaestion, his playful demeanor clearly in full bore. "Git downstairs. Use the charge handle to shock the walkway until it's safe. God's speed, poncey and heeb!"

They did as instructed, climbing down the ladder into a mechanical workshop filled with vacuum tubes, vices, presses, and other machinery. A spiral staircase led further down.

The tower moved again, rotating as they ran. Emmett's rifle went off several more times above, each shot accompanied by a vicious insult that speculated as to the validity of each enemy's lineage.

Once at the bottom, Hephaestion lifted the barricade bar. As soon as he did so, the door burst open and several ninja piled onto him. His sword wasn't out, and though his shield was whole, it was affixed to his back. So he used his *head*, and broke the nose of the nearest ninja with a headbutt. Following up with a swift forward kick, he drove the lot of them backwards through the door with all of his weight.

Over their shoulders, he could see nearly a dozen warriors, their swords flashing as they cut down the damned clutching at their feet, trying to secure a path to the tower. The nearest ninja found his footing instantly, and several others had explosives in hand.

"Hit the lever!" Yitz yelled, pushing Hephaestion aside with the large Colt in both hands.

Hephaestion spied the charge lever on the wall by the door, and swung it upward by its rubber handle as Yitz fired into the crowd. Sparks erupted, causing ninja and condemned alike to convulse in a macabre dance just before several of the explosives went off, chunks of flesh soaring and searing into the river.

Hephaestion pulled the lever back down and pushed Yitz through the door first, then followed, swinging it shut behind him.

As both men ran, Hephaestion called over his shoulder. "I'm clear, Emmett!" He drew his shield from his back and turned to face the tower from the safety of the shore. Several arrows zipped by, and Yitz took cover behind him.

A dragon airship hovered above, much like the one that attacked Mom, and from it dangled ropes with streams of ninja pouring down onto the watch tower.

They could still hear gunfire, so Emmett clearly remained in the fight.

Two more airships approached from upriver, their gunports open. One looked as if executing a flanking maneuver on the tower, ready to volley it in a pass.

As several gliders came silently swooping toward Hephaestion at the edge of the wood, Yitz fired the Colt. It wasn't as loud as the other pistol, the kick less significant, and its accuracy was startling. Only Yitz's lack of practice was to blame for the rounds he missed, but by the time the pistol was dry, two gliders had swerved and crashed into the river to be consumed by the souls below.

But more came. The fronts of the gliders were bladed, and as their pilots' feet hit the ground, they flung the gliders forward into Hephaestion, his shield saving him.

He didn't want to leave Emmett. The walkway fell back into the river. A throwing star glanced off of Hephaestion's chest, and two crossbow bolts struck a tree next to him, one narrowly missing Yitz's head as he reloaded the pistol from the bandoleer.

The tower exploded, detonated from within, tearing apart the airship hovering over it and bringing the whole thing down into Styx in the most spectacular explosion Hephaestion had ever seen. Emmett would be proud, and Hephaestion permitted himself the brief and pleasant thought that if Emmett regenerated before his enemies, the ninja would make a marvelous artistic medium.

The two other airships approached, and shafts of beaming light canvassed the suicide wood and tower's remains through the billowing smoke and leaping fire.

"We have to run!" Yitz pleaded.

Hephaestion obeyed, the trees providing them concealment.

CHAPTER 37

Hephaestion wished he was like Adina so he could have hurtled fiery salt spears into the airships. Or maybe he could have been like Boudica and called down lightning from Heaven to cook their crews. If he had been Minu, maybe he could have soothed the enemy.

But he was nothing, possessing no power beyond what others had lent him. Feeling as helpless as the trees surrounding him, he stumbled on frantically through the terrain, his toes catching on the roots and his knees banging each time he slipped.

Quivering with frustration, he leaned against a tree as the sound of the airships droned above, their lamps stabbing through the leaves above, searching.

Yitz noticed his comrade had stopped and, pistol at the ready, he pulled back and stood next to Hephaestion as he keenly scanned the trees. A smile came to Hephaestion when he realized that Yitz was actually guarding him, protecting him while he caught his breath and gathered his senses. This tiny, unassuming man was as brave as any warrior when a friend, or any soul for that matter, was in need.

Hephaestion pulled out the astrolabe and got their bearings. Picking out several trees in the distance, he had a direction to work toward.

"This way," he whispered, and the two marched off.

That's when the fire started. The two dragon ships began hurling giant flaming jars of pitch into the wood. They crashed through the branches and shattered on impact, the liquid flame splattering and splashing in blazing plumes. The trees caught fire, and smoke started spinning about, kicked up by the airships' propellers.

Hephaestion held his breath as Yitz gagged and coughed, and when they finally reached his intended clump of trees, they examined the astrolabe again to judge another azimuth. Flame crawled up the tree trunks nearby while waves of heat distorted his vision.

They had to keep moving, as the fire circled around them from where they had come. It was forward only from here on. Soon it became too dark to navigate, and they could only move in one direction: the one with the least fire.

Hephaestion became disoriented, trying to avoid the walls of heat erupting around him. He lost track of Yitz, and frantically called out his name into the curling smoke as he stumbled.

The trees began to thin, and he couldn't see the astrolabe in his hands clearly. He spotted a break in the smoke and rushed forward, the ground suddenly smooth and even, hoping Yitz had found the same opening.

Clear of the wood, he stood high on a ridge overlooking what had once been the boiling river of blood known as Phlegethon.

But there was no river. It was dry, or nearly so.

Hephaestion scanned the horizon and saw that it had been dammed with enormous generators and turbines, portions of its boiling blood funneled and piped into nearby stone buildings. Steam rose from each structure, accompanied by the sounds of clanging metal and uneven machines. The entire landscape was a giant foundry, crawling with people hauling crates and pushing carts and yelling and tripping and arguing.

Several long, rolling logging machines sat in various stages of construction by the dry river's bank. Atop those already completed rested giant swiveling cannons, mounted onto their backs. 'Tank' was the word Boudica had used, and having now seen them, Hephaestion understood their glory and horror.

Once he'd observed all the motion and noise of the industrialized hellscape, Hephaestion's gaze settled on the more mundane: a low row of wooden rafts built of suicide wood. Barges, to be specific: flat on the bottom for dragging through the woods to the river Styx for crossing. He had the same idea himself when Alexander and he had to cross the Hydaspes. Was this tactic common among armies now?

No one looked up toward Hephaestion. A few laborers gave the burning trees behind them a half-glance or a shrug before returning to work, but that was all. Occasionally, a whip would crack, someone would bark an order, and the steel hammers would continue their

work. It was an army, a war machine so focused on its self-construction that the world around it could burn without notice.

Before Hephaestion, standing tall on a carved pillar of red stone by the dry riverbed, was the statue of a man on a horse. Smoke and steam obscured it, but it seemed familiar. It haunted him. Hephaestion was so intent on discerning its form that he didn't see the samurai approaching as he wandered closer to it, transfixed, until it was too late.

Laborers parted as the samurai moved in slowly, their hands resting on their hilts, approaching from all sides.

With the burning woods at Hephaestion's back, the samurai closed in loosely around him, each keeping several steps back. Behind them, between Hephaestion and the statue, stood Father Franco looking stoic and fulfilled, his quarry finally cornered.

Hephaestion understood he was surrounded, but he couldn't leave the presence of the statue. He drew his sword and adjusted his shield on his forearm, then dropped the satchel at his feet, shedding the weight. Within his peripheral vision he counted six samurai in total, each armored in their traditional trappings of Bushido warfare. All laborers had moved safely away, their smelters and anvils unattended, perhaps having the first rest they had ever seen.

In unison, all six samurai silently drew their katanas, placed their left foot forward, dug the balls of their feet into the mud, and took a battle stance. Through their eyes, Hephaestion stood at the end of each of their blades.

One shouted and charged, and Hephaestion knew that wasn't where the first attack would come from. Turning his shield toward him, he faced the opposite direction, where a second samurai had charged silently from behind, blade low.

Hephaestion blocked the loud attacker with his shield, and deflected the stealthy one with his blade, Boudica's burning edge sparking along the Japanese steel. He then lashed out and kicked in the knee of the samurai he parried, and with the full force of his spinning body, slammed his shield into the one behind him, knocking him down onto his back. Snarling, he drove his blade into both of them before they could get up.

The remaining four charged together in a coordinated blaze of flashing steel and shouts.

Hephaestion's cuirass glanced several blows, and his shield deflected the rest of the attacks. Their katanas were long and fast, but his burning blade disoriented them, and after a few moments each of the four fell back out of his reach to regain their footing.

He stood bloody among them, knicks and slices shallow in his skin.

Father Franco folded his arms patiently, and they immediately came at him again.

Hephaestion blocked them as best as he could, but this time several slices got in deeper, and one carved into his outer thigh, his leg going numb and unable to hold his weight. He tried his best to return their attacks, but they retreated again before he could riposte.

Bleeding seriously from his leg and side, Hephaestion knew where this was all headed: he had no chance. The astrolabe would be captured, his heart would be ripped out and jarred, and that would be his eternity.

They came again, but Hephaestion shifted his tactic and charged one at random. His shield piston crushed the man's helmet, skull along with it, while he overran his enemy. Hephaestion could not survive being surrounded again.

Shield up, he then charged the opposite direction, slamming into the nearest samurai and bowling him over. With a precise heel, Hephaestion stomped the downed swordsman's throat in as the remaining two both stabbed him directly though his midsection. They swiftly withdrew their blades and danced away from him as he staggered, shield barely higher than his waist.

Father Franco didn't stir.

The two remaining samurai took flanking positions opposite Hephaestion, one with his katana high and the other with it low. They feigned a strike to test Hephaestion, but he didn't flinch. They feigned a second time, and he *still* didn't flinch.

Before they came a third time, Hephaestion lashed out with his blade, but he stumbled, the blood loss and injuries catching up to him.

One katana sliced into his sword arm, and the other drove directly into his chest. His thighs came unstrung, and Hephaestion fell onto his knees. The two samurai backed off a moment, and one looked to Father Franco for direction.

The priest resolutely nodded in return.

His gaze drifted about and, as he tried to think straight, settled beyond the Jesuit to the statue high above. It was visible now; either the smoke or Hephaestion's mind had cleared. Perhaps, like a distant star in the night sky, he had been directly staring at it so it was obscured from him.

The statue was of Alexander, his sword raised in a pumping fist into the air, on horseback. Had someone commissioned such a thing? Were there other statutes of other military legends about the

Phlegethon's edge? Was the *entire* river dammed in spots to build this war machine army before him? Did Alexander know of this? Was his likeness used against his will to inspire the murderous damned to build a metal army?

The horse. The horse, perfect down to the braids in the mane, was Bucephalus — as only Alexander and Hephaestion had known him. The eyes were the same, as well as each knick in the hooves. Only Alexander could oversee this statue.

Hephaestion's shield slipped from his grasp, and his sword fell, sizzling into the mud.

"With honor," the samurai standing over him whispered just before decapitating him.

CHAPTER 38

"Alex? Don't leave," Hephaestion said, his eyes sunken from the fever. He was on the mend, but still too weary to leave bed on his own, and just outside the chamber doors hovered various doctors and medicine men from all corners of the empire. He'd been sick for a week, during which Alexander had barely left his love's side... up until now.

"You're doing better, Paty!" Alexander said, already dressed and ready for the music festival in the city of Ecbatana, renowned for its instruments and musical competitions. Alexander was to be a judge, despite knowing little about music — the emperor of the world needed to be the judge of all things, at least in the eyes of many. "There's a race later today, a causal one, but I have to win it all the same. I must be there."

Alexander could never say no to a challenge.

"They can postpone the race." Hephaestion rested his hand on Alexander's arm. "We can stay here, and you can read to me the correspondence." He was too proud to say how much he needed Alexander's presence. Something was wrong in Hephaestion's gut, and despite the fever having dropped and the pain having eased, his instinct told him not to be alone.

Simply put, he didn't want Alexander to leave. He wanted to hear his voice and see his face. The opulent, black marble bedroom was nothing. The hanging tapestries and wooden masks and other decorations were nothing. Hephaestion wanted to be like boys again, lying in the hay, listening to the horses flick their tails. Having Alexander's head on his chest would put everything right, fix whatever

was wrong in his gut, and then they could both go together to the music festival the next day.

"Paty... I *have* to go. You said so yourself, that a king can't be a king on the campaign trail. Here I get to be with the people and show everyone how much of a king I am, not just a conqueror. This is something you wanted me to do!"

Hephaestion caved, as always. He smiled and nodded, touching his love's face. Alexander was so handsome, his green eyes crinkling as he pecked at Hephaestion's fingertips with his lips. Spry and boyish despite the scars and arrow wounds of a dozen cavalry charges, the man was very much the god others claimed him to be.

"I'll be back soon," Alex said. "I promise."

He gave a final, tender kiss to Hephaestion's forehead, and walked out. When the physicians flooded back in, Hephaestion demanded solitude and ordered them out with a ferocious shout. If he didn't have Alexander with him, he preferred to be alone. No other soul would do until Alexander returned.

Ulfric once said the first death was always the worst. He was right: it was the scariest and loneliest. Hephaestion couldn't remember it or recall if it had been painful, but he remembered it as the saddest, most solitary moment of his life.

Then, he waited in Purgatory... waited and waited for Alexander... waited for him to return from his festival of victory... waited for him to return from the finish line.

When Hephaestion had no more 'wait' left in him, he came here, to Hell, only to find the prison holding his love had been broken open, its contents spilled about in the mud like a looted village, all under the shadow of Alexander pumping his fist high into the air with his sword gripped tight.

CHAPTER 39

Father Franco waited anxiously in the interrogation tent. Chained upright to a pole at its center was Hephaestion, his head having grown back, but his eyes not open and heart yet to beat again. His personal compliment of samurai stood erect along the sidewalls of the tent, their armor still bearing the scorch marks of their battle with Hephaestion. Each stood as unmoving as a statue.

He was pleased with his samurai. Father Franco had earned the Provost General's attention early on, and when given command of the small detachment of ronin, it had been a great honor. Such warriors could allow a man to do great things in the name of Christ.

Now that Hephaestion's head had grown back entirely, the General Provost would come and inspect the prize and deliver accolades to Father Franco.

The tent flap swung open, and Franco's master entered surrounded by four robed and mysteriously hooded figures, their hands folded into their cloaks. They were his personal escorts, bodyguards, and record keepers, and he rarely went anywhere without them. The entire camp would obey their orders to the letter.

Charismatic with a trim gray-speckled beard, the Provost General strode in making it clear that he owned everything in sight, including all of Hephaestion's items on the far table. With mild interest, he poked and prodded the astrolabe, ruffled through Gil's documentation, and tinkered aimlessly with the heart ripper.

"Ah, it is truly him." The Provost General examined Hephaestion's still face up close. "You have saved us a tremendous amount of trouble,

Lord Hephaestion. We are grateful you came all the way down here to deliver yourself to us." He mocked the Grecian, his head still low in the state of after-death. "You even delivered a clever little instrument to contain you. I like it far better than our more crude tools."

"What shall I do with him, your eminence?" Father Franco asked.

"We have a steel jar for him, more of a sphere, really, and once it is welded shut he'll be safe and sound."

Father Franco nodded. "Alexander will be kept in line knowing that we have a little metal ball that contains the heart of the man he loves most in all existence. Hephaestion is the best collateral we could ever have hoped for." He wanted to make it *clear* that he had done marvelously for his lord.

"True," the Provost General said flatly while his four attendants waited. "But there's hardly need, is there?" He offered a condescending smile. "Anyhow, take the heart, give it to one of my attendants here, and then I'll seal it away. You did well, Father Franco."

Bowing low, Franco accepted the compliment.

With that, the Provost General marched out.

One of his robed attendants split from the pack and silently stood off to the side near Hephaestion's things.

Father Franco sighed. "Who would like the honor of ripping out his heart?"

The samurai remained silent.

"Is this manipulation how you plan on getting into Heaven?" Hephaestion asked, his eyes now piercing Father Franco. The priest gasped in alarm, each samurai's hand instantly finding their sword handle. Despite being chained to the post, Hephaestion managed to be threatening.

"All humanity will conform!" Father Franco fired back, a stern finger pointed. "And through conformity we will be saved. I will repent, as will the Provost General and all others, as we are entitled to do. But first, we must bring the rest of condemned humanity to its knees, Hephaestion!" He frothed, still energized from the scare. "No more enabling them to wallow in sin. No more pity or sympathy like what the Buddhists provide. The Jesuits are the *light*. We are the light! First that light may come from a cannon's barrel, but eventually it will come from Heaven itself."

"And what of Alexander?" Hephaestion snapped.

"Alexander? Heh... this was largely *his idea*."

Hephaestion squinted at Franco as though he had spoken another language. "I... what...."

"Now, my vows forbid me to ever touch a weapon or the blood of another." With that, Father Franco turned to one of his samurai and jerked his head in the direction of Hephaestion's things on the table behind him. "Take his heart, and be quick with it!"

"I would reconsider that, good sir," the robed figure said politely, breaking its silence. "I have a far better proposal to offer you, one far more beneficial."

Franco spun about to face the robed attendant. "I don't... your grace, you heard the Provost General. Why would you tell me not to follow through on his direct orders?"

"Oh! Oy, I'm sorry," Yitz said, sliding back his hood. He then pulled his revolver from under his robes aimed it at Father Franco's heart. "I wasn't actually talking to you. I was talking to *them*."

Yitz kept his weapon on the Jesuit, but looked to the samurai. Before continuing, he made certain to attain direct eye contact with each of them. "I was hoping to speak to you without your white master, but it is what it is, am I right?" Feigning a casual air, Yitz shook the robe off of his shoulders and kicked it with his foot off to the side. "You know, gentlemen, my wife is back in New Dis looking after the displaced souls from your ward — those unchristian, those unwilling to convert, unwilling to obey...." Yitz lingered for effect. "Those in need of *help*."

The two nearest samurai began shifting their weight, slowly moving to Yitz's sides. He only had a few moments before they'd spring on him. His next sentence would be everything. "What part of the Bushido code stands supreme: obedience or honor?"

They halted.

"He is just manipulating you! It's obvious!" Franco protested.

"You're God-damned right I'm manipulating you. I'll do anything to save New Dis, my wife, and *our* freedom. Even if you want my head, I still have to do what I can for us. You are part of my *city*." Yitz turned his attention back to Father Franco and cocked back the pistol's hammer. "Manipulative or not, ulterior motive of not, I'm right and all of you know it. Free Hephaestion!"

Hephaestion cleared this throat, his voice distant but resolved. "You take me to Alexander and I can end all of this. I can end it all."

All eyes floated to the bound warrior on the pole.

Father Franco was red with rage. Then a katana slipped through the priest's heart from behind, and he fell to his knees with a whimper. The samurai didn't do him the honor of a beheading, opting instead to step casually over his twitching body.

They immediately unshackled Hephaestion and helped him down.

"Thank you. From one warrior to others, thank you," Hephaestion said, suppressed misery in his voice.

Yitz packed Hephaestion's satchel and carried his cuirass over to him.

With muted awe, Hephaestion asked, "How did you manage to get those robes and play yourself off as one of the Provost General's servants?"

"Submissive silence. That's all the Provost General expects. He didn't even notice I replaced one of his men. People are functions to him." Yitz winked. "So what now, Heph? What's the plan? How do we bring this all down?"

The samurai stepped nearer, attentive.

Hephaestion thought, sorting through the slippery and ugly truths in his mind. Had Father Franco lied just to hurt him? Did Alexander know of all this? Was Alexander the commander of this army, and if so, was it against his will, or did he do so willingly?

The airships. Hephaestion gasped as the horror of it all sank in. The airships had been scouting over the pit for as long as they had needed, surveying the terrain from above. All the smoke from the foundries had obscured their operation, and the tanks would be rowed across the river Styx, take Old Dis as a staging ground of operations, and then they would march in their full force into New Dis and take all of the circular city, including the docks. All of Hell would be under one regime, Alexander at the head of the army.

No, not Alexander. He would lead the campaign, but no.... Someone had to have fished him out first. Someone had to dam the river. Someone had to have the vision, someone who wanted conformity, to conquer all.

The Jesuits. They converted Japan to limit their threats within the city, so it would be easier to siege. Promising ascension to all that fell into line was their recruiting technique. *What was it Father Franco said in*

the railcar? Something about being of the same mind and conformity, but also "soldiers of God." Was that their path to Heaven they promised all others? Promised Alexander?

No, they would have to promise each murderous soldier Heaven through conquest, but not Alexander. He needed no such promises. Alexander needed only the challenge, to know that a city existed that was not his.

He needed only to know that war awaited.

The Provost General had said it perfectly. "Have you seen him?" And he had even said it with a smile. Hephaestion knew exactly what the Jesuit's leader meant. How many nights had Alexander bounded around the war table, planning with boyish glee? How often had he delighted in training the shock troops until morning's first sun? What was better on the Earth for Alexander than war? What meant most to Alexander above all things?

Hephaestion accepted, in quiet heartbreak, that it wasn't *him*.

Despite the rage and anger brewing in his throat, the frustration and embarrassment crushing his chest like a vise, he felt crippling fear most of all. He was so afraid that Alexander would walk into the tent at any moment and hold him, and he would buckle. As always. Alexander would cry and sob with joy and just be so glad to see him again. He would plead and charm and entice Hephaestion to follow him — into New Dis, and perhaps even to siege Purgatory itself.

Would Alexander's metal army tear down the white clock? Would his men burn Minu's pillows? Would the soldiers overcome Adina and Gottbert and Boudica, leaving Yitz and Albrecht at their mercy? Alexander's entire army wasn't Greek countrymen either, but Hellbound monsters, each and every one of them. Once, when questioned by Cleitus about the loyalty of Alexander's army on Earth, Alexander declared, 'I march with the army I have.'

Clearly, Alexander's current army was malicious, bloodthirsty, eager, motivated, and horrifyingly armed. And at any moment, he could walk into the tent, touch Hephaestion with his lips, and add another soul to its ranks.

Hephaestion just didn't have any strength anymore, having spent everything he had while waiting in Purgatory. Now, after all the sacrifices of others and trials of his own, he'd learned that Alexander was still exactly as he had always been.

Father Franco's assassin wiped his blade clean with the crook of his elbow, and said, "We will escort you to the command tent."

"Yes..." Hephaestion's spine felt like it was collapsing, but he still strapped on his armor despite his quivering hands. He knew what he had to do. Adina, Yitz, Boudica, Albrecht, and so many others in pursuit of their own existences were at stake. How many temples would be filled with the dead this time? "You get me close to Alexander. Just get me close so he can see me."

"You will assassinate him?"

"No, I'll challenge him."

CHAPTER 40

Like a royal escort, the samurai surrounded Hephaestion and led him from the interrogation tent. They traveled along a walkway made of ground bones and stone, and walked past bunkhouses, training pens for soldiers, and armories.

Grunts and snarls came from all directions as men lifted cargo, heaved ropes, and shoved each other. Those that trained slaughtered and spit, larger men brutalizing smaller ones by tearing them open as they screamed, learning how to kill both flamboyantly and effectively.

Alexander was training these men to slaughter and terrorize, not fight an opposing standing army. They had siege weapons such as tanks and cannons, but no major infantry. They would break the walls of each enclave and swarm it like pillaging thugs.

As Hephaestion walked on, a head taller than his samurai escort, with Yitz at his side, several soldiers looked his way. He was cleaner than everyone around him, and his Songhai cuirass stood out as distinct among all of their red and grungy battle gear.

It occurred to Hephaestion that the men he'd fought in the Glutton's circle must have been deserters from this army, and the skinless man in Dis could have been a forward scout of some kind. Either way, these men were brutes. More than a few looked halfway to becoming hulkish beasts, not unlike the Ushers.

A crowd slowly gathered around them to gawk. Hammers paused and shouts ceased. The samurai took no notice, merely escorting Hephaestion with purpose toward a tall flag in the distance, but people began to follow.

Embroidered on the flag, a white horse reared up with its front hooves kicking — the traditional flag for Alexander's command tent. Hephaestion had spotted it from afar hundreds of times during his life, and it had often evoked a smile. Any place under that flag had been home.

Beyond the forges and armories stretched a large, long field of mud, with posts driven deep into the ground. Trireme-looking airships drifted above, nearly a dozen of them tethered to those posts. Between each hung smaller airships, the size of longboats, clearly meant for transporting shock troops. War had indeed changed, but Hephaestion could still discern the strategy.

Crew members from the flying war machines craned their necks over the railings of their decks to watch the samurai pass, Hephaestion and Yitz center within them, as the crowd followed.

Curious whispers hit Hephaestion's ears. Then he heard his name. *A fellow Greek that recognized me, perhaps? Either by sculpture or by personal acquaintance?*

The tent came next, a large, multi-room affair just like what Alexander and Hephaestion traveled with during their campaigns. A tall, armored guard of copper complexion stepped forward, arm out to halt the advancing samurai. The guard had most likely earned the position by being almost seven feet tall with tusked teeth.

The nearest samurai drew his sword, the blade in full swing before leaving its sheath, and took the guard's head clean off in a singular motion. The samurai next to him kicked out his foot, perfectly catching the falling head, and launched it clear over the tent.

Never had Hephaestion seen a more precise and spectacular display of intimidation before.

Once at the mouth of the command tent, flickering torch light deep inside, Hephaestion cleared his throat. Nearby decorative cauldrons of bubbling Hell-steel provided the only other sound. The wooden porch looked sturdy and simple, but the muddy ground before it looked like the best place for a fight. The samurai looked to him, and Hephaestion responded with a nod, flexing his arms outward indicating that he needed dueling space.

The samurai turned toward the gathered crowd with authority, commanding them to back up. Most onlookers did so, and any that hesitated died instantly, before their sundered bodies even hit the mud.

The whispers surrounding Hephaestion increased, and he heard his name again and again. With his shield at the ready, his knuckles white

with a tight grip, he drew his sword. The wave of heat made him wince, and his sweaty skin prickled.

He banged his sword and shield together three times in the proper rhythm.

Silence dominated everything within a league, only the hissing cauldrons foolish enough to make noise.

Wide-eyed, Alexander emerged from the tent clad in white leather armor. He was beautiful and looked as virile and delicious as the day he'd left Hephaestion on his deathbed.

Apparently, Alexander's mourning for Hephaestion had been legendary, but Hephaestion didn't care. He'd only wanted Alexander to stay with him.

Alexander's face erupted with joy, his green eyes sparkling as if all his prayers had been answered, his arms out and open as he took a step toward Hephaestion. Then he saw Hephaestion's eyes mired with tears, and the challenge's seriousness became clear to Alexander.

Never before had Hephaestion seen such hurt in a man as Alexander exhibited just then. His arms drifted down to his sides, a baffled agony on his face.

Alexander's lips pursed to form the question, 'Why?', but the word never came. He knew Hephaestion had come to fight, and not for a playful sparring match—Hephaestion had never been good at concealing his intentions.

Hephaestion was glad Alexander didn't speak. One word from him would make every joint of his surrender like a marionette cut from its strings.

Two runners brought Alexander his spear and sword, while a third brought his shield. It was round, an intricate portrait on it of Hephaestion's face. Alexander adjusted the strapping on his sword, hoisted his shield bearing Hephaestion's visage, fingered the spear in his hand, and rolled his shoulders.

When Alexander finally made eye contact with Hephaestion again, he found that the tears were gone, eyes swollen and red with enraged resolve.

Hephaestion stepped first, slowly creeping toward Alexander's right.

Alexander corrected, his shield forward and his spear hand back, thrust at the ready.

The samurai all moved in unison, keeping the combat space clear of any interlopers.

Yitz watched, arms folded, his one hidden hand resting on his pistol.

Alexander jolted forward a little, testing Hephaestion's nerve. Hephaestion was jumpy and flinched, so Alexander did it again, his spear tip slipping past Hephaestion's defenses and deflecting off of Emmett's jaws.

As the two men continued circling each other, Hephaestion spied the Provost General emerging from the tent to investigate.

Alexander had always beaten Hephaestion. He had beaten him at taming horses and flirting with girls and sparring and planning and leading.... Alexander had always been the best, the first, the one celebrated beyond all human measure.

Alexander knew this too, and it must have been on his mind when he charged in to strike at Hephaestion.

It was on Hephaestion's mind too, when Alexander blazed at him with shield forward and spear aimed, but Hephaestion knew something Alexander did not.

Hephaestion had always held back.

With sheer ferocity, Hephaestion leapt into Alexander's attack, shield pointed out and piston poised. A noise like a hollow hammer cracking against an anvil echoed over the masses as the pressure-powered device struck Alexander's shield dead center. Alexander stumbled backward, desperately trying to keep his footing, but Hephaestion pushed on, not allowing Alexander to get his stance again. He bashed Alexander's shield aside and sliced the searing blade into his love's exposed forearm, severing it completely. Then he grabbed Alexander by the collar with his shield hand, and bellowed as he buried the burning blade into the conqueror's gut. All Hephaestion's weight crashed down, pinning Alexander to the royal tent's wooden porch.

Sputtering and sizzling, Boudica's blade was finally tempered by Alexander's blood, and it burned no more. Alexander's shield spun slowly, face-down in the mud like a bowl, the remaining arm inside filling it with a reflective pool of blood.

Hephaestion knelt next to Alexander, his color fading.

"I came for you," Hephaestion choked, his hand on Alexander's pallid face. "And I find *this*," he chastised through his returning tears.

Alexander nodded in shame. "I am what I am," he said, gargling blood through his teeth.

"I love you," Hephaestion sobbed.

"I love you, too," Alexander forgave.

Hephaestion tore Alexander's armor open with clumsy hands weak with grief, then took out the heart-ripper.

For the first time in Alexander's entire existence, he willingly accepted defeat and closed his eyes.

The Provost General stepped forward, his hands out in mid plea just as Hephaestion drove the ripper in, twisted it, and ground it. Alexander's eyes rolled up toward Heaven as, with a final wrench and tug, his core came free, the arteries like dark roots violently pulled from the ground, bloody and in the grasp of the wretched device.

Before he could lose his nerve, Hephaestion stood and walked over to one of the molten cauldrons, and dropped the heart ripper holding Alexander's heart into it.

The heart incinerated instantly, fusing with molten steel and ash, burning into nothingness. It would take centuries to reform, if at all. Alexander was *gone*.

Hell was doing the worst thing you could ever imagine, but doing it willingly.

"Do you realize what you have done?" the Provost General cried, hands clenching the air before him.

With numb emptiness, Hephaestion almost gave a macabre laugh at the question. He lifted Alexander's spear from the mud, claiming it as his own, pointed the tip at the Jesuit leader, and announced to all ears, "I am Lord Hephaestion, and when Alexander died, he was asked who would inherit the empire. Do you all know what he said?"

Several nods came from the crowd. Many had heard of Alexander's famous words, uttered on his deathbed. Alexander had answered his surviving generals with only, 'Whoever is strongest.'

With that, Hephaestion dug into his satchel and handed the nearest samurai the astrolabe. "Take your flying machine that brought you here, and return this to Queen Sungbon of Songhai. Please go with my gratitude and blessing. Don't stay here, for this army will tear itself apart in a few hours and be nothing but *ruin* within a day." Despite his attempts to sound dignified, his heart was so broken that his voice squeaked and cracked.

His knees reluctant, he marched down into the dried riverbed and across to the other bank, Alexander's spear helping him walk as stunned witnesses kept clear of him.

Yitz ran to his side, lifted up Hephaestion's free arm, and pulled it over his own shoulders to support his friend.

CHAPTER 41

In the distance behind them, cannons blazed and explosions rumbled like a rolling storm. Hephaestion hoped that the samurai had gotten away in time. Given the nature of Alexander's army of abominations, they would largely prey on the weak first, and the samurai were anything but. Most likely, by now the siege weapons had turned on each other, and ancient rivalries among the murderous damned had resurfaced.

With Yitz supporting his one side, and Alexander's spear supporting the other, Hephaestion's knees had come unstrung from sorrow and shock, his body unable to sustain its own weight. His body weakened with every step, toes dragging, his emotions so muted and dulled that he was grateful to *feel* less and less. Neither joy nor hope nor future existed now.

Only one thing remained: his promise to Yitz and Adina. He had to find Gil. Nothing else mattered. Someone had to walk away with something from all of this.

The mud firmed up as they moved farther away from the war camp and its heat. After several leagues, the air became crisp and ionized, and the ground soon felt solid beneath their feet. A wind howled in the dark ahead where no light flickered.

They were approaching the Malebolge. Down in there, no light from Heaven would reach them, and much like an oubliette, it was a place of forgetting. At the bottom of that icy pit lurked Cocytus, the lake of frozen tears that drained from all of Hell's damned. In the center of that frozen lake sat Lucifer himself, Chief of all the Hated, imprisoned as a paragon of sin.

The ground began to slope upward, and each step required all the more energy. Hephaestion dug the weighted end of the spear into the cold ground with each forward stride, and eventually he and Yitz stood at the very lip of the crater of the Malebolge. A wall of wind blazed upward before them, firing out from the abyss below. He had originally intended to climb down one of the infamously narrow staircases along the cliff face, two leagues downward, to safely reach the bottom. But his misery was making his judgments for him, and with an outstretched hand he held out his spear, point downward, and let it go. It sped against the wind and descended into the black.

Yitz gripped him tightly. "Easy there, Heph," he said. "Where do we go now? How do we get dow —"

Hephaestion shrugged free of Yitz and walked forward, arms out, embracing the abyss's impending afterdeath. He wanted to be swallowed by the maw of nothing, to *feel* nothing, and to *be* nothing. Forward he fell into the black, wishing to fall forever and never land, leaving Yitz behind.

His fall slowed, impeded by the wind constantly tussling him about and pushing against his descent. When he finally landed on the frozen plateau of Hell's loneliest region, leagues below the crater's edge, his spine shattered, his skull cracked to pieces, and his blood froze as it poured from his wounds.

CHAPTER 42

Yitz sighed, not entirely surprised with Hephaestion's dramatic descent. His friend did have the tendency to do things the interesting way. Rolling his eyes, he resolved to take the slow way down and gather up the pieces.

Nearby stood a marker of frosted stone. On it, a jagged arrow pointed downward, indicating a staircase. It was likely one of many, carved into the sheer sides of the crater, each spiraling down at a consistent descent, ending at the lake's surface below.

Despite the howling cold air that blew up from the depths, Yitz couldn't help but feel the warm tingle of excitement. Soon he would see Gil. He would see his boy.

Standing next to the stone marker, he saw the stairway curl into the darkness below, each step no more than a foot across and hanging from the wall precariously. Yitz briefly considered the fast way down. After all, he had already managed to shoot himself in the heart.

As he cautiously lowered his foot, his frigid fingers clinging to the rocky crag, he prayed to be strong like Adina. If only God had chosen to send her instead of him, Hephaestion would have been better off, safer, and whole. Adina made everything better, because *she* was better.

Struggling with the second step, Yitz didn't pray for Adina's strength; he instead prayed in gratitude to God for making Adina.

The third step was almost as easy as the fourth....

CHAPTER 43

Hephaestion's death had been too brief, and he hadn't dreamed of Alexander. Instead, he'd dreamt of a swiftly spinning star, blindingly bright and beautiful, seen from all corners of existence.

He loved the star, and felt its warmth energizing the single planet that orbited it. At first the planet appeared lifeless and void, but the star's warmth breathed energy into it, and oceans flowed and volcanoes burst and clouds blew.

The beautiful planet marveled in the light of the star, but the star grew hotter, searing with might, and the planet began to char. Its trees withered, waters boiled, and magma devoured the surface. Gravity kept the planet fixed to the star, unable to flee despite the motion of its orbit. The star increased in power, demanding more of its orbital.

Yet the planet moved faster along its orbit. It spun around and around, rotating to the point of being a blur as it managed to increase its centrifugal force.

Finally, the planet, in a surge of momentum, broke free and flew away into outer space, the damaging burn of the star becoming a distant ember.

He slowly opened his eyes. His body had corrected itself, and his heart must have just started anew. Armor cracked and torn, shield filled with dents, his body had mended but his eyes didn't seem to be working. At first, he thought he was blind, but in truth, there was simply no light for his eyes to see by.

This was Hell, and Hell was just... *nothing*. Or perhaps Hell was knowing that, despite all the nothing, you had a promise to keep.

Hephaestion had failed entirely. Alexander was gone, more gone than he'd ever been before. While Hephaestion had waited and waited

for his lover, Alexander had been playing with his toys, building his army, and fulfilling his personal and selfish desires of conquest.

All of this had been a terrible loss: dragging Ulfric and The Bonny Sweetheart into the sea to spend months looking for a glutton; the hackneyed attempt to get past Minos; the protection from Adina; the kindness from Minu; the guidance from Boudica; and even the newfound bravery from Yitz — all a loss. All of it had been effort and care and love wasted on the worthless endeavor known as Hephaestion.

Perhaps I could just lay here. But in the back of his mind a thought crept in. What if this wasn't *his* story? What if this wasn't about Hephaestion or Alexander at all? What if all of this was about Gil, a son needing to simply hear his parents loved him? Would Hephaestion allow his wallowing to prevent Gil's story from continuing? Was even this crushing heartbreak enough to prompt Hephaestion to forsake a promise to good people?

His joints found their place again, and Hephaestion rolled to his knees. He figured Yitz would have landed nearby somewhere. The wind hissed in his ears. His shield had become bent at the bottom and, no longer able to be bisected, now fused into a round whole.

He could hear through the grinding wind a singular, constant humming, a bright vibrating note, as if played by an instrument. It surrounded him with its tiny, alluring song. He scanned through the blindness in all directions until he saw a flickering light, so small as to be almost imperceptible. If he focused too hard, it vanished before him, so he unfocused his eyes, adjusted his disheveled armor, and lumbered toward it.

The icy surface of the ground was smooth with long flowing ripples that emanated from the nearby cliff-face of the crater. It was like the lake had been frozen as it rippled from an impact at its center. The origin of the giant craterous formation of Malebolge, according to legend, was that it first formed when Lucifer was cast down from Heaven. The impact from the fallen angel was apparently so significant that the entire pit of Hell formed. While its specific machinations remained a mystery, all sources agreed that at the very center of this frozen lake was Satan himself.

And... down the devil's spine was the only exit, a crawl space leading to a cave right along the back of the very beast himself — a cave that led to the first two stars seen by man.

Hephaestion soon saw that the light was a flickering flame, held high by a figure sitting with their legs crossed. The singing note that Hephaestion heard was actually coming from his spear, lanced into the ice directly next to the man.

Yitz. It's Yitz. Hephaestion smiled; a feat he feared would be impossible for him. As he drew closer and saw the windburn on Yitz's face, and the intact state of his attire, he realized that Yitz had managed the stunning feat of actually climbing down. As impressed as he was before with his friend, he was even more so now.

The torch Yitz held had been fashioned out of the bandoleer wrapped tightly into a cone, the documentation on Gil and gunpowder used as fuel.

They both regarded each other, Hephaestion standing and Yitz sitting, next to the singing spear.

"You're a self-absorbed jackass," Yitz chastised. "I could be with my son somewhere right now, but I had to wait for *you.*" His voice carried no humor.

Hephaestion nodded, humbly accepting Yitz's assessment of him. "I'm sorry, and thank you for waiting for me."

Yitz stood up, grunting with cold and bitter discomfort. His eyes then flitted to the spear, encouraging Hephaestion to take it up.

The song ceased when Hephaestion gripped it, and it came free with a strong tug.

As they stepped forward, the ground perfect and reflective, the frozen damned encased in ice came into clear view. Some were completely submerged beneath their feet, while others were frozen from the nose down, their heads exposed to the gnawing wind. Occasionally, they would see someone with an arm free of the ice, their body encased at an angle. With their free arm they would tear at the heads around them, pulling hair out and denying any measure of warmth to those they were imprisoned with.

Beyond the torchlight, long shapes stalked, eyes shimmering and careful to keep their distance from Hephaestion and Yitz. Perhaps they feared the light, or perhaps they feared a soul with purpose.

Occasionally, they had to be careful how they proceeded, as thin lines in the lake's surface indicated a new rotating ring. Whenever they traversed one, they held onto each other and jumped together, just like in the queen's throne room. Each spinning ring contained a different kind of betrayer: a false counselor toward a leader, or perhaps a parent that betrayed a child.

Yitz said, "I know Gil is being held in the next circle, bit I have no idea where we might find him." He swallowed hard, eyes wide.

Hephaestion understood. The journey so far had been a parade of human misery, torment, and irreversible regret. Yitz was probably

bracing himself for the heartbreak of seeing his boy's eyes among them, not knowing if he could tolerate it.

Hephaestion found a random head, knelt down, and looked the trapped soul in the eyes. It wasn't Gil. "Do you still have the picture?" he asked Yitz.

Numbly, Yitz shook his head while pointing at his torch.

Hephaestion nodded. "We'll look one by one if we have to. Would anyone know his name? Maybe know where he is?"

Yitz cleared his throat, and with a booming voice much larger than his frame, he bellowed, "I have come to see my son, Gil Isserles! Blink twice when we come by if you know him!"

"I know him," a smooth voice called from the darkness.

Yitz stumbled and nearly dropped the torch.

In the weak light, Hephaestion could see only a pair of black boots in the distance.

"Why do you seek him?" the man queried.

Yitz straightened himself as Hephaestion adjusted his shield and renewed his grip on his spear. The voice was hard to hear, prompting the men to slowly walk closer.

The voice's owner didn't stir, allowing them to approach. A man in all black, with a long cloak chewed threadbare by the wind, stood before them. He wore a jester's cap, the bells on the conical tips frozen and only making a sad *tin* sound with each gust of wind. He wore a black mask over his face, carved like a skull, obscuring his whole visage except for his lower jaw. His trimmed beard was covered in frost.

"Why do you want to see this man?" he asked again, placing one of his gloved hands on the bladed metal whip coiled on his belt.

"I am his father," Yitz said.

"You bring light here."

"I couldn't see without it."

"You bring warmth, too."

Yitz didn't know where this was going. Did the man want an explanation for his bodily warmth?

"I can't... *not* be warm," Yitz finally offered.

The man in black stepped forward, easing his hand from the whip. It seemed as though he had once dressed for a costume party. Everything on his person appeared to be playful and luxurious, everything except the ferocious whip at his side.

He let his gaze wander over Yitz. "If I take you to this man, you will tell him that you love him?"

"Yes."

"Why?"

This question baffled Yitz, and he simply didn't have the strength of mind anymore to deal with *anything*. "Because I *do*!" He laughed, his desolate voice echoing off of the heads of thousands watching from the dark.

Both men stood there, regarding each other, and Yitz tried to ignore Hephaestion, whose body language suggested he was preparing for a flanking strike if the man became hostile.

"This torch won't last as long as I will," Yitz snapped impatiently at the masked man.

"I am Montressor, the guard of this place. I will lead you to this man, and you may speak to him, but if you try to free him or offer him any more light or warmth than that torch, I will end you a *second time*." His cloak snapped in the wind as he spun on his heels and started leading Yitz and Hephaestion deeper into Cocytus.

With difficulty, Hephaestion and Yitz kept up as the man's boots deftly avoided each head from memory.

Soon, not even a quarter-league, the man stopped and pointed to his feet. "He is here. Gil Isserles."

Hephaestion nodded in thanks, and the masked man backed up, but stayed within both hearing and striking distance.

Yitz trembled as he approached, sinking lower with each step.

His frozen hair had been molded by the wind, and Gil was frozen from his lips down. Snot had frozen his nose solid to the ice, and his eyes blinked furiously, the cold film over them melting away from the friction.

Yitz dropped to his knees and palms, and examined the unfrozen upper half of Gil's head. He had come through Hell hoping to be able to wrap his arms around his boy. His body ached to sit his little boy on his lap again, with Gil's tiny head tucked under his chin.

"Gil? Boy? Is that you?" His voice quivered.

Gil's eyes glazed with moisture, and then he was instantly recognizable to his father. Yitz gasped and delivered a flurry of kisses

on his boy's forehead. The skin was so cold that it burned Yitz's lips. Gil's eyes welled up, his brow crinkling as his sobs of joy struggled to break free of the ice.

Montressor reached for his whip and prepared to swipe, but before he could loose it, Hephaestion placed his spear tip at the man's throat.

"Don't," Hephaestion commanded. He straightened up as his body suddenly filled with renewed blood and strength, and used the spear tip to hold the caped warden's chin high. "I'm a Greek with a spear. Do you want to see if you have a chance against me?"

Hephaestion allowed a moment to pass, making *certain* Montressor knew he was being spared.

Yitz's sobs filled the silence between the two men.

"It's my fault, Gil. My fault," Yitz croaked in confession. "Too much of me in you, and not enough of your mama. She cries for you at night and says your name in her sleep. And it's my fault!"

Montressor's hand eased from his whip.

Hephaestion lowered his spear, but still kept his grip on the weapon firm.

"You violated my terms," the warden said. "Let those that damned themselves suffer as they *must*. Offer no comfort!"

Hephaestion sighed. "We're not here for Gil," he whispered. "Not really. We're here for his parents' sake."

"The damned are my concern, the ones who got away with it." The masked man seethed.

"Trust me," Hephaestion said with weary humor. "I don't think they *did*. Besides, you aren't here for them so much as you are here for *you*."

Hephaestion meditated a moment on his last sentence, realizing how true it was for himself as well.

Yitz's sobs cooled. He pulled off his yarmulke, licked the underside of it furiously, and used it to wipe his boy's forehead as clean as he could. Then he fixed his kippah clips into Gil's hair and fixed the Yarmulke to his frigid head.

Yitz appeared vulnerable without it, the bright bald spot at the top of his head shining in stark contrast to his dark, wavy hair.

With one last, solid, tender kiss to Gil's forehead, Yitz held his boy's head in his hands. "We love you, my Gil. Mama and I forgive and adore you, even now. Frozen and cold and sinful, we love you just as much as the day you were born." He pulled away as he stood, but maintained eye contact with his son. "We're on the rim above—" He pointed. "—and we wait for you and pray for the day we hold you again."

Gil's eyes clamped shut as if to contain his shame.

"You are worth it, my boy. Your mama and I would have no other son than you."

With that, Yitz turned and walked away into the gloom to sob alone.

Montressor crossed his arms and glowered at Hephaestion.

"Is Lucifer that way? Farther out?" Hephaestion asked while pointing with his spear into the nothing ahead, toward the center of Cocytus.

"Will you forgive *him* too?"

"I might as well, but his spine is my way out."

"Then head in that direction, toward the center of the maelstrom."

Hephaestion walked on, easily finding Yitz sitting on a rock some distance away. He felt taller and energized, and as he walked past each head in the ice, he made eye contact with them and offered a small smile of kindness.

Yitz sat with his face buried in his hands, shoulders heaving.

Hephaestion sat next to his friend, put his arm around him, and resolved to sit next to him for however long he sobbed, eternity or otherwise.

It turned out to be no more than a minute.

"All right," Yitz choked. "All right, let's go home."

The two men proceeded, steadying each other's steps as they walked among frozen limbs and splintered black ice. Chunks of frozen volcanic rock gradually became more common as they approached Cocytus' center, and the wind's sting became more cruel.

After stepping over several more circle partitions, some moving at greater speeds than others, they felt a shift in the air. The wind was much stronger now, pounding at their bodies and forcing them to cling to each other for footing. Yitz's torch blew out and flew from his hand, but tiny lightning strikes on the horizon guided them.

Forward they went into the grinding winds filled with dust and pebbles, deafening them with its roar. In the dark above, illuminated by the occasional flicker of discharged electricity, resided The Fallen One. Like a massive windmill, Lucifer's six wings pounded frantically in the black, his lower half frozen under the lake's surface. Lucifer was said to forever be trying to break free of the ice, but his wings caused such wind that he froze himself into place, fulfilling his cycle of eternity.

When Yitz and Hephaestion came to a small crag, Yitz began climbing down immediately, but Hephaestion was transfixed by the giant being before him, its wings fluttering like a desperate moth trying to reach a distant lamp. He gazed up through the swirling electrified gloom, and could see the tiniest suggestion of light above. Even here, at the bottom of the universe, Heaven could still be seen if one looked hard enough.

Clearly, Lucifer could see and feel it, his wings hammering away to return.

To return like a rogue planet missing its star.

"Heph!" Yitz commanded from the rocks below. "Move!"

Hephaestion shook free of his trance and obeyed, following his friend's descent down. Jagged crag after jagged crag jutted from the ground, bringing them closer to their exit. *Banding together.* Hephaestion used his shield to deflect the brunt of the wind upon Yitz, and both men pushed on, crouched low. After another quarter-league, they came directly under the wings, the wind not as strong here despite the ear-bursting pressure.

A minute flame flickered nearby, the remnants of a burning flying machine, one of the troop transports that had chased them in Dis, and which had crashed down near the devil's backbone. Someone had braved the winds to get here, smashing their vehicle into the ice, and several burned and broken bodies lay strewn around the wreckage. Tracks led away from the crash, leading Hephaestion and Yitz directly to the giant hole through which they had intended to exit.

Both men looked at each other, understanding that they were not alone.

As they came to Satan's spine, the flanking dark muscles pulsing with each pound of the wings, Hephaestion peered below. A wooden ladder had been staked into the ice and unrolled downward. Someone had made the descent already, and upon close examination of the airship, he had a good idea exactly who.

CHAPTER 44

Provost-General Eggert van der Meer stood fuming as his remaining loyal men slumped casually along the walls of the cave, waiting for Hephaestion's eventual arrival. The howling wind on the surface of Cocytus above was little more than a whisper here, but despite the calm air and beautiful crystal walls of the cave, the Provost-General was in complete inner turmoil.

Alexander had been the key to everything. Only a leader as charismatic and ferocious as he could compel the wrathful to fall in line behind him and march into New Dis. The plan was to cause chaos, usurp Sun Tzu, and then swoop in with the Jesuits and Japanese to reestablish a stable government. The Provost-General was reaffirmed in his plan to seize New Dis in Christ's name when Hephaestion surfaced. Clearly, van der Meer had God's blessing for such fortune to occur. With Hephaestion as an available bargaining chip, he could neutralize Alexander after the conquest, uncomplicating his ascension to becoming de facto leader and spiritual figurehead of New Dis.

No more faux mercy from the Buddhists and other Heaven bound. The city would have become a Christian state. Thousands, or perhaps even millions, of souls would have ascended under his guidance, and in doing so, Eggert van der Meer would finally have his place in Heaven.

But after Hephaestion annihilated Alexander's heart, and even before he'd marched out of sight, the army had turned on itself. Tribal conflicts and slights from past lives had erupted, and soon the machines began smashing into each other. Centuries of work and plans were reduced to a rioting massacre in less than a literal *minute*.

Father Franco was nowhere to be found, and what few men seemed loyal to the Christian cause secured the nearest airship for van der Meer and aided his escape. He'd promised those men that they could move on to Purgatory. It was a lie, but the Provost-General decided long ago to commit any minor sin, even if it meant sacking Sodom, to lead the multitudes into Heaven.

And so he stood, arms crossed, with a dozen men waiting for Hephaestion to attempt his exit through the cave at the base of the devil's spine. It was a gamble, but the Provost-General knew it was the only way out, and if Hephaestion never came, he could at least point the waiting men deeper into the cave, to the exit that led to Purgatory's shores.

All eyes suddenly turned to the dangling ladder, its visible rungs twitching like a string from a spider's web. Was there prey? Was it Hephaestion descending?

The Provost General's staff, the top adorned with a golden cross, clanged loudly as it fell and landed on the lip of the cave. He had left it in the airship above.

Every man in the cave sprung to their feet, clubs, axes, blades and rifles ready. The Provost-General stood as a statue, eyes keen on the cave's opening.

Several men near the front, clad in red steel, crept near the entrance, their heads craning upward to see if the ladder had an occupant. For a moment, the Provost-General was disappointed, thinking that Hephaestion had slipped and fallen during his descent, and all that remained of him was the staff he'd stolen as a prize.

Then Yitz swung from the ladder, upside down and dangling with his feet in the rungs, revolver in hand. He fired six rounds from a pistol and four men fell bleeding onto the cave's floor.

"Him!" van der Meer shouted as the men charged forward. "The Jew is nothing! Throw him out!"

Hephaestion dropped from somewhere above Yitz, shield and spear at the ready, and landed on his feet. Bullet shells tinkled on the cave's icy floor around his friend as Yitz frantically reloaded while dangling upside down.

"There! Bring me Hephaestion's heart!" the Provost General cried.

The eager warriors charged in, eyes wild with promises of Heaven, at Hephaestion. The first one received the flat of Hephaestion's shield, his teeth knocked out and nose shattered. Another crazed follower moved in, and Hephaestion caved in his chest with the piston, flopping him back into his comrades. The remaining men hung back, eyes glancing about each other as they looked for leadership and bravery among themselves.

Yitz spun his revolver's cylinder and snapped it shut, ready to fire.

Hephaestion looked like a wind-burned hero of epic tales.

In stark contrast, no bravery showed itself among the Provost-General's men as Hephaestion pushed forward like a one man phalanx, grinding his shield into their mass as he stabbed with his spear.

Yitz supported him by firing aimed rounds over his shoulder.

Hephaestion alternated his grip between underhand and overhand positions, and his attackers couldn't anticipate or counter any of his thrusts. Some men fell clutching their empty eye sockets, while others held their intestines in as they begged for quarter, only to receive it with a bullet to the head... compliments of upside-down Yitz.

Hephaestion had soon plowed through them like fallow soil, and now stood over his work, searching the fallen for any signs of motion, and ended them quickly by jamming his spearhead into either their throats or their hearts.

Yitz seized the moment and clumsily undid his legs from the ladder, and jumped down into the cave. The pristine crystal terrain now shimmered red with bloody handprints and viscera.

Hephaestion, his shield slick with gore, then approached the perfectly still Provost-General, both men fuming with fury.

"You will never know peace from me," the man of Christ threatened.

"Then you'll never know Heaven," Hephaestion retorted as he wiped his bloody spear tip off on van der Meer's robes.

Having said and done what he had to, Hephaestion walked past the bitter man and deeper into the cave, in search of the two first stars.

Yitz followed behind, handing the golden cross staff to the Provost-General. "You forgot this," he said flatly as he moved by.

Relieved not to be the victim of violence, van der Meer exhaled. His fury was still palpable, but he was out of immediate danger for now. His knuckles whitened as he gripped his staff in frustration and rage.

He gathered himself and surveyed the ruins of his entourage, and saw a man in black standing at the foot of the cave, a bladed whip in hand.

CHAPTER 45

Hephaestion and Yitz trudged on shoulder to shoulder, the cave growing wider and darker, the light behind dulling into nothing.

Spear forward, Hephaestion tapped its steel tip to guide his way. Soon they had no sense of up or down, but only forward. Even if they turned around, they wouldn't be sure if they were heading back or not.

Hephaestion wondered what there would be for him, now. He'd known Alexander since childhood. He sat next to him while learning from Aristotle, and held onto him when they rode Bucephalus together. They bloodied and pleasured each other as they grew into men, and there was no corner of Hephaestion's existence that Alexander's eyes hadn't seen.

A terrifying uncertainty rose in his chest. He had known, every single moment of his life, exactly what he wanted, where he was headed, and what he waited for. Every moment had been dictated by the existence and light of his love. And now... what?

Green eyes... Hephaestion thought about Alexander's green eyes, and the hurt those eyes held when he realized Hephaestion had come to end him was haunting.

No one would ever call Hephaestion 'Paty' again. That pet name, that particular *affection*, would now be lost to the world like an untended monument—always there, but gradually obscured by overgrowth. Hephaestion held back his panic, his chest heaving, as he tried to accept that he would never smell Alexander's hair again.

I tore his heart out! I tore his heart out and fed it to molten steel!

Hephaestion belonged in Cocytus as much as Gil, frozen in agonizing stasis for his betrayal of his soul mate and king.

Two tiny spots, like distant eyes, appeared before them. The cave was wider now, and with Hephaestion's spear unable to find the walls, only the two spots of light guided them. They were so dim and far away that if he tried looking directly at them, they'd vanish. Hephaestion had to unfocus his vision and continue toward them... step after step.

At any point he could just sit down.

At any point he could feel that his promise was fulfilled and Yitz could move on.

He could stop.

But he didn't.

The lights became brighter, now clearly stars in a distant sky that gradually became purple up ahead. A gentle *shush* came from them, soothing his angst and guilt. The sound rolled in and out, and the cave's floor gave way to wet sand. His boots sank in and the sound of surf poured into both his ears, echoing off the cliff face above.

They were in Purgatory.

Stories had told of those unworthy, who would be lost in the cave along Lucifer's spine. Hephaestion, feeling confident that he himself was worthy, had hoped to carry Alexander's heart with him to salvation. But perhaps if he had taken Alexander's heart this far, they would both be lost to the dark tunnels forever.

What would that have been like, watching Alexander regrow from his heart only to find himself in black emptiness, Hephaestion explaining his failure to him?

Foamy water splashed his boots beneath a sky adorned with the flicking delight of stars. Vines hung on the nearby rocks, and tufts of long grass jutted from bulging patches of sand.

"You look like *hell*, Hepher! And is this your friend?"

Hephaestion leapt, spotting the hulking Ulfric sitting by a large, brass optical scope aimed at the sky. Just as always, the very sight of the kindly man brought Hephaestion faith in humanity.

"W-what... how did you..." Hephaestion stammered, his footsteps heavy with wet sand.

Yitz bent down, scooped up water with his cupped hands, and washed his face.

"This one's wife can be persuasive," Ulfric said. "She sent message for me to come here, so I took some time to enjoy the stars while waiting for you. I knew you'd make it." He jumped down, arms open, and

scooped up Hephaestion with a flurry of pats on the back. "We missed you. It's been a while. A second war even came and went. Earth's gone crazy, and a lot of busted people are flopping onto the rocks every day. We could use help guiding them." Ulfric's beaming smile moved back and forth between Yitz and Hephaestion.

"I'd just as soon return to my wife, good sir," Yitz said, straightening up with a stoic look on his face.

"Fair enough. I'll see to getting you transit. And you, Hepher? Are you game? Want to come back with me and see to the throngs of poor people pouring onto the rocks?"

Hephaestion looked up at Ulfric wearily, pondering the question. For all of his existence, Alexander had been at the center... and now he was gone. That entire *universe* had vanished. Hephaestion was no longer a satellite to greater man, circling his love like a planet would a star. He'd become a rogue, drifting in the void.

So what now?

Would he orbit another star?

Was there an ideal that would burn as bright as a sun?

Was there something better?

THE END

BOOK CLUB GUIDE

1. In your opinion, is the afterlife in *Trampling in the Land of Woe* either fair or unfair? How did you form this opinion considering your personal background, experiences, and culture?

2. This novel is set in an afterlife based firmly on Dante's *Divine Comedy*. Why do you think the author chose a predominantly Catholic setting for these novels to occur in despite the main characters being Jewish, Iceni, Zorastrian, and ancient Greek?

3. Was Hephaestion's quest always doomed to begin with? Was there a way he could have saved Alexander or salvaged the situation? If so, why did Hephaestion instead decide to end Alexander's rulership?

4. Compare Yitz and Adina's relationship to that of Hephaestion and Alexander. Taking Hephaestion's flashbacks into account, how do these two relationships differ?

5. Ulfric is, in effect, a recovery sponsor and mentor for Purgatorians. Given the brief time he has in the novel, do you think he is effective at this?

6. Why do you think people in the afterlife regenerate from their hearts and not from any other organ? How did the author's choice here impact the conflict between Hephaestion and Alexander?

7. What secondary or minor character in this novel would you like to know more about? Whose back story would you like to know more about?

8. There are five books in this series, and *Trampling in the Land of Woe* is the first. What do you think the other four books are about? Or... what would you *like* them to be about?

ACKNOWLEDGEMENTS

I would like to recognize the following for their contributions to this book:

1. Ally Bishop, the believer in this story.
2. Aleksandr Dochkin, for producing the fantastic artwork used on the cover.
3. David Lane (aka Lane Diamond), for fantastic polish.
4. Kabir Shah, for taking Aleksandr's artwork and turning it into a great book cover.
5. Dante Alighieri, for inspiring the imagination.

Trampling in the Land of Woe was brought to you by David Lane, Evolved Publishing, and the letter H.

~ William LJ Galaini

ABOUT THE AUTHOR

Having lived up and down the East Coast, William Galaini finally settled outside of DC after a charming stream of career failures that ranged from the hospitality business to the military. After marrying his college sweetheart, writing became his vehicle to pull his life together. Six novels, four cats, forty pounds, and one son later, you now can find him here at Evolved Publishing.

His work focuses on character revelation and multifaceted conflicts nestled within science fiction and fantasy settings. The influences that echo in his writing include role-playing games, classic literature, world history, and his personal experience. To recharge, he naps on the couch under his mother's afghan, surrounded by his cats.

For more, please visit William LJ Galaini online at:
Website: www.WilliamLJGalaini.com
Goodreads: William LJ Galaini
Facebook: @WilliamLJGalaini
Instagram: @WGalaini
Twitter: @WGalaini

WHAT'S NEXT

William always has at least one book in the works, including the fourth book in the "Hellbound" series, *An End to Ice and Sorrow*. Please stay tuned to developments by subscribing to our newsletter at the link below.

www.EvolvedPub.com/Newsletter

MORE FROM
EVOLVED PUBLISHING

We offer great books across multiple genres, featuring high-quality editing (which we believe is second-to-none) and fantastic covers.

As a hybrid small press, your support as loyal readers is so important to us, and we have strived, with tireless dedication and sheer determination, to deliver on the promise of our motto:

QUALITY IS PRIORITY #1!

Please check out all of our great books,
which you can find at this link:
www.EvolvedPub.com/Catalog/

Thank you!

TRAMPLING IN THE LAND OF WOE

Hellbound – Book 1

A Novel by
WILLIAM LJ GALAINI